BECAUSE

BECAUSE

Book One in the Time's Song Series

By R.K. Slade

Published by Marching Band Is Awesome
www.marchingbandisawesome.com

Author's Note: The story contained within these pages is a fun romp through the high school marching band camp setting and swirls in a big helping of music history, band jokes, and general music nerdy! Many of the situations are based on real life people and events that I experienced, and the historical information is as accurate as humanly possible while also taking liberties to craft a great fiction!

Join the advance reader team by signing up for my email list: http://bit.ly/rksladelist
Early copies, giveaways, and opportunity for input into future projects!

Dedicated to my fellow band and music geeks who make up one big forever family.
Once a band kid, always a band kid.

*"Music should strike fire from the heart of man,
and bring tears from the eyes of woman."*
~ Ludwig van Beethoven

First Movement: Sonata

1

IT'S SO HOT out here today.

I close my eyes for a few seconds. It feels like forever since we took an actual break.

Water.

In my mind, I see a big tall glass of water. Then, like a changing scene from a nature documentary, it transforms into a bubbly stream. Then the vivid frame in my head morphs into a rushing waterfall surrounded by lush green plants with butterflies fluttering about. I can almost hear the birds singing.

Water.

I have a water bottle, but when we're working out here in the sun all day, we can only take a break when the director says so. Those few, short refreshing minutes can't come soon enough. I can't stop thinking about the cool, thirst-quenching liquid. I lick my lips as discreetly as I can.

It's only the third day of two grueling weeks of all-out torture. It's voluntary, though. We all willingly signed up for this. Not a single one of us out here on this grassy field wants to quit. The sticky August heat makes it hard to breathe, like something is pressing against my chest. The occasional gnat buzzes around my head, but I won't move when I'm standing at attention.

I'm like a statue, you little devil insect. Can't make me move, won't make me move.

It's hard work keeping my elbows out and arms high. Hours of holding my trumpet at the proper horn angle are beginning to take a toll. My arms are on fire.

Even though I'm wearing a lot of sunscreen, I can still feel my skin baking. My chops, the muscles around my mouth, feel like mush, so fatigued from playing my instrument for hours. My feet are tired from all the marching and standing. It feels like I've been walking around on this field forever, but it's only been two days and a few hours.

This is band camp.

"Hey, Rigs," Chewie thinks he's whispering.

Yeah, not so much. He's the worst whisperer ever. His real name is Charles, but for as long as I can remember, he's proudly gone by that silly nickname. He's not even a Star Wars fan. He says his dad gave him that nickname when he started growing a peach-fuzz mustache when he was ten years old.

"Rigs, psssst. Rigs!" Chewie says.

Only my close friends call me Rigs. I'm pretty introverted, so I don't really have a lot of friends.

It's kind of cool, though. We found out last spring before school got out for the summer that our opening show would be Beatles themed. I mean, we're literally playing the song *Eleanor Rigby*, the song that I was named after.

My parents were big fans of the Fab Four from Liverpool. When Mom found out she was pregnant, they decided to name me after their favorite song, *Eleanor Rigby*. Dad really wanted to call his baby girl Eleanor - Ellie for short. But Mom got her way, and the name Rigby won out. So that's me, that's who I am, Rigby Raines...

Mom.

I try not to linger on that memory for too long. The pain is still too close to the surface.

Even though I'm standing at attention, I turn and sneak a peek over my right shoulder to see what Chewie wants. He's standing there looking goofy with that massive sousaphone. I don't understand why he likes lugging that monster around all day. It's like a big tuba that's been unwound and then reconfigured just so that tuba players can wear it for parades and marching band.

"Riiiigggsss!" Chewie is relentless. "Can I have some of your water? I left my canteen on the sidelines." His sweaty, moppy brown hair is in his eyes.

Of course, he's the only person in the whole band who actually brings a military canteen to practice and then forgets it on the sidelines.

Typical Chewie. It's hot here in Georgia in the summer. Like, almost one hundred degrees, and muggier than you think, hot. We don't get many water breaks, though. I have a small water bottle that hooks onto my belt bag. Yeah, don't laugh, it's a small fanny pack. It's practical.

"One more time!" Mr. Zimmer, our band director, calls out through his crackling megaphone. He's pretty cool, but I'm sick of hearing those three words. Over the next two weeks, we'll hear them again and again.

We're working on learning new formations. Once we get a shape down, we head back to the previous form, get set, and then while the director counts out loud, march back into the new shape. It takes hours and hours of this to get the finished "drill" onto the field for halftime shows, but it's worth it.

"Here you go, Chew." I hand him my canteen as we head back to our previous spots. He has to be quick to sneak a drink in between sets. We're not always on the same part of the field, but our marks in this section of the show are close to each other. As we continue to learn this drill, each section of the band will occupy different areas of the field as the music changes. It's like a set of pictures that moves with each part of the song. All of the members of the band are individual dots that make up the whole picture.

"Thanks, Rigs," he pants. "It's hot out here today." He heads back to his first dot a few yard lines over. I'm standing at mine waiting for Mr. Z to call out the next command. A few yard lines over, a guy in the clarinet section that I never really talk to is wearing one of those hydration packs It's got a long rubber tube that comes over his shoulder. He can take a quick sip anytime he wants. It's like he's got the holy grail of summer band camp strapped to his back. Water on demand.

That's actually pretty smart. Chew should really get one of those.

All this thinking about water has me so thirsty right

now. I reach down for my water bottle. It's not there.

What the...where's my water bottle? Crap! Chewie still has it!

"CHEW!!" I call. "You've got my water..."

"RIGBY!" A piercing voice stops me in my tracks. It makes my skin crawl.

I turn uneasily to see Taura Jacobs staring me down with eyes like icy daggers. She's the trumpet section leader, and basically the band's self-proclaimed queen. She knows everything about everything and everybody seems to think she's so great. She's giving me the stank eye like I just insulted and slapped her.

I don't know why she always singles me out. I'm basically a nobody in the trumpet section. I like it that way. I hate being in front of people. I think I'm too nervous, or anxious, or something. The only time I ever played a solo was that time during concert band that I accidentally played during a rest. The whole band was silent and I honked out a right note at the wrong time. I was so embarrassed that I wanted to hide in my band locker.

"GET BACK TO YOUR SPOT AND QUIT TALKING TO THE SOUSAS!" She snaps. She looks like a grumpy cat when she's hissing out all those bossy orders.

She's always been so harsh to me. Such a bully. Cruel at times. I don't know why. Maybe it's because I'm shy. Maybe it's because I can't ever come up with anything to say back to her. She's been the bane of my existence since we all started band together in the sixth grade.

Her family moved in from somewhere else. She just kind of swooped in and became the popular girl. She carried herself like she just knew she was better than everyone else. And instead of everyone seeing her for the witch she is, she became everyone's role model. It's like everyone was mesmerized by her even though she acted like she could care less about them.

Taura has that look that makes people like her. She's actually pretty. Tall and lean. Her outfits are always color-coordinated. Her ponytail is constantly in a perfect bow or flowing flawlessly out of the back of her color-coordinated baseball cap. Even in middle school her hair was perfect. What kind of seventh grader has model status hair? Taura, of course. I can't stand it. I have to wrestle with my straightener for what seems like hours to get this frizzy, ginger hair to behave.

Taura acts as if everyone else is beneath her. I mean, it feels like she cares more about the *idea* of band than the actual people in it. To top it off, now she can officially boss me around and get away with it. Mr. Zimmer made her a section leader. Somehow he thinks she's perfect. I guess he didn't get the memo about her. I don't know how he can't see what I see.

She's such a jerk.

"Ok, Taura." I mumble softly. My ears are burning. I'm embarrassed. I hate being singled out for anything. It makes me extremely nervous. I wish I could just stand up to her...but I can't.

I've never been able to. I'm not brave. I'm not bold. I'm not fearless. And at the moment, I'm just shy, quiet, and scared to say anything. Just me.

Just Rigby.

2

ONE OF THE reasons I love band camp so much is that it takes my mind off of the grief. I lost my mom to cancer last year. It's been rough.

Her name was Juliet. They named me Juliet, too. It's my middle name. My trumpet was actually hers. She played it in the marching band when she was my age. It's literally the most important thing I own. I don't know what I'd do if anything ever happened to it. It's my only tangible connection to her.

When I was in fourth grade, she gave me this trumpet. Sometimes, on a rainy night, when we didn't have anything better to do, we used to pull out old photos of her in the marching band. We laughed at how funny and cute she looked in her uniform. There were even pictures of her conducting in front of the band. She was the drum major, the leader and field director of the band, her junior and senior years.

For as long as I can remember, I've been playing the piano. She was my first and only teacher. She taught me everything I know about music. We would sit at our family piano for hours on end. She used songs by the Beatles to teach me how to play. Songs like *I Wanna Hold Your Hand* and *Hey Jude*.

Over the years, I progressed to the more complex classics. She would have me play Bach and Mozart. I even tackled Beethoven's piano works. I think that, out of all of them, Beethoven is my favorite. There seems to be such emotion captured in his compositions. The pieces were difficult, but I mastered them fairly quickly. My mom was a great teacher.

Now she's gone.

When she slipped away, my world turned dark. It seems like I'm always under a storm cloud. She was like true north on my compass. I feel completely lost. I just don't understand why it had to be her.

Dying of cancer is not a pretty thing. We got the diagnosis, and then seven months later she just faded away. She didn't even seem sick before. But they say that's how it goes. I don't even know who "they" are.

Now it's just me, dad, and my music. I haven't really touched the piano, though, since Mom...since she left. My anxiety seems to have gotten worse. The marching band has been kind of therapeutic, though. I can get lost in the trumpet section. It's like I'm invisible.

Band has really been the one thing that allows me to experience somewhat of a distraction. They say music heals, right? I'm able to exist in all my weirdness right in the middle of a big crowd of people, but all I really have to focus on is playing my own part, marching with the correct foot, and being where I'm supposed to be on the field.

Without Mom, I feel so lonely at times...but I also can't stand big crowds. It's kind of a paradox.

All I have ever wanted was to make her proud of me. I

ended up being so much like my dad, though. Quiet and shy. He calls it extreme introversion. Mom balanced us out, though. She was the life of the party and was born to be drum major.

Chewie really tries hard to keeps tabs on me. Sometimes it's annoying, but I do love him. I mean, I'm really lost right now, but he has been there for me. I guess other people know about what happened with my mom, but nobody really tries to say anything.

I mean, what do you even say to somebody like me?

So here I am, standing on my dot with my cherished, old trumpet. It's not as shiny as it used to be. The second valve sticks at the most random times. When I tried out for marching band this year, it got stuck right in the middle of my C scale. I sounded like a duck.

Yay, me.

I guess that's why I'm last chair, the bottom of the trumpet section. Fine by me. But sometimes I actually dream of being like my mom. Out there in front playing solos and leading the band. But I don't think I could ever do that. I would probably die of stage fright or have one of my panic attacks.

One time in seventh grade the band director thought it would be a good idea to make everyone run through their individual parts to check and make sure the section had the music down. It was just during a rehearsal but when it was my turn to try it I froze. I literally sat there staring at the music as the room started to spin. My hands shook and my eyes watered, and I thought my heart was going to pound out of my chest. It was my first legit panic attack. It was so scary. Nobody said anything, or tried to help me out of the awkward silence. I'm just not cut out for the up-front stuff.

That's what really makes it tough, though. I WANT to be drum major, standing in front of the band conducting the music. I WANT to play solos. I WANT to follow in my mom's footsteps. But every time I think about it I get so nervous that I can't function. Maybe it's because I'm shy. Maybe it's anxiety. I don't know. I just can't handle it. And it tears me up inside because I want it so bad.

Have you ever really just wanted to make someone proud of you? You know, because you love them so much, and your world would not be right if you couldn't make them smile? That's how I feel. Except, my mom's gone, and I'll never see her again. It leaves a big hole inside.

All I've wanted since I was little was to be like her, to see her smiling in the stands as I followed in her footsteps. It's like I'm stuck between two really big things. I'm too scared to try out for drum major, but I really want to, more than anything, because it would make her proud. This really sucks.

Maybe next year.

3

THE TRUMPET SECTION is lined up across the front hash marks now. Those little white lines mark off each individual yard and make it really easy for the band to find their spots. I'm standing on the left side of the field at the 30-yard line. The guy next to me is named Reggie, but we don't talk much. Well, *I* don't talk much. For three days, he's been quoting Harry Potter and asking everyone if they want to be in his fantasy Quidditch league. He's on his dot between the 30 and the 35-yard line.

The next person is on the 35, and it continues like that through fourteen trumpet players. Taura steps in and out of the form to bark orders at the freshmen and makes a point always to include me in her rants. She has a talent for singling me out.

God, I wish she would just leave me alone.

If it's not one thing, it's another. It's like Taura knows every single button to push, every word to say that will totally wreck me. I get so flustered around her. She's so confident. I'm not.

What really stinks is I KNOW that I'm as good a trumpet player as anybody here. Jason, the guy two spots over from me can barely play a G over the staff. But he's ok. He's been nice to me so far. Carlos, one of the freshmen this year, plays jazz like nobody's business, but he kind of keeps to himself. And then there's Kayla. She tries really hard, but for some reason always sounds like she needs to empty her spit valve. Taura, the leader of our pack, is pretty decent, though. She...

"Rigby!" Taura snarls at me snapping me out of my thoughts. "Quit daydreaming and get in your spot. If Mr. Z yells at the trumpets again because you're off in la-la land, you'll pay in push-ups."

Push-ups.

Like this is some sort of military boot camp. Well, apparently Taura seems to think it is.

Cracked notes? Push-ups.

Crooked lines? Push-ups.

Taura wakes up on the wrong side of the bed that morning? You guessed it. Push-ups.

Oh, wait, that's actually every morning. Taura is the very definition of the wrong side of the bed when it comes to me. I still can't even really put my finger on the exact moment that she started bullying me. I don't remember a particular reason. She has just always had it out for me.

I think I could take her, though. Right here and right now. I could run up to her right now and just lay her out. It would feel so nice. I imagine raring back and punching her in the face. I envision her wobbling on her feet and then hitting the ground hard like a fighter who has taken too many punches to the face.

I literally chuckle out loud.

"You think that's funny, Riii-gby?" Taura mockingly stretches out the syllables in my name.

"Um," I stutter. "No, I was just thinking about..."

"INCOMING!" The voice from behind us sounds like a squawking goose mixed with a young bear cub. Poor Chewie, 16-years-old, and his voice still cracks all the time.

"HEADS Uhhhhhhh..." Chewie warns.

BAM! My water bottle hits Taura square in the nose.

Oh, crap!

She grabs her face and doubles over, dropping her perfectly polished silver trumpet into the soft grass of the field. She immediately starts sobbing as a red stream of blood begins to pour from her nose like a faucet. She's dazed and stumbles, blinking her eyes rapidly as tears begin to blind her.

Crap. Crap. Crap. That has got to hurt!

There's a part of me that is enjoying this. Taura screams as she trips over her trumpet and loses her balance. We all hold our breath for a split second as she flails wildly trying not to to step on her instrument. We're all thinking the same thing.

Not the instrument!

Down she goes. Like a sack of potatoes. She hits the ground with a dull thud and for about five seconds her sobbing stops. Her eyes go wide. The wind is knocked out of her. Nobody knows what to do.

"Owwww!" She gasps loudly, finally catching her breath after a few seconds. The sobs tumble out of her like quick, chirpy hiccups.

That has to hurt. The whole trumpet section is now

gathered around Taura trying to help. Carlos is offering a towel. Kayla is trying to get Taura to lean her head back. Reggie is just standing there with a shocked look on his face. Jason is pacing back and forth nervously.

"I am so sorry! So very sorry, Taura!" Chewie says as he runs up with a shocked look on his face. "I was just spinning that bottle around on my finger, and it must've slipped. It got so much air...so much air."

It's one of those metal bottles with the carabiner clips on it. Apparently Chewie was trying to see how fast he could get it to spin on his finger, and he lost control of it.

"Shut up, you...loo...oo...serrr..." she sob whines. "You're soo...oo dead."

Why am I enjoying this so much?

I am smiling on the inside. I must be smirking on the outside, too. Taura's teary eyes catch mine for a split second, and she knows. She sees my satisfaction. She can tell that I'm enjoying this. It infuriates her. But she can't do anything about it. At least not with a busted nose that's bleeding everywhere.

In her stare, in that split second, her eyes go from hurting and embarrassed, to furious and determined. I'm not sure how or when she'll attempt to get revenge, but she will. I can see it in her angry eyes. She always has to have the last word. She is always right.

Just for this moment, though, I'm content in knowing that for once she's the one that's embarrassed. Somebody is the center of negative attention and it's not me.

4

WHEN IT'S A clear night like tonight, I like to wake up before dawn and slip out of my bedroom window and sit out here on the roof. It's perfect for some alone time. I can just listen to music and think. I like to look up at the sky and just think. This last year, I've been out here more and more. I guess I'm trying to get away from dealing with all the emotions of losing Mom.

The sky is dark. The stars are like billions of tiny Christmas lights strung all across the sky. A meteor streaks overhead with a faint hiss and sizzle. I see them often on summer mornings before the sun comes up. They make me think of Mom.

Maybe she's somewhere out there, across the universe, in a better place, smiling down at me right now. I try not to think about it too often.

It's been a long three days since the water bottle incident. Taura is ok. She looks like she's been in an MMA fight, but other than some swelling and some killer raccoon black eyes, she'll be okay.

She hasn't said much to me. But I can sense that something is rumbling under the surface there. I'm a little worried that she'll cook up some cruel and unusual punishment for me. I'm not going to lie, I've been looking over my shoulder for the last few days.

Taura knows that the bottle thing was an accident, but

it was MY bottle, and I didn't do anything to help her when she was down. Even though I tried to hold it in, she saw the look of contentment on my face. To her, that's probably worse than just outright throwing a punch.

Another meteor streaks across the sky. I pull out my phone and plug in my headphones. I push play. The *Moonlight Sonata* starts.

How appropriate.

It's one of the first classical songs I learned on piano. Beethoven. It's one of his most recognizable pieces besides the famous symphonies he composed. In my history class, we briefly talked about the history of Western music. You can't talk about the Romantic Era of music and art without mentioning the significance of Beethoven.

As a pianist, he changed the way composers wrote for piano. As a composer, he pushed the boundaries of the period before him, the Classical Era. Without Beethoven, you wouldn't have the Romantic Era, which gave us music that was much more intense and passionate.

The *Moonlight Sonata* is dark and melancholy. It's simple and full of deep emotion. There is a passion in the notes that you can't find listening to the radio today. I'll never really understand how composers can fill a song with such feeling. Every time I hear this piece, I want to cry. I guess, because of my connection to Mom, the song is more of an emotional experience than just another smarmy pop tune on a playlist.

Lightning flashes in the distance and a few seconds

later I hear a far-off rumble. Summertime lightning storms are pretty common here. But the timing is surreal.

My heart aches.

Sometimes it feels like there is a thunderstorm inside my chest. I cry a little, but I don't really know how to get it out. Part of me wants to go to the piano and just play...but it just doesn't feel right. It's too soon. Too many memories.

My phone vibrates with a text notification.

It's Chewie. Love that kid.

"its early i know. was thinking about u. jus wanted to c if u were ok"

I text him back that I'm fine. He wants to know if Taura has said or done anything to me since the incident. I tell him back she hasn't yet, but that I'm worried she might try to murder me with her perfectly organized flip folder.

"lol. u cray cray," he replies.

Honestly, I'm not sure how I feel about his text vocabulary. It's almost like he's a 13-year-old girl with a new phone. But I love that he takes the time to check on me. I ask him what he's doing up so early. He says that he couldn't sleep and that he is watching Beatle's remix videos on Youtube.

He's always trying to impress me with anything related to the Beatles. He knows that I love the Fab Four. He's a great friend. The kind you always want around. I'm thankful for him. Without Chewie, I think I really would be alone. I mean, sure, I'm surrounded by over a hundred other people in the band who probably think of me as a weird step-sibling or something. But even in that band family, I think the way that I'm wired allows me to be pretty much a loner.

It's not that I don't feel like I'm a part. I do. I think I just have such a hard time with the chaos of the crowd. It drains me. The times I can come out here by myself, looking up into the sky into the bigness of the night, are when I recharge. The only way for me to feel like I'm being energized is to withdraw away from people. I guess dad is right...I'm a total introvert.

Chewie's face pops up on my phone as it vibrates to let me know he's calling. I tap the green button to accept the call and hear that he's got me on speakerphone. The noise in the background is hard to make out.

"What are you listening to, Chew?"

It sounds like a robot, a computer, and an old record player got together to make some music. I recognize John Lennon's voice in the song Imagine, but the rest is hard to make out. Seriously, some things are better left as is.

"It's dubstep, Rigs." Chewie is proud of his latest YouTube remix discovery.

"Chew, you gotta leave that stuff alone," I laugh out loud. "It's bad for your soul!"

Although his taste in music is seriously questionable, his timing couldn't be more perfect. I need a laugh, and he's usually the one that makes me chuckle.

"Chew, I gotta go, but I'll see you bright and early at camp Monday." I'm glad to have the weekend to relax before the second week of camp begins.

Movement catches my eye. Down below, in the dim light of the streetlight, a shiny black sedan creeps by slowly. I haven't seen this car in the neighborhood before. It's a nice ride. I instinctively shrink as low as I can against the rooftop. I don't know why, though, because they probably can't even see me up here. There's usually not much activity at this time of the morning around here. It's probably somebody's mom or dad off to catch a super early business flight at Hartsfield-Jackson International Airport.

Off in the distance, the lightning continues to light up some dark clouds. A few seconds later thunder rumbles in response. I feel flutters in my stomach as I turn *Moonlight Sonata* back on. I need to go back inside. But for a few seconds, I close my eyes and take a deep breath, inhaling the promise of a new day that lingers in the pre-dawn air.

5

So MUCH FOR *bright and early!*

I woke up late this morning, so I am in a rush to get to camp. Dad is already at work and I guess I forgot to set my alarm. I dash out the door.

My school is about eight minutes away with no traffic. But today at 9:12, it seems like everyone is out and about and I'm catching every single red light on the way there.

My old Camry gets me there as quick as it can. The paint is fading, and the dome light doesn't work. The driver side inside door handle fell off a few months ago. My dad ordered a replacement from Amazon. The color is close, but it doesn't match. At least I don't have to reach outside my window to open my door anymore. But she's my baby. And I love her.

I pull into the almost full parking lot at the practice field, and I can see that everybody is already gathered on the field for sectional warm-ups.

Ugh. I'm so late.

I'm expecting push-ups. Lots of push-ups. I'm guessing Taura will be waiting for me ready to dish out the pain. I guess I deserve it this time, though. Being late is not acceptable. Mr. Z always says, "Early is on time, on time is late, and late is unacceptable!" I think it's a quote or something. In band, it's true, though. It's a way of life.

The only open parking spot is on the opposite end of

the parking lot. I park and shut off the engine. As I open the door, I hear the noise of over one hundred musicians noodling on their instruments.

It's 9:21. Twenty-one minutes late.

I'm grabbing my stuff - my flip folder that has all my stand music in it, my towel and water bottle - and scrambling out of the car. I shut the door and run about three steps before I realize I don't have my trumpet.

Smooth. You MIGHT need your horn, Rigs.

I turn around and grope around in my belt bag for my keys. I haven't buckled it around my waist yet, so it swings awkwardly as I fumble around for the keys.

Lip balm...no. Valve oil...no. Keys? Yes, keys...Got 'em.

I open the trunk and pull out my trumpet case. It's well worn. My mom used this old trumpet during her whole high school and college band career. She saved her own money for several years in middle school to buy this instrument before she went into 9th grade. It's seen a lot over the years!

I should probably take the case with me and get my trumpet out on the field like everyone else, but I'd rather just grab my horn and go.

C'mon, c'mon. Go. Go.

The left latch sticks sometimes, so you have to wiggle it just right to get it open. It comes open with a loud pop. I grab my mouthpiece, put it in my trumpet, push the case back in, and close the trunk. For a split second, I have this weird feeling about leaving it in the trunk, but I don't have time for that this morning. I sprint across the parking lot, trying not to drop anything, and hoping that I'm not missing anything important.

As I step onto the green grass of the practice field, the band has already broken into sectionals. The clarinets are over to the left and behind them, the flutes and piccolos set up in their circle. We have two piccs in our band. Everyone teases them because they have a hard time playing in tune with the rest of the band, but generally speaking, our piccs are REALLY good.

The trombones are attempting to make a human pyramid at the back of the field. I honestly don't know why. But hey, does anyone ever really understand what goes on in the trombone section?

The percussion section is in the far right end zone. Each subsection of the drumline is grouped by the type of drums, but they are all in one big semicircle. The bass drummers are all in a line from largest to smallest. The four tenor drummers are on the other side. The snare line is in the middle. The whole semi-circle is facing the lead snare who is their section leader. The cymbal players are off to one side practicing their visuals. They'll spin and flash their cymbals to emphasize different parts of the drum rhythms and it takes a lot of practice to get them all to be in sync.

The saxophones are grouped over by the mellophones. They are two separate sections, but most of the time, their music is very similar, so they tend to gravitate towards each other. I'm not even sure if it's intentional or not.

Chewie and the sousaphones are lined up on the 50-yard line practicing their dance moves. In our band, the sousas get a little special treatment. Sometimes when we hit a formation where everyone is marching, the sousas will get to stand there and rock back and forth. When they are all synchronized, it actually looks really cool.

Chewie is the smallest person in his section. But he more than makes up for it with his great sense of humor. He is hilarious. Not only does he make me laugh, but if there's a group of people laughing somewhere, you ca bet that he's usually the center of attention.

He's wearing a blue tank top that says, "This Is My Band Camp Tank Top" in big bold white letters. It's funny because it's so literal. He found it on one of the marching band Facebook pages he follows. Every day he sends me a funny meme or two that he sees on the page. They're clever, sometimes stupid, but always amusing.

Chewie has even started making his own memes. He says his specialty is combining band jokes with movie quotes. Sometimes he really nails it. Most of the time he has to explain them to me.

"Very good of you to join us this morning, Miss Raines," Mr. Z motions to me without looking up. He is looking at a clipboard with sheet after sheet of halftime show drill that will be taught to the band today.

"I am so, so sorry, Mr. Zimmer." I'm so embarrassed. "I got here as quick as I could. It won't happen again."

I'm staring at my feet and fidgeting with my trumpet valves. I don't look at most people directly in the eyes when I'm talking to them. And definitely not in a situation like this. Mr. Z chuckles, though, and I look up.

"I like you, Miss Raines. Let's not make a habit out of this, mmkay?" He still hasn't looked up from his clipboard, but he's got a friendly smirk on his face. "I'll let it slide this time, but I don't think your section leader is too happy right now."

He's right. Taura is waiting for me to join the trumpet section. She's standing with her hands on her hips. She isn't happy. She's got kind of a hit-with-a-water-bottle-embarrassed-by-the-outcast-who-is-also-late-to-camp thing going on with her face. She turns to start warming up the trumpet section.

This is it. I'm going to die a horrible push-up induced death and be buried on the 50-yard line. I'll never be heard from again.

Directly in between where I am standing next to the front ensemble with all its marimbas and xylophones and where the trumpets have gathered is a group of about twenty color guard members. That presents a dilemma. I can either walk around them or through them. Maybe if I walk right through the middle of the whirlwind of spinning flags and tossed rifles, I'll catch one to the head and be knocked unconscious. I decide to take my chances with the color guard.

Yeah, that would be nice. I can hear it now. "Breaking

News: Local teen musician, Rigby Raines, was knocked out in a freak rifle tossing incident in which she also successfully avoided confrontation with her nemesis, the self-proclaimed band queen, Taura Jacobs. More details at eleven. Let's go on scene to our roving reporter Brian for a fun story about kittens."

6

I MAKE MY way without incident through the gauntlet of the color guard to where the trumpet section is gathered. No concussions from spinning rifles and I wasn't impaled by a falling flag of doom. The trumpets are just finishing a warm-up of long slow notes.

Taura is standing there with her arms up and eyes closed as she conducts the last few long swells. I can't help but think that she looks like one of those big wacky inflatable balloon men you see at a car dealership, arms flailing everywhere.

With the dramatic flair of a muppet, she cuts off the last note and stays frozen there as if the end of the warm-up is the end of a famous orchestral performance of some epic symphony. She's really so full of herself. But then again, Mr. Z thinks she's something, I guess, or else she wouldn't be the trumpet section leader.

I clear my throat softly, hoping not to shock her out of whatever trippy zone she's in. Maybe she'll at least open her eyes as I approach.

"Uh, hey, Taura. I'm sorry I'm late." I feel like I'm standing in front of a firing squad. "My alar..."

"Can it, Raines." She snaps, eyes still closed. "Nobody cares about your irresponsibility."

"But, I..." The words come out in a jumble. "I...I didn't mean to..."

"RIG-BY!" She cuts me off again. She must have eyes in the back of her head. "Gah! Just shut up and get in line. I don't care about your stupid excuses."

I take my place next to Kayla, the spit valve girl. I think about telling her she needs to empty it, but that would probably just be rude. Besides, Taura is the one who is coming down hard on me, not Kayla.

Taura calls us to attention. "Trumpets...ten-HUT!"

We all snap sharply and rigidly into formation, being careful to position our elbows just right. I'm holding my horn at the perfect height.

"Ladies and gentlemen..." Taura walks behind us. I can't see her face, but just by hearing her snarky voice I can tell she's got a smug smirk on her face. "It looks like we're going to need to tighten up some weak links in our section this year."

Although my eyes are facing straight forward, I can feel her arrogant sneer burning into the back of my head.

"For whatever reason," she hisses, "it appears to me that this section needs more discipline. See, when one person is late, ALL of our time is wasted. When one person disregards the rules, we all suffer the consequences."

Oh, crap. I do not like where this is going.

"Trumpets, you know that next year I'm going to be drum major. It's pretty much a guarantee," she continues. "For now, though, I'm stuck with you. And because I'm devoted to making this band the best band in the state, I want you to know that I'm going to be hard on you day in, and day out."

She walks around the end of the line, making her way to the front again. I'm trying my best not to lock eyes with her. One thing about Taura that is actually positive is that she really is committed to being the best. Sometimes I think she doesn't realize how harsh that makes her come across to others.

"I'm running a tight ship here, and we'll all be the better for it." She stops directly in front of me.

"Trumpets!" she shouts in her best drill sergeant voice. "Who was late this morning?" It sounds more like an angry mom yelling at an umpire at a little league baseball game. You know the one, the mother who goes ballistic when her kid that she thinks is safe is called out.

"RIGBY!" the trumpets offer loudly in unison.

"That's right," she says sternly. "Rigby Raines. How many push-ups does she owe me?"

Nobody says anything. On the very first day of band camp, she laid out all her ground rules - 10 push-ups for every minute that somebody is late. We all thought she was joking with us. She wasn't.

"Taura...uh..." I can't seem to think in complete sentences at the moment. "I...I think I was only about 20 minutes late this morning..."

My heart begins to pound faster, and my palms get clammy with nervous sweat.

"Twenty-three minutes, by my watch," she jabs mockingly. "That's two hundred and thirty push ups that you owe me, Raines." She's dead serious.

I clench my jaw. I'm trying to look tough, but inside I feel like a scared puppy. I take three steps forward until I'm looking her square in the eyes. For a split second, I think that I could just head butt her right here and now and run into the woods on the other side of the practice field. She knows I'm thinking about it. She squints her eyes and stares back at me with a gaze that could freeze hell. She takes a step forward, and we're nose to nose.

I'm not really a fighter, so I look down. I wasn't really ever going to throw down on her anyways. I would probably faint if I ever actually got into a real fight. I just wish she'd just leave me alone. I take two steps to the right and drop down on the grass to begin my push-ups.

"One...Two..."

My arms are already burning. Chewie had tried to get me to work out with him over the summer. He and his dad had been going to some new gym across town where they flipped tires, swung kettlebells and threw around medicine balls. It sounded awful. Now, I wish I'd taken him up on the offer, because THIS, this is awful.

"Three."

My whole body is trembling as I try to push up off the ground to get a fourth push-up done. I hear a few snickers from the trumpets. A few people are actually trying not to laugh out loud. Taura ignores them.

"Oh, Raines?" Taura's mocking sing-songy voice stabs through my embarrassing push-up torture, and I collapse onto the ground. "I think you misunderstood me."

What is she talking about?

She kneels down and hovers over me like a vulture about to tear apart its dinner.

"I said 'When one person disregards the rules, we all suffer the consequences,'" she actually uses quote fingers when she quotes herself.

Son of a biscuit...

"Thank you, Raines," she snarls smugly, "for those four beautifully lame, but oh-so-amusing, push-up attempts. But, because of you, EVERYONE is doing push-ups this morning. Trumpets, assume the high plank position!"

Everyone groans and looks at me as they set their instruments down in front of them. Each person begrudgingly walks their feet back into the plank position. Taura hasn't taken her eyes off of me. I just want to dig a hole and bury my head under the grass.

It's not enough that she hates me, now she's going to turn everyone else in the section against me.

"Two hundred and thirty push-ups divided by thirteen trumpets is about seventeen per person," Taura calculates out loud. "But, since I like round numbers, let's round it up to twenty per person."

"Rigby. On your feet," she barks. "I want YOU to count them out. Begin!"

"One."

I hate this.

"Two." Twenty push-ups aren't enough to kill anybody,

but just enough to get everyone pissed off for the day.

"Three. Four"

"Five."

Taura stands there looking smug, pleased with herself as the section muscles out another few pushups. She's the only one enjoying this.

"Six. Seven. Eight. Nine."

"Ten."

Everyone except Reggie, the Harry Potter guy, is starting to struggle. He's like a machine. I would have never guessed that.

"Eleven. Twelve. Thirteen. Fourteen."

"Fifteen. I'm sorry, guys," I offer sincerely.

After five more push-ups, there is an audible grumble that moves through the trumpet section. I want to crawl in a hole. It's bad enough that I have trouble enough making friends as is. If they only knew the real me, not the stuttering, shy idiot that shows up whenever I'm in front of people maybe I'd have more friends.

Now, my own section literally hates me.

7

I AM CRUSHED.

All I really want to do is just play my part and make some good music. I'm not trying to rock the boat or make enemies here. But Taura is making it impossible for me. I can't even imagine what band would be like if SHE were the drum major.

Probably like the Apocalypse. Death and destruction raining down on everyone.

It's been a few hours since the push-ups. I've been hoping the trumpet section would forget about it. No such luck. Everyone seems to be turning a cold shoulder to me.

After a long morning of marching and working on our show drill, our drum major, Ellis, calls out through his megaphone that it's time for indoor music rehearsal. He is a senior who really knows his stuff. He's actually one of the coolest people in the marching band. This summer he marched with a drum corps called Carolina Crown. Their show theme was truly phenomenal.

He is always the life of the party. Of course, I haven't really ever worked up the nerve to have a conversation with him. Maybe one day before he graduates and heads off to college I'll work up the courage to say hey to him. Last year, I stood off in a corner of the band room while he showed a few of the trumpets how to dance the Lindy Hop. It's a cool form of swing dancing that my two left feet are definitely too uncoordinated to learn. It's times like that when I wish I was more outgoing. Instead I usually just hang off to the side watching everyone else have fun.

Everyone starts gathering their belongings from the sidelines. We'll head in for an hour or so and then break for a late lunch. Like a big herd of buffalo, we start rumbling towards the school buildings. The band room is just on the other side of the parking lot.

Chewie walks up with a bounce in his step. I don't understand how after a long morning in the sun he still has the energy to skip around like he does. And that's while he's still carrying his heavy sousaphone.

I'm not really feeling up to company at the moment. I can't get the push-up scene out of my head. Maybe I'm over-reacting, but I can't help but feel like everyone in the section is aggravated with me. I really just want some space to walk across the field alone, but I can see that's probably not going to happen.

"Hey, Rigs." It sounds more like a song than a greeting.

"Hey, Chew. What's up?"

"I saw your section doing push-ups earlier," he says with an inflection that makes it sound more like a question. "What happened?"

"I really don't want to talk about it right now."

"Aww, come on Rigs," he says with a goofy smile on his face. The way he's tilting his head to the side makes him look like a big goober.

But he's still kind of cute.

What was that? Did Chewie just look *cute* to me? Of course not, he's like my brother...my best friend.

"Not now, Chew," I stew moodily.

He walks behind me and starts to play a bouncy tuba march in time with my feet as I'm walking.

Seriously!?

I stop in my tracks. I turn around to give him a death stare. He immediately stops and smiles at me like some kind of weirdo.

"CHEW! I will literally hurt you."

As soon as I start walking again, he picks the tune back up and makes it even more bouncy and obnoxious. Over in the parking lot, a shiny black car rolls slowly through the rows of cars. It's really nice. Blacked out windows and rims. Something seems familiar about it, but I can't put my finger on it...

Oh my gosh, Chew!

"Chew-ie!" I snap. "What part of 'I will hurt you' are you not processing?"

Although it's annoying, his friendship feels like a warm blanket that wraps around me when my world is most cold and lonely. I can't stay annoyed at him for long. I can't help but love Chew. He's always cheering me up. He goes out of his way to see me happy.

I glance back quickly to the parking lot. The blacked-out car is nowhere to be seen.

That's odd.

I turn around, my back to Chewie, for the third time.

But a sneaky glance over my shoulder and I can see him move his face back to the mouthpiece. I look down at my feet quickly so he won't see me trying not to smile.

Chewie resumes my walking soundtrack as we head toward the school. He follows me a hundred yards to the band room playing that silly tune. The whole way there I'm doing everything I can to keep from smiling.

8

THE BAND ROOM buzzes like a noisy beehive. People are finding seats in their sections. The woodwinds take their places up front. The brass files in behind. The drum line occupies the space behind everyone. They've set up their drums on stationary stands, so they don't have to wear harnesses inside.

Some folks are playing. I can make out A Hard Day's Night, Yesterday, and of course, Eleanor Rigby. I guess they are making one last attempt to get the show music memorized before Mr. Z goes section by section and checks to see if everyone has learned their parts.

My worst nightmare.

I walk sideways to my spot at the end of the trumpet row. I feel like I'm walking on a tightrope. If I lose my balance, I might stumble and land in someone's lap.

Last chair, third trumpet. It's lonely down here by the baritones and trombones. I like it, though. No pressure to perform. Sometimes I wonder if I disappeared would anyone even notice? Don't get me wrong, I love contributing my part. In fact, I'm not sure I could physically ever handle playing way up in the first trumpets during a concert or half-time show. I think my anxiety would get the best of me.

Taura and all the first trumpet elites sit all the way at the other end of the trumpet row. Carlos and Jason are down there playing Paper-Rock-Scissors. Kayla is actually emptying her spit valve at this very moment. I wouldn't believe it if I didn't see it with my own two eyes. I look down the row past her and notice that Taura has taken her seat in the first chair seat. She stares at me with a menacing look on her face.

Whoa! Wasn't expecting that!

I turn away instinctively and realize that I probably look like the biggest doof in the world. I slowly turn back and make a casual gesture with my arms as if I'm stretching. Maybe I can sneak a peek and see if Taura is still giving me her infamous stank eye. Maybe I'm just imagining things. I just want to make sure I'm seeing what I think I'm seeing.

Sure enough, if eyes were guns and stares were bullets, Taura would be committing a world-class drive-by right now. She's staring holes through me.

Crap.

I look down quickly, fidgeting with my valves and tuning slides. I left my trumpet case in my trunk, so I pull out a mini bottle of valve oil that I keep in my handy belt pack and start reading the label. Hmm. It says "Mineral Oil." Good to know.

Aaaand, there's nothing else to read.

A slight panic settles over me. My heart starts beating faster. Taura really gets under my skin. I just want to go home. I want to be on my roof, in the moonlight, listening to Beethoven and texting Chew. I'd give anything to be home at the piano sitting next to Mom playing Hey Jude. I want to be anywhere but sitting here as the band room starts feeling smaller and smaller.

Mom. Why now?

A low rumble from outside signals the possibility of another summer storm. Thunder. It sounds angry, like random rolls on the timpani. It's unpredictable. Slowly, one by one, drop by drop, rain starts falling. The roof is metal, so it's loud. It builds in intensity, and I close my eyes. I'm trying my best not to freak out in front of everyone. I fight back tears, but as the sound of rain crescendos, so does the pain.

Of all the times I could have a panic attack, why does it have to be here and now? I'm surrounded by a ton of people when all that I really want is to be by myself. I need space. The room is closing in on me. And Taura is at the end of the row killing me softly with her gaze of doom. The silver lining is that at least she looks funny with her black eyes from the water bottle incident.

I try to find solace in the humor of her looking like a raccoon, but even thinking about that isn't holding back my emotions. It isn't working. I pick up my folder and flip through my music, but I don't really see anything. My eyes are watering, and everything is getting blurry. I can literally hear my heart pounding in my ears. I can't breathe. I need fresh air. I need to leave.

That's it, I can't do this. I'm leaving now...

Tap. Tap. Tap. The sharp sound snaps me out of it. Mr.

Z taps his conductor's baton on the music stand at the front of the band room.

"Ladies and gentlemen," Mr. Z says from the podium, calling everyone's attention to the front. "Before we get started I've got a few announcements to make."

The chaotic din of the room dies down as each section settles down. Instruments are resting in laps and eyes are forward now.

"First of all, I'd like to say a big thank you to everyone in this room today for all your hard work."

Focus on Mr. Z, Rigs. Focus.

I can feel my heartbeat slowing down. The world around me begins to stop swirling. Mr. Z's voice has a calming, in-control effect on me.

"...last week was a great start," He continues. "I'm excited about this morning's work on the field. We're making great progress. After lunch today, we'll head back out and hit it hard some more."

Everyone shuffles in their seats. The band seems to kind of buzz for a few seconds as people make comments to the person next to them.

"Listen up," his voice commands respect.

You can tell just by listening to him that he loves being a band director. He loves the students, the music, and the halftime show.

"I want to have all four songs plus the percussion feature on the field by Friday and you guys are working hard to make that happen. Great job, everybody."

The band erupts into a boisterous clamor as everyone shares their thoughts with the person next to them. With over one hundred people in our band, Mr. Z has learned to allow a few seconds of these outbursts before he tightens the line back up.

Tap. Tap. Tap.

Mr. Z reels everyone back in again, and it hits me that right now I feel normal. No panic attack. No freakout. I am feeling normal again.

Thank you, Mr. Z.

As the room falls silent again, he is about to say something, but he pauses for a second. He's gathering his thoughts. It takes longer than usual.

"Folks, I've got a very hard announcement to make right now." He's rubbing his left temple as if he has a headache. "Ellis, would you please join me up here."

Ellis walks slowly but confidently up to the front. He looks strangely unhappy. Too serious. Something is up.

I look over at Chewie across the room. He shrugs his shoulders and mouths the words, "I don't have a clue."

"This weekend we got word that Ellis and his family are moving all the way across the country. His dad got a new job. Sometimes things like this come out of nowhere. Although it will be a new adventure for him, we're sure going to miss him."

Ellis looks like he's fighting back tears, but he holds it together. He nods silently.

"Because this is so sudden, and something we weren't

prepared for, it is a huge shock." Mr. Z is visibly upset, but trying to keep things smooth for the band.

I wonder if he knew this morning when I showed up late. Of course. He had to have known. Maybe that's why he didn't look up from the drill clipboard.

"So, as you all know, this leaves us with very big shoes to fill. We'll need to pass the torch on to a new drum major. Ellis will be with us through this week, and then he and his family will be on a plane to the West Coast."

The room is entirely silent except for the sound of rain on the roof.

I'm stunned at this news. I don't know what to think. I guess I'll never get to know Ellis as well as I thought I might could have. But even more so, it begins to dawn on me that the drum major position is now open. Like, this year, right now, open.

Holy tryouts, Batman!

As Mr. Z continues to explain the details, my mind is a blur. A tryout for replacement drum major will be held this coming Friday. That's four days from now.

FOUR DAYS, PEOPLE!

There's a small part of me leaping for joy. This is my chance. I can do this. It's time to step up and make Mom proud. This is the opportunity I've been waiting for.

No. There is absolutely no way.

And then she shows up. The other part of me, the sad and dark part. The one that speaks loudest most of the time. Who am I kidding? Taura is a shoo-in for drum major. Why do we even need to have tryouts? Why am I even getting my hopes up?

I sit silently. I'm overwhelmed and speechless. I feel like I've just been hit by a ton of bricks. Why is life so unfair? I just wanted a year where I could exist in band without Taura being the actual drum major. I can't even imagine how bad it's going to be when she's drum major. And that is going to start a lot sooner than I had hoped.

9

ON HER FACE, Taura has the most self-satisfied smile I've ever seen. She just can't help herself. She knows that she's the most likely replacement for Ellis. At least, in her mind, and maybe everyone else's mind, she's the one, the clear choice, the perfect candidate.

She's got this far off look in her eyes like she's in the best part of a great daydream. She probably imagines herself in a drum major uniform. She's standing tall on the podium, arms outstretched as she conducts the band with some sort of phenomenal cosmic power. She likes to think of herself as a high and mighty musical deity bringing goodwill and cheer to all of us underlings on the field. She is large and in charge.

Wait, a minute.

I snap out of it with a chuckle, realizing that I'm just projecting my disdain for her into that little daydream. She's probably not that bad, right? I mean, Taura has to have at least one decent bone in her body, doesn't she?

I shake my head to focus and realize she's staring at me again. Her left eyebrow is cocked, and she's got this I-told-you-so kind of a look on her face. This time, it's not just smugness in her look. She's rubbing it in. That smile on her face is saying, "Don't even think about it, Loser."

Gah, that arrogance...there ISN'T a decent bone in her pretentious body.

She knows that this development isn't making me happy. In fact, I can see in her smug smile that it's making her happy to know that I am struggling.

I don't think I'm anywhere near her level when it comes to potentially leading the band, but her rubbing it in my face like this makes me want to at least sign up for the tryout. Admittedly, she probably IS the best candidate to replace Ellis. But, dang, I always had hoped she would just move away. Why does Ellis, the best drum major ever, have to be the one whose family has to pack up and move all the way across the country?

I gather my things and stand up. The band is kind of milling around getting ready to head to lunch. A few people are just talking, but just about everyone wants to go up front where Ellis is and speak to him. It's the right thing to do. He's getting a lot of hugs and high fives.

"RIGATONI!" Chewie seems to materialize out of thin air behind me.

"Chewie! Gah! Don't do that!"

"Can you believe it?" he asks excitedly. "What do you think about all this?"

Chewie knows just about everything about me. Our late night conversations over the last year have made us pretty close. I don't know how I'd have made it through this without him. He's always there for me.

Of course, I've held a lot back. He knows that I struggle with my shyness and anxiety in sticky situations. We've talked about my hard times dealing with losing Mom. But,

I don't think he realizes how much I want this drum major position. I don't know if I've ever even mentioned it to him.

"Rigs!" he exclaims. "This is YOUR chance!"

How does he do that?!

He *DOES* know. He really knows me. He must be like my long lost twin or something. This connection is starting to weird me out.

Now's not the time, Rigby. Note to self: think about Chewie later.

"I may be overstepping here, but I'm pretty sure this is like divine invention or something," he says.

"Intervention, Chewie." I can't help but smile at his slaying of basic English. "It's intervention."

"Whatever, Rigs! That's beside the point!" he continues. "This is destiny!"

"You're out of your mind, Chew." I'm resigned to my fate. "I'm pretty sure I could never make it past the interview round of tryouts."

Man, do I really sound like that? Am I actually that unsure of myself?

"Girl, you've got this. Believe me." Something in his eyes catches me off guard.

I can't breathe for a second. It's like he sees into my mind. How is it that this goofy best friend of mine is reading my mail? What does he see in me? For the last year, I've been nothing but dark and withdrawn. Hardly a good friend. I barely let him in. And yet here he is standing by me when I can't even believe in myself.

"You can do this, Rigby," he says.

"I don't know, Chew." I really want to so bad. But I don't know if I could stand up to Taura like that.

"You. Can. Do. This." He says again with his hands on my shoulders.

I. Can. Do. This.

It sounds good in my head. I can do this. Maybe I can. I *AM* my mom's daughter. I am a great musician, even if nobody else knows it. I can stand up to Taura. I can do this audition. Heck, maybe I can even win it.

"You're right, Chewie. If I don't go for it now, I probably won't have another opportunity. It has to be here and now."

He's smiling. I'm feeling a weird flutter inside my abdomen. I'm not sure if I'm about to throw up. I think it's nervousness, but it feels a little different. This might actually be excitement stirring inside me.

I need to take action, so I decide to go and talk to Ellis right now. It's my "first step." Mom always used to say that it was the first steps of the journey that were the hardest. It's so true. And it's those first steps that will lead to the second steps.

I set my trumpet down in my seat making sure to place it just right, so it doesn't slide and scratch the bell. I head to the front to speak to Ellis. I have no clue what to say to him, but I'm determined to say something.

Chewie is tagging along behind me. I take the long way around the band room to avoid Taura. Out of the corner of my eye, I can see she's still sneering at me.

She's so going down.

"Hi, Ellis." I'm a nervous wreck. "I'm Rigby."

"Hey Rigby, I know who you are." He's cool, and collected, but serious after the big announcement. "You have the best red hair in the band."

"Ha, for real?" My cheeks are getting hot, and I'm sure my face is starting to look like a big strawberry. "I hate that you've got to move so far away like this."

"Me, too." He's probably already heard this and responded a hundred times in the last few minutes.

"Hey man, I hate to see you go," Chew interjects.

"Thanks, bud."

CLANG.

The sound of metal hitting metal and then the floor brings the whole room to a silent pause. He looks up and around us sharply. Something in the back of the band room has got his attention.

I turn to see Taura, getting up clumsily from the floor. She looks over at me. For a fraction of a second, she still has that smug look on her face, but it quickly turns into what looks like feigned shock.

"Oh, my God, Rigby!" she exclaims. "I'm SO sorry!"

What's going on?

"I didn't see your trumpet sitting there on the chair. I was trying to get around all the chairs to go to my locker. I must've bumped your seat and then the trumpet just fell out of the seat, and before I knew it I tripped trying to catch it, but I accidentally stepped on it..."

"Wait, what!?" My world seems to be caving in on me again. "I don't understand..."

She picks up the mangled metal mass of tubes that used to be my mom's trumpet. It's destroyed. Literally destroyed. There's no way that this was an accident. She had to have knocked it out of the seat and then stomped on it intentionally. I can't believe it.

I knew she would be gunning for me after the water bottle incident, but I had no clue she would stoop this low. I can feel a lump in my throat as I run to the back of the room to grab my trumpet out of her hands. I think my heart is literally breaking.

"Give that to me!" the words spill out in a sob. "Get your hands off of it."

How could this be happening? Why is this happening? What did I do to deserve all this?

I don't understand how anyone could be so cruel. After everything that has happened today, my heart can't take any more. In some strange way, I feel like this trumpet is my only connection to my mom, and now it's destroyed.

"I know you did this on purpose!" I say through clenched teeth, as tears fill my eyes.

"Rigby," she says in manufactured shock. "I am appalled that you would even think that. It was totally an accident."

Ellis and Chewie are beside me. Chew puts his hand on my right shoulder.

"Rigby. This is...This is crazy. What's going on?"

"Taura," Ellis inquires. "What happened here?"

As Taura goes on to explain her version of what she calls an *accident,* my world starts to spin again. I can't catch my breath. Everything seems to be a blur. I tune everything out. There's nothing she can say that would convince me that this was not intentional. I know that she did it on purpose.

I collapse to the floor with this busted heap of metal, my trumpet, Juliet's trumpet, pressed to my chest. I give up. She's done it. She has beaten me. This hits me where it hurts the most and she knows it. All I want to do is just lay here and cry. I just want my mom, and this instrument, this sad, shattered mess of a trumpet is really all that I have left of her.

10

"Tick...Tick...Tick..."

A tiny clicking cadence sounds from somewhere on the edge of my hearing. The sound ticks in a constant rhythm, like a far away drummer counting off a song that never starts. It just keeps ticking.

The last three hours have been a blur. I'm fading back into awareness. My vision is blurry, and my chest hurts from crying. I'm sitting in Mr. Z's office while the rest of the band is out on the practice field. Chewie says that I was an incoherent babbling mess for about thirty minutes.

Why wouldn't I be? The trumpet that Taura destroyed was basically the only real connection I have left with my mother. I'm not even sure how she did it. Nobody really saw anything. By the time I had worked up enough courage to go up front and say something to Ellis, most everyone had already come by and given him a hug. That just left Chewie and me, and of course, Taura in the band room.

"Tick...Tick...Tick..."

What is that ticking sound? And where in the world is it coming from?

Chew and Ellis tried to convince Mr. Z that Taura had intentionally knocked the trumpet over. But since they hadn't actually seen what happened, they couldn't definitively say that she had done it on purpose. Taura protested passionately. Her faux horror and fake apologies were enough to convince Mr. Z that he couldn't really be sure what had happened.

I couldn't believe it. I'm still sitting here literally not believing it. This is one of those situations where I can almost justify saying the words "I can't even." Chewie says it all the time, and I punch him in the arm every time he uses that phrase.

You can't even what?!

After Mr. Z had looked my trumpet over closely, he determined that there probably wasn't much hope for any sort of repair work. It is absolutely demolished. He said that it would probably cost more to fix it than it would to find a decent replacement.

I already knew it, though. As soon as I saw that mangled mess of metal, I knew that I'd never play it again. And that's why I collapsed. That's why my heart broke. That's why everything just went dark.

"Tick...Tick...Tick..."

The constant click of that little drummer is getting louder and louder. It feels like it is now in the room with me. I'm not sure what is making the sound.

I wish that I had dropkicked Taura in the head. Heck, I'd even be happy if I had slapped that smug smirk off her face. She had only flashed that self-confident look for a split second before becoming the most remorseful human in history of the world.

I can't actually remember how many times she said: "I'm so sorry." Chew says it was a hundred or so. There are not enough apologies in the whole universe to make up for what she did.

"Tick..."

I swear if I find whatever is causing that sound, I'm going to smash it into oblivion.

There's an empty cheeseburger wrapper, and a half finished tiny container of fries next to me on the couch. I think Chew brought me this kids meal when he came back from lunch. I haven't ever been in Mr. Z's office. I just peeked in every so often while passing by. It kind of feels like a secret place where only the marching and concert band elite gather. It's like the holy of holies or something... but in a musical sense.

So, now I'm just sitting here looking at my feet. Anger. Sorrow. Confusion. Defeat. All of these feelings are scratching at my heart and mind right now. I can't focus. I feel like I've lost so much.

The weird thing, though, is I don't really want to think about it right now. I don't want to be sad. I don't want to miss my mom so much. I don't want to grieve. I don't want to have to deal with all that emotional pain. I don't want to...and nobody's been able to make me.

Why?

Because that means I have to admit that she's gone. For real gone. It means I have to let go of her. And I don't want to lose her. Even after a year, there's a part of me that is still waiting for her to come home from the hospital. Like it was all some bad dream. I mean, she's my mom.

My mom.

"Tick...Tick...Tick..."

The ticking is close, coming from above and behind me. I realize it's coming from the wall.

The clock, Rigby. It's the clock.

I chuckle at myself. I rub the back of my neck with my left hand and my temples with my right hand. I have a headache from all the crying earlier.

Suddenly, the bell rings. It's not really a bell, though. It's a loud digital tone that blares through the school's hallways to signal the changing of classes. Well, if classes were in session that's what it would do. I have no clue why it just sounded. Classes are not even in session until next week. Nobody's even here.

It's enough to jolt me out of my haze.

"Miss Rigby?" A deep, gravelly voice from across the room scares the crap out of me. "Miss Rigby Raines?"

"Ahh!" I scream. "Whoa, dude, you sacred the...well, you really scared me."

An old man is standing in the doorway. He's leaning a little to the left like he's tired of standing. His hands are behind his back. It's almost like he's standing at parade rest, but gravity or old age won't let him stand up straight.

His dark green work coveralls are covered in grease stains and paint splatters. He looks like all the other maintenance crew members I've seen around the school, except I've never seen him before.

He's got an old, faded red Georgia Bulldogs cap on, but

I can see that his hair is white. The front edges of the bill are worn and frayed. It matches his face perfectly, though. He looks like he's been around a long time. His skin is leathery and wrinkled, the years showing in crows feet and laugh lines.

His old brown eyes are intense, and something about them makes me feel safe. They have a twinkle in them that you don't see in young people's eyes. He has a lot of what I've heard older people call crow's feet around his eyes. I bet he's seen a ton of stuff around here.

"Uh, can I help you?" I ask nervously.

He smiles a big toothy grin. Except he's missing one of his upper front teeth. If I had to guess, I'd say he was in his late eighties, maybe even nineties. But something about his smile makes him seem like a much younger man.

"Time will tell, Rigby Raines," he answers happily with a seasoned, rolling southern accent. "Time will tell."

"Umm. Oookay?"

I'm trying not to be rude, but I don't even know what that means. The last thing I need right now is to be sitting here with a complete stranger trying to figure out senior citizen riddles. I'm not even sure what he's doing here.

"I'm sorry, sir." My voice cracks. "Do you need to see Mr. Z? I'm waiting for him to get back and help me with my instrument."

Mr. Z needed to get the band out on the field and into hard work mode before he could come back in and deal with my situation. He apologized to me but said he'd be back in as soon as he could.

I crack every single knuckle on both hands. It's a nervous habit that I've been trying for years to kick. So far, I've not had any luck.

"You mean this instrument?" He says, holding up Juliet's trumpet, my baby.

It caught me off guard for a split second because I wasn't even sure where it was. I lost track of it when I kind of blacked out.

But, there it was. So sad. Still destroyed. Still mangled. And still reminding me that Taura had beaten me before we ever even made it to tryouts.

"Hey, that's mine!" I blurt angrily. "What are you doing with it?"

"Miss Rigby," he says gently. "I'm here to help YOU."

He shuffle-walks over to the chair in the corner and attempts to sit down. I'm not sure if I should try to lend a hand or not. He lets out a triumphant sigh as he plops down into the seat.

"Help ME?" I inquire.

"You've been down for a while, and I'm here to help you get your feet back on the ground," his words bounce like the lyrics of a song.

More riddle talk. But such familiar riddle talk.

"See now, I was sent to make sure that you got the right replacement for this poor trumpet." He's holding up the smashed trumpet.

This old man is both creepy and reassuring at the same

time. Creepy because I have no idea who he is or what he wants. Reassuring in some strange way because I feel like he could be my grandfather.

"Who are you?" I ask.

"My name is McKenzie." He says with dancing eyes. "Pops McKenzie."

11

"FOLLOW ME, MISS Rigby." Pops teeters and wobbles as he struggles to get up. "I've got something important I want to show you."

"Okay." I get up and follow him out of Mr. Z's office.

He shuffles slowly across the band room. What started out as a big formation of neat rows of black plastic chairs in a large semi-circle, is now scattered and unorganized. When the band leaves the room, it's like a stampede.

Because the doors are open, we hear that the band is running through show music now. The driving rhythms of A Hard Day's Night are filtering in through the doors. As terrible as this day has been already, I really wish I was out on the field making music with the band.

I wonder what happened to Mr. Z. I guess he sent this old dude to help me find a replacement trumpet. Part of me just wants to go home and be done with all this, but there's a tiny little voice in the back of my mind that knows that if I just leave, then Taura will get the last laugh. And as hard as it is to swallow, I just can't give up so easily.

We exit the band room through the double doors that lead into the school hallway. There's a part of me that's wary. I know you're not supposed to just randomly go with strangers, but I'm pretty sure I could walk away from this old timer if I need to. I'm following about five steps behind Pops. He's not setting any land speed records.

I think I trust him. I don't know why. Even so, I start thinking about how to leave a message to my loved ones.

If something happens to me tell Chew that...

It suddenly hits me. Chewie? Charles. Why is *HE* the first person that I think of in this situation? What's that all about? We've been such good buddies for such a long time. Like, really good friends, nothing more.

Something is different this year, though. His eyes. There's something about his eyes. And that goofy smile. There's something in the way he smiles that makes me just pause. I mean, I'm not saying that I'm in love with him or anything. That would be weird.

I literally love Chewie like a brother. He is totally my best bud.

If you asked me if anything was growing there between us, I'd say I don't know.

I really don't know.

But now, in this moment, it seems like there's something in me that just wants to be with him. Maybe I'm losing my mind.

Gah! What the heck! This is so weird!

Pops is humming a tune that I can't really make out. He's moving slower than molasses as we make a left and head down past the cafeteria doors. At the end of the hallway, we head out into a courtyard that is pretty much off limits to students. Across the small concrete space, there is an old rusty door. Nobody really knows what's behind it.

It's just known as "the red door."

I've never seen anyone come out of it or go into it. It's not marked by a number, so it's not a classroom. It's not marked maintenance, so it's not a custodian's closet. I never really thought about it until now, but a wave of anxiety washes over me as it becomes apparent that's where we're headed.

"Hey, Pops?" I ask anxiously. "Where are we going?"

"Time will tell, Rigby," he answers. "Time will tell."

Ok, now I'm officially starting to freak out.

"Uhh, You said that before, Pops." I'm not sure I want to find out what's behind that mysterious door.

I can hear it now. "Breaking news tonight. Rigby Raines, local teen musician, and resident high school idiot was never heard from again after she followed a complete stranger that she had only just met minutes before into a mysterious portal that leads to who knows where. More details at eleven. How's the weather, Brick?"

Pops looks at me with those kind old eyes and I see a genuine concern. His half smile is reassuring, but I'm not sure I want to be reassured right now. He pulls out his keys and begins to unlock the door.

"Miss Rigby," his voice is full of care. "I ain't ever gonna hurt you. I'm here to help you. When I was young like you, I never needed anybody's help in any way."

Wait, is he quoting the Beatles right now? I'm pretty sure that's a Beatles song.

"Uh, ok." I'm not sure where all this riddle talk is

leading. "What's in that room?"

"When I was your age, Miss Rigby, I could wail with the best of 'em." He's got this far off look in his eyes. "I've got something I want to show you."

He pulls the door open and looks back at me.

"A trumpet? For me?"

"Rigby, you've got to be patient. Time will..."

"Ughhh!" I let out an exasperated sigh. "Oh, I'm sorry, I didn't mean to do that out loud! You keep saying that!"

We both laugh out loud. His eyes are twinkling. He laughs a hearty, throaty laugh that makes his eyes water. It makes me smile.

12

POPS TURNS AND holds the door open for me like a kind, old gentlemen. I take a step toward the door.

Here we go.

As I walk into the doorway, a rush of cold, dank air hits me. It smells like something old. It's dark. I can't really see anything, so I pause after two steps.

Pops shuffles in and hits a switch. It takes a few seconds, but after a few flickers and a dangerous sounding hum, the room is lit up by a crisscrossing strand of what looks like patio lights with round bulbs. They give off a yellow glow. It makes the room look like an old photo.

There are floor to ceiling shelves against the left and right walls. Each level is stacked high with all kinds of boxes and instrument cases. Guitar cases. Drum cases. Wind instrument cases. There are probably a hundred instruments crammed on those shelves.

"Wow, Pops."

As my eye adjust, I see that this is not just a storage room. There's a cot, made up neatly, on the far wall next to a sink and a mirror. This is actually someone's living space.

"Pops, do you live here?" I turn to face him.

He's humming again.

"I live wherever I am at the moment, Miss Righy," he offers warmly.

More riddles.

"Do you sleep here, I mean?"

He has that far off look in his eyes again. The lighting makes him look much younger as he smiles.

"I take a load off here, ev'ry now and again."

He rubs his hands, the thumb of one hand in the palm of the other, the other four fingers holding the backside of his hand. It reminds me of my grandfather's constant arthritis flare-ups.

"Here, now," Pops says with a determined smile. "I think it's somewhere in here."

His shuffle is less pronounced, and it actually seems that he has a bounce in his step as he walks over to a shelf housing a bunch of smaller instrument cases. There are so many of them.

"I believe this is the spot where I left it," he says with a furrowed brow.

He looks up and down the shelf, scanning from top to bottom and left to right.

"No, no. That's not it." He's searching for something specific. "It's gotta be up in here somewhere."

I glance to my right and notice a picture hanging on the wall over the cot. It's a black and white photo, so it's old. It's a young man in a military marching band uniform. I step closer for a better look.

"Oh, that's me, Miss Rigby," he exclaims without even looking over. "I must've been 'bout your age."

In the picture, he's holding a trumpet under his arm. He's smiling that same really big toothy grin, and I can see the same twinkle in those same big brown eyes, just on a much younger face.

"Pops, you're a trumpet player?"

There's a dusty hourglass on the back of the sink. It looks like the kind you find in board games, but it's bigger and made out of brass and glass.

"Oh, not so much no more." He suddenly seems sad. "'Bout twenty years ago I came to realize that I couldn't push my air anymore. Had to give it up."

"Oh, no. What happened?"

"Well, Miss Rigby," he chuckles, "that's what happens when you go and get old like me."

Oh, no, Rigby! Go ahead and just start chewing on your foot right now.

"Aww, Pops!" I'm embarrassed. "I didn't mean to pry!"

"It's all about time, Rigby." He's shaking his head and seems to be more serious now. "Time."

All this stuff about time!? I'm not sure I get it.

I'm wondering if he's trying to teach me some sort of weird sensei lesson. He's the master, and I'm like Rigby-san, the "grasshoppa" apprentice. This is so weird.

"AH! Hotdang!" He dances a little jig as he pulls out the most raggedy looking case I've ever seen. "Knew it was over here somewhere."

He carries it with both hands. The handle is broken. It's only attached on one side. It's old. Leather. It's so worn. Pieces of leather are just hanging off of it. The corners are old tarnished brass. There used to be some sort of badge on it, but there's only an oval where it used to be.

Pops gently sets the case on the bed and then just stares at it for what seems like an eternity.

Open it, open it!

"Miss Rigby," he says with both hands clasped in front of his lips as if in prayer. "This is MY baby. Over the years, we've been through thick and thin."

"Can I see it?"

"Whether you see it, will be up to you," he says seriously. "Like I said, time will tell."

Oh. My. God.

"Time will tell?" I can't seem to get past that with this man. "Time will tell WHAT?"

"Yes, time. It will tell you when you can see it." He seems to be lost in thought. "You'll know when it's time."

I'm pretty sure if he says 'time' again my brain is going to explode.

He reaches slowly to unlock the clasps, first the left side, then the right side. Each one snaps open with a pop. He places his hands on either side of the case and slowly opens the top.

I can't see the trumpet because there is a velvety red fold down flap covering the instrument. The smell of brass and plush velour hits me. It's a smell I'll never get tired of. Mom's trumpet case smells the same way.

Pops steps to the side and motions me over. I look up at him, and he encourages me with a big smile and a nod.

Now I understand why he moved with such intentional

care when he carried it over and set it here on the cot. I'm about to look at an instrument that hasn't been played in decades. And by the looks of the case, this horn could be almost a century old.

"Pops, is this the same one that's in the picture?"

"It sure is, Miss Rigby."

I step up to the case, lean over and pull the flap aside.

Wait a minute. That's not a trumpet.

The instrument I'm looking at isn't a trumpet at all. It's a cornet. An *old* cornet. It's basically the same thing as a trumpet. Most people don't even know there's a difference. The only real difference is that a trumpet is a cylindrical bore, and a cornet is a conical bore. It's wound a little different than a trumpet, so it makes the whole instrument shorter. You play it the same, but a cornet sounds warmer than a trumpet.

"This is a cornet, Pops." It's more of an irritated question than a statement.

"Sure is, dear," he says oblivious to the fact that I thought I was going to see a trumpet.

I pick it up. It's cold to the touch. The silver is worn off in many places, leaving a bunch of dull, green-grey areas. There's nothing beautiful about this instrument. It just looks like an old, tarnished cornet.

My heart sinks a little. I guess I was expecting something a bit more impressive.

"Miss Rigby," he says with a trembling hand on my shoulder, "This here instrument is my pride and joy."

His eyes water again.

"I want you to have it."

"Oh, Pops, thank you so much." I'm trying not to be rude. "But I need a *trumpet* for marching band."

I had hoped when he said that Mr. Z sent him to help me replace my trumpet that I'd get something decent. Not this. I'm sure it's seen a lot during its life, but I'm also sure that it's seen better days.

"Young lady, what you need right now ain't in the form of a trumpet or a cornet. It ain't brass and valves."

He's going to give me a speech. I can feel it. I brace myself for a lecture about values and priorities.

Here we go...

Instead, he happily zings me with one more confusing riddle about time.

"When time stops, time starts," he says with a grin. "And then you'll have everything you need."

13

I'M HOME NOW. A lamp on my nightstand casts a dim glow in my room. The old cornet is sitting in its case on my desk. I haven't opened it since I got home. I can still hear Pops chuckling to himself as I left. Honestly, I'm embarrassed to take the cornet to practice tomorrow. Now I'm wondering if this is her ultimate prank on me.

Is Taura behind this?

Of course, that's ridiculous, but I can't help but be a little paranoid. I can't stand the idea of her getting the best of me, so I'm determined to show up tomorrow and use this tired old cornet if I have to. Well, at least until I can get Mr. Z to give me a real trumpet.

Above my desk is a vintage black and white poster of the Beatles in suits walking on a city street. Paul, looking like he's in the middle of saying something, is a bit goofy, but cute. George is looking at the camera as if he's waiting for me to say something to him. John is staring intently off to the side, probably thinking about something profound and amazing. Ringo is, well, he's bringing up the rear, just giving off those awkwardly cute Ringo vibes.

Next to that poster hangs a large portrait of Beethoven. He's holding the Missa Solemnis score in his left hand and a pencil in his right hand. The bright red kerchief around his neck looks like an oversized neck tie. It's hard to believe people actually dressed like that. His hair is gray and wild like he's been outside on a windy day. I like the way he looks. He's handsome in a weird way. His hazel-eyed gaze is deep and intense.

Sometimes I think it's funny that a person can be so drawn to such different things. I mean, who loves the Beatles AND Beethoven. Most people my age are into One Direction or 5 Seconds of Summer, but I really can't get into that sort of thing. The music they make is fun for sure, but I find something deeply satisfying about music that's been around for decades or even hundreds of years. Maybe that's why nobody wants to hang out with me.

Well, everyone but Chew.

It's time like this that I miss Mom the most. Sometimes I catch myself thinking I could just run downstairs and find her in the kitchen and talk. But then I remember she's not here. And she won't be ever again. After she died, I remember being so numb. But so sad at the same time. It's like I was so sad that I didn't know how to feel at all. It's like my emotions, or whatever controls them, just broke.

There's a part of me that just wants to open up and let everything out, but I don't know how. It's like being paralyzed, but on the inside. Sometimes I want to scream at the top of my lungs. Other times I just want to sit and stare into nothing.

Tonight, I'm really feeling it because all I want to do is talk to her about how frustrated I am about my trumpet and this cornet. I really had my hopes up. I don't know what I was expecting, though. Some sort of magical trumpet that would play itself and wondrously erase all my fear and pain? An enchanted instrument that would help me win drum major tryouts while simultaneously granting me the ability to roundhouse kick Taura in the jaw?

Heh.

Wishful thinking, I guess.

I can't say that I'm not curious about the cornet, though. It seems to be calling to me from that worn out case. I do wonder how it sounds. A part of me wonders what it was like when it was new.

I wonder if Pops was any good with this thing back in the day?

After an hour of mindless Netflix watching, curiosity gets the better of me. I get up and stand in front of the case. I purse my lips as I stand there motionless, pondering what it would be like to open the case and just play the thing. I slowly tilt my head from side to side.

"Snap. Snap."

I pop open the latches on each side and open the lid. I move the plush cover to the side and pull out the cornet. It feels pretty good in my hands. The mouthpiece fits into the lead pipe with a metallic clink. I place my fingers on the valves and press them rapidly a few times.

"Whoa!" It feels like butter underneath my fingers.

The action of the valves is smooth and fast. I use my left ring finger to push out the third valve tuning slide. It works beautifully. No sticking at all.

I bring the cornet to my mouth, inhale deeply, and then

hesitate right before it touches my lips.

EWW! I've gotta clean this thing!

I mean, I'm no germ freak or anything, but I figure it won't hurt to give it a good wipe down. I can't find my disinfectant spray, so I just run the mouthpiece under the bathroom faucet with some hand soap. I give it a good shake to get the water out of it and dry the outside with a hand towel. That should do the trick.

Back in my room with the door closed behind me, I raise the instrument to my lips. The mouthpiece is cold to the touch.

From the first buzz, this old cornet sounds like gold. The sound is so warm. I run up and down a C-scale, and the room seems to brighten a little. I pause and look around. Nothing seems out of the ordinary, but I swear whenever I play a note, the room gets a little brighter.

No way.

I play a low C. I hold this note for a few seconds. My eyes dart around the room trying to verify if the room is actually getting brighter when I play.

No, I must be imagining it.

Either way, I FEEL the room getting brighter. I just feel better with this instrument in my hands.

Another C. This time, an octave higher. My skin tingles. I can't help but smile. There IS something about this instrument, but I can't put my finger on it.

Maybe I'm just projecting what I WANT to happen.

"Bum-bum-bum-baahhhh." I play the notes of

Beethoven's Ninth Symphony. "Bum-bum-bum-baahhh."

Glorious.

I noodle around with the trumpet solo from Penny Lane from the Beatles. It comes out flawlessly. Everything I play comes out perfect. The tone is warm and at the same time bright. I can't explain it. Somehow it sounds exactly like how it needs to sound. Every song, every scale, every note I play not only sounds awesome, but it makes *ME* feel better, like I'm floating musically.

Holy moly. This thing rocks!

I can't wait to go to camp tomorrow and play this awesome cornet. I can't believe I had such little faith in Pops. He KNEW this cornet was going to make me amazing. I can't explain it, but this is going to rock I can't wait to see the look on Taura's face when she hears me wailing on this thing.

14

IT'S GETTING LATE, and I've been playing everything I can think of for the last hour. This cornet is amazing.

My chops are done. My mouth feels like mush. But it's been the most remarkable time of playing ever. It's like this old cornet knows everything about me. I'm convinced that it anticipates my every musical thought.

Out of the corner of my eye, I see something shimmer in the cornet case.

What was that?

I must be seeing things again. Even though the room feels brighter, the light is low. There is only one lamp on. I'm staring straight at the case, and nothing is happening. I think I'm losing my mind.

I set the cornet down on my bed. The case looks normal. I bend over and move my face closer to get a better look. I don't see any...

"Whoa!" I jump back. A wave of light shimmers quickly across a little brass knob in the top left corner of the case.

This is weird.

I reach out slowly to touch the little brass knob. I'm not sure what it is, but I bet if I pull on it a hidden compartment will be revealed. Most cases have this sort of thing for storing miscellaneous items for your trumpet like rolled up music, extra mouthpieces or valve oil.

My finger barely touches the knob, and I feel a quick

surge of warmth run up into my arm.

Ok, now that IS weird!

I pinch the knob between my index finger and thumb. It's hot to the touch. I have no clue what is happening, but after the day I've had, nothing is surprising anymore. The warmth spreads through my arms into my body then wraps around me like a cozy blanket, and I feel more at peace than I have in a long time.

I let go, and the warmth fades. I touch it again, and it starts back up again. Pinch. Let go. Pinch. Let go. I do this literally ten times.

The shimmering light has spread out to every piece of brass on the case. The corner pieces and clasps are now shimmering. And that's when it hits me...this thing IS magical. I turn around to look at the cornet expecting to see it glowing brilliantly.

Oh. That's odd.

Nothing. The cornet is not doing anything. No light. No warmth. Just an old cornet.

I turn back to the case. The lights are dancing all over every piece of metal. And then it hits me. I grab the cornet and put it back in the case and almost immediately it starts glimmering. It is beautiful. The CASE!

YES! A magic...case?

I have a magic case? I'm baffled. This has got to be the oddest discovery in the history of humankind. I mean, stuff like this only happens in Harry Potter or Doctor Who, right? And even then, it's something cool. You know, like a wizarding wand or a sonic screwdriver, not an old raggedy instrument case.

What good is an enchanted case? Don't get me wrong, it's cool and everything, but it doesn't make for a great once upon a time story at all.

I can hear it now..."Once upon a time, there was a fair maiden named Rigby who discovered a wonderfully mysterious and powerful magic...cornet case."

Where's the epic romantic flair in that? At least give me a magic cornet that banishes orcs or defeats dragons! Just then the little knob flickers again.

WAIT A MINUTE! Rigby, you're an idiot!! Open the hidden compartment!

I set the cornet aside and reach back into the case to pull the knob. It seems stuck. I tug on it a few times and on the third pull, it pops open. Light bursts into the room and my suspicion is confirmed. Whatever is IN the case is creating the light, not the case itself.

I peer into the compartment. I can't make out what's inside because the light is flickering and shimmering. Every time Chew pulls out his iPhone flashlight and shines it in my eyes, it feels like this. Bright, very bright.

I reach into the compartment, and my fingers brush what feels like a rough wooden box. I cover my eyes with my left hand and pull out the box with my right hand. As soon as I bring it out of the case, the shimmering light suddenly disappears.

I see floating black blobs and twinkling stars. It takes a

second for my eyes to adjust. In my hands is what appears to be a small, wooden pyramid. It has four sides like the pyramids in Egypt, but it is shaped a little different. It's taller than it is wide at the base. I set it on the desk. It stands about eight inches tall.

What IS this thing?

I turn it around and inspect all four sides. They all seem to be exactly the same except on one side, which appears to have a latch and tiny hinges. It must be the front panel. Sticking out of the side on the right of the panel is what seems to be a key of some sort.

I flip open the latch and gently open the panel. There is a long, odd shaped metal piece that has a small and dense metal weight on it. There are handwritten numbers on an old paper label behind the metal piece. I pull the metal piece to the side to get a better look at the numbers.

It moves to one side with a click and then comes back to the other side where it clicks again. It continues clicking back and forth a few times before I stop it. I've never really seen anything like this up close, but I'm pretty sure that it's an old-fashioned metronome.

The numbers are different tempos. The metal arm ticks from side to side and creates a clicking tempo to which a musician can practice. The key sticking out of the side allows you to wind up the mechanism so that it will keep going for a while.

This thing must be pretty old.

I set it down on the desk and return the cornet to the

case. There's no more light shimmering on anything. If this thing IS magical, I wonder what it does? Obviously, it makes things light up, but it also seems like I played better just a few minutes ago.

I bring the metronome over to my nightstand. The red letters on my clock say "12:46 A.M." so I've got to try and get some sleep. I lay down on my side so that I can look at this wooden metronome. I reach over and move the weight to the middle of the metal arm. I wind the key a few times, and the arm ticks from side to side quickly.

"Tick.Tick.Tick.Tick." The sound is mesmerizing.

There's no telling how many people have rehearsed their music over the years with this metronome. It has probably seen all kinds of musicians. Beginners. Professionals. Everything in between. It's fun to imagine who all has practiced to the clicking.

"Tick. Tick. Tick."

I reach over and move the weight up to the top, and the ticking slows way down. My eyes are getting heavy. The clicking cadence reminds me of the clock in Mr. Z's office from earlier.

Is this somehow all connected?

I'm trying to replay the day's events in my mind. My eyes are closing. I'm fighting a losing battle against sleep.

"Tick. Tick. Tick."

What did Pops say about time?

"Tick...Tick."

The metronome seems like it's slowing down. I'm

trying to put it all together, but I can't focus. My eyes are crossing. I'm so tired.

No, no, no. I need to figure this out.

"Tick."

The metronome clicks one last time. I need to know what this is all about.

Maybe in the morning I'll have a talk with Pops and see what he...

I give up the fight and let sleep take me.

Second Movement:
Adagio

15

IT'S MORNING. I still have my eyes closed, but I can feel warm sunlight hitting my face. I slowly open my eyes. I rub my face but can't seem to get my eyes to focus.

Ugh. I distinctly remember closing the blinds last night before I went to bed.

As the world around me comes into focus nothing makes sense. I'm not in my bedroom. This room looks like some sort of old hotel room or something. Everything looks vintage and antique. The light is streaming in from the window in rays.

What is this? Where am I?

I bolt upright in shock. This is definitely freaky. The room I'm in is like an old bed and breakfast or something. Totally not my bedroom. I'm racking my brain trying to remember what must have happened the last day or two because clearly I must be missing something. I run through a mental checklist of all the possibilities.

Did dad surprise me with a trip?

Are we on a mini-vacation or something?

What day is it?

None of this seems to make any sense. I pull the heavy floral-patterned quilt off of me and swing my legs to the side of the bed.

What the heck!?

I'm wearing some kind of frilly nightgown! But it's NOT

cute at all. It has long sleeves and covers me from my neck to my feet. I feel like a granny in this thing.

What is going on?

Nothing adds up. Birds are chirping outside the window. It is strangely peaceful. Low dull thuds echo outside the window as a horse's hooves clop along on the ground. The pounding sound is getting quieter. It must be moving away from the house.

I stand up and slowly creep over to the window. The wooden floor creaks. Sheer curtains at the window are moving gently in the morning breeze. Looking out the window, I can see that I'm not on ground level. I'm two stories up.

The air is fresh and slightly cool, a stark contrast from the hot and humid air that I'm used to. The sun is not that high in the sky, so it must still be mid-morning.

Where the heck am I?

The scene outside the window spreads out to the horizon like a postcard. Vineyards stretch out until the countryside becomes green forested hills and then hazy blue mountains.

To my left, a man wearing black gallops away from the house on a dirt road. The sound of the horse's hooves get fainter and fainter. I can see glimpses of him between the trees that line the drive.

Now he's gone.

The courtyard directly below me and in front of the house is cobblestone. It's a large area that is fenced in by a tall gray stone wall. There is a big iron gate that leads to the dirt drive.

"Guten Morgen, Fräulein!" a young boy working in the courtyard calls up to the window.

Uh...

"Good morning, to you, too," I answer hesitantly, but I hear the words as "Guten Morgen, du auch."

Wait, a minute! That sounds like... uh, German? But I don't speak German! What's going on?

I step back quickly from the window. I'm officially perplexed now. I don't seem to be in any immediate danger. That young boy acted like he knows me. I can't piece together what's going on at the moment. But I do know that I can understand German.

"Hello, my name is Rigby," I whisper.

But I hear, "Hallo, mein name ist Rigby."

What? SHUT THE FRONT DOOR!

"I play piano." It comes out as, "Ich spiele Klavier."

I totally understand it, though. That's what's so weird. I'm speaking a foreign language that I've never learned, yet I comprehend every word.

"Chewie will never believe a word of this!" I whisper gleefully to myself.

The words sound like, "Chewie wird nie glauben, ein Wort davon!"

I kick my feet up and dance a little jig in my oversized old lady nightgown. The wooden floor creaks a little bit. I went to sleep last night and then woke up a master of the

German language.

I am the master of foreign languages, hear me roar!

World domination here I come. I wonder if I can transfer out of my regular Spanish class to German. I would totally ace it.

THIS IS SO LEGIT.

Suddenly I stop dancing. On a stand in the corner, there's a tall mirror. The reflection that I see stops me in my tracks. I'm not actually seeing myself in the mirror. The person staring back at me with wide eyes and an open mouth is not me.

Holy crap. Who am I looking at?

I step closer to investigate. The reflection moves as I move. I lift my hands above my head, and the person in the mirror does the same. I stick my tongue out, and the reflection does the same. The girl in the mirror is definitely moving like me. But there is so much that is not me. The face is different. The hair is long, curly and brunette. The eyes are dark. The body I'm seeing is not the one I've seen every morning my whole life. The reflection is not me, but at the same time *IS* me.

Where'd MY face go? Where's MY red hair?

How can I be seeing an entirely different person in the mirror when it is clearly me? Maybe I'm dreaming. That has to be it. The metronome probably affected me in some way. If I can find that metronome, and restart it, maybe it will knock me out of this weird dream!

Wake up, Rigs, WAKE UP!

I turn to the small table beside the huge antique bed. The metronome! It's there, just like I left it on the nightstand back in my own bedroom. This isn't making any sense. In two quick steps, I bound over to the table and pick up the metronome. I wind it up.

C'mon. C'mon. Wake up, wake up, wake up.

Nothing happens. I pull on the metal arm. Still nothing. I shake the unresponsive wooden gadget hoping to get it working. Nothing. I pinch myself on the arm. Still here. I shake my head and rub my eyes trying to wake myself up. It doesn't work. I'm still here.

Wherever here is.

16

I STUMBLE BACKWARD and bump into a wooden wicker rocking chair. I catch myself but step on the edge of my gown. Down I go. I let out a short shriek as I tumble awkwardly to the floor. I land on my side with a thud.

The metronome miraculously hits a corner of the quilt, before sliding harmlessly to the floor. I see it come to rest out of the corner of my eye.

The pounding of footsteps hurrying up a staircase rumbles through the wooden floor. I feel the vibrations through the boards as I lay there dazed. The footsteps pause outside the door.

"Julietta?" A bubbly voice beckons through the door. "Julietta? Are you hurt? What's going on in there?"

The voice is female, and the words are German, but like before, I understand every word perfectly.

Who the crap is Julietta?

I try to work my way up to a sitting position. I didn't bump my head or anything, but I landed awkwardly, and I think I might have rolled my ankle or something. It hurts.

"Julietta?" she calls. "I'm coming in!"

My mom's name was Juliet. MY middle name IS Juliet. This is too weird.

The door swings open. A young woman a few years older than me is standing there looking concerned. She peeks in trying to see what's going on. The outfit she's wearing looks like it's from a movie like Sense and Sensibility or something. Her curly brunette hair is swept up. Her dress is long and the front is cut low. If I wore something like that to school I'd get sent home.

I grab a handful of the quilt trying to get my footing so I can stand. She hurries in around the bed to help me.

"Oh, Julietta!" she exclaims, her dark brown eyes wide. "What happened?"

Either she's crazy or I am. I know I'm not Julietta, but maybe I look like this Julietta she thinks I am. I did look different in the mirror.

"I'm ok," I answer. "I just slipped."

"Here let me help you stand." She reaches out and puts her shoulder under my hand.

"Thank you, uh..."

"Josephine!" A stern female voice calls from downstairs. "Josephine! What's going on up there?"

Josephine. The young lady helping me up is named Josephine. Good to know.

"Nothing, Ma-ma!" Josephine calls over her shoulder as she helps me sit on the side of the bed.

"I think I rolled my ankle, Josephine."

I must look anxious because Josephine tilts her head to the side with a big smile.

"Oh, Julietta," she bubbles. "It's only your first day in the country here at your cousins' house and you've fallen out of bed and gotten yourself hurt."

My first day here. I still have no clue where here is.

"Josephine," I ask. "When are we going back into the, um, the city?"

Maybe she'll say what city, so I can at least get my bearings and figure out where I am.

"We're here on holiday, so we won't be going back into Vienna for a while," she offers. "But you'll love the countryside here!"

Vienna. Ok, Vienna. Wait, a minute! Like Vienna-all-the-way-around-the-world-in-Europe-Vienna?

This is turning out to be the coolest dream ever. I can't wait to tell Chewie about it when I wake up.

But there's something too real about all this. It doesn't seem like a dream. In fact, in most of my dreams, I'm usually tripping and falling all over my Dinkles in front of the whole football stadium. I usually wake up right after I ruin the halftime show.

"Can you walk on it?" Josephine asks.

I stand and put a little pressure on my foot to test my tingling ankle. It hurts a little but feels ok. I step lightly across the room.

"I guess I just landed on it the wrong way," I say.

"Well, it's nearly lunch time!" she chirps. "We need to get you dressed!"

She flings open the doors of a tall wooden wardrobe that stands against the wall.

"Let's see, what shall it be?" she says perusing the options. "Well, you only brought three dresses so which one suits you today?"

There are three dresses hanging there in the wooden wardrobe. A royal blue one, a dark green one, and a fiery red one hang in a row on wooden hangers. A few pairs of fancy leather shoes line the bottom.

The blue dress is nice. The green one is probably going to look the best on me and my pale self. The red dress will totally clash with my...

Wait a minute! My hair is brunette now. I can totally pull off that red dress! Heck yeah, let's do this!

I lean back towards the tall mirror just to double check that my new body is still there.

Yep. Tall, dark and handsome.

"Um," I say awkwardly. "Can I wear the red one?"

"It is your dress, Julietta! Red is an excellent choice for you, dear!" Josephine can't be but a few years older than me, but she seems so mature and refined.

"We want to look our best when we meet our guests of honor this evening!" she says cheerfully.

Guests? This is getting more and more complicated with every minute. WAKE UP, RIGBY! WAKE UP!

But I don't wake up. I'm still here, caught in this dream. I'm putting on a red dress that makes me look like a character from a Jane Austen novel. I'm somewhere near Vienna and apparently I'm going to be introduced to some very important people today.

I can hear it now. "Breaking News: Local teen, Rigby Raines, wakes up on a different continent thinking she's dreaming only to find herself caught up in an elaborate

cosplay with people who are fascinated by Pride &
Prejudice characters. We're not sure what's happening,
but we'll have more details at eleven. Over to you, Champ,
for our action sports update."

17

AFTER GETTING ME dressed and all dolled up, Josephine leads me downstairs to see the rest of the family gathered in the dining room. I've got to figure out who everybody is so I don't make a fool of myself. From what I gather, Anna "Ma-ma" Brunswick is the head of the household. She appears to be a strong-willed woman. Therese is the first-born and oldest sister. And then there's Charlotte, the baby of the family. Josephine says that her brother Franz, the only son, is away on business.

I wonder where their dad is?

Ma-ma explains that they'd moved here to Vienna from Hungary about two years ago to seek more opportunities for the children in the family to broaden their education in music. Josephine married a Count named Joseph Deym right after they moved here. That makes her a Countess.

A freaking Countess!

All this talk seems so weird to me, but they speak casually about courtships and marriages like it's just a part of everyday life.

This is all feeling so real.

The table is set with elegant dishes and glassware. There are platters of meat and vegetables. In between the large serving plates and bowls are some loaves of bread and sweet red wine fills every cup. It reminds me of Thanksgiving at my grandma's.

That really stings. Thanksgiving won't be the same without Mom.

Candles are placed throughout the spread, but they aren't really needed in the daytime. Sunlight filters in through the two large windows. On the opposite wall, there is an ornate fireplace. The mantle is decorated with small ceramic bowls and pitchers. There are paintings on the wall framed with elaborate golden frames.

This room is amazing. I feel like I'm in a museum.

"What year did you say you all moved here?" I ask.

I'm trying really hard to figure out where all of this is taking place. And if I can just narrow down what year this is supposed to be, maybe I can wrap my brain around it a little better.

"Seventeen Ninety-Nine, child," Ma-ma answers.

So 1799 was two years ago. That means it's 1801 now.

1801. The date seems familiar to me, but I've been learning so much in history classes the last few years, that sometimes it's hard to keep the dates and events organized in my head.

Mozart? Is it Mozart?

No, it couldn't be Mozart, he died in 1791. That was ten years ago. Well, ten years ago IF this isn't just a dream and I'm actually sitting here in Vienna in the year 1801.

Maybe it's Haydn that I'm thinking abou...

"Julietta," Ma-ma interrupts my contemplation. "Why don't you and Josephine walk the grounds this afternoon. You can take in the fresh air and see the countryside around the cottage."

"Ok, ma'am," I say. "That sounds great."

I really just want to be back home marching on the practice field with Chewie, Ellis, and as much as it pains me to think, even Taura.

"Wonderful!" Josephine bubbles with excitement. "We'll surely have an adventure!"

18

I'VE BEEN SITTING in the bedroom for the last half hour waiting on Josephine. I'm not sure if we're going to be changing clothes for our little countryside expedition, but she calls to me from the front courtyard. I move over to the window and look out to see her standing there with her hands on her hips.

She's wearing the same clothes, but with a big floppy hat tied under her chin with a big scarf.

"Come on down here!" she says. "And bring your hat!"

There are only two hats in the big wooden wardrobe. The closest one will do. There are a few scarfs on a hanger. I grab one that I think matches.

Here we go, Rigs. Or should I say, 'Elizabeth Bennet.' I'm sure Mr. Darcy will be waiting for us in a fancy horse-drawn carriage or something.

Typically, you can find me wearing some jeans and a black tee. I usually like to rock some old school black Chuck Taylor high tops. But here I am looking like a character out of a nineteenth-century romance novel, getting dressed up to go galavanting around the Austrian countryside with Josephine the Countess. If you had told me yesterday that I'd be doing this today, I would have said you were crazy.

Actually, I think I'm going crazy.

I still don't know what's happening, but I'm playing

along. If this is a dream, I'm sure I'll eventually wake up. If this is not a dream, well, I'm not really sure what it is then.

When I finished lunch with the Brunswick family, I looked all over my bedroom for the cornet that Pops gave me. I thought for sure if the metronome was here, then the cornet would also be here. No such luck. I haven't been able to find it anywhere.

The metronome still isn't working. I tried winding it again. It will wind and wind, and then wind some more. It just won't tick. Not even manually. I can't explain it.

"Julietta!" Josephine calls again. "What in the world are you doing up there?"

"Coming," I call back across the room toward the open window hoping she'll hear me.

A minute later, I step outside into the sunny courtyard to meet Josephine. She helps me tie my hat to my head. The only hats I ever wear are my baseball cap at band camp and my shako during halftime shows and marching competitions. You should see me trying to stuff my hair up into that thing. My favorite part is the feathery plumes we wear on top of the marching shakos. They look like ruffly, sparkly chickens.

This floppy hat feels so weird. The front of the hat droops down over my eyes. Josephine fixes it, so the sides fold down, and the front and the back make a scoop so that I can see in front of me.

"Let's go!" She takes off running and giggling. "You're going to love it out here!"

Seriously?

"Coming." My ankle still feels a little tender.

Right out of the gate the drive heads off to the left towards a forested area off in the distance. Before you get to the forest, there is a long, straight stretch of road. Full, leafy chestnut trees stand like soldiers guarding the way on both sides of the drive. The branches reach out and touch each other over the road forming a shady canopy. It reminds me of the big oak trees we have in Georgia.

"Don't stay out too long," a voice calls out from the house. It's Therese, the older sister. She seems nice, but also a little bossy.

"Oh, don't you just love nature?" Josephine asks as she skips along.

"It *is* nice out here." I can't remember the last time that I went outside just to spend time in nature.

It really is nice. The weather is perfect. A few fluffy clouds drift overhead. The sun is high in the sky, but the shade of the chestnut trees keeps the road cool.

We walk for a while and make small talk. If I had to guess, I'd say we've covered about half a mile. Josephine always seems to have something to say about everything. She's very positive and is full of energy. It's starting to wear on my introvert self, but I convince myself that I get to reinvent who I am since I'm in this new body.

Time to get out there and be outgoing!

"So, uh, Josephine," I ask with false bravado. "What's your husband, the Count, like?"

"Oh, the Count?" She turns and faces me. "He's a very agreeable man. I do admire him so."

"That's cool, I mean, uh, that's nice."

"That's an odd saying." She turns and looks at me with a curious expression.

"Yeah, I mean, yes it is." I'm trying my best to be this Julietta that Josephine sees me as.

C'mon, Rigs. Time to channel your inner Jane Austen.

As we come to the end of the chestnut-lined drive, a wide clearing opens up for a few hundred yards before becoming a forest. From the house, this grassy area is difficult to see because the chestnut trees are so tall and full. I'm seeing it up close now for the first time, and it's beautiful, more scenery that looks like a painting.

Millions of tiny wildflowers stretch out across the meadow. It's a lot different than back home. My yard is basically spotty grass and a few tall pine trees that drop like a million pinecones and a ton of pine straw everywhere. When I was young, my parents made me pick up pine cones for my allowance. I hated it.

All those dang pinecones just for a few dollars and tiny puncture wounds all over my hands.

It's amazing how the simplest things can trigger the most random memories. Of course, these days, most of my memories take me to a dark place because they remind me of Mom. But I'm ok with a memory now and then, especially if it is prompted by something that looks like this meadow. If the clouds weren't moving lazily across the sky,

I'd swear we were looking at a painting.

The air is crisp. The sun is warm. A few butterflies are fluttering from flower to flower. The chirpy melodies of birds singing drift from the forest into the clearing. I only hear the sound of nature. No cars. No sirens. No machines. It's weird, actually.

"Come on, Julietta," Josephine bubbles as she takes off into the meadow in a sprint. "The weather is divine today!"

What have I gotten myself into?

This is not really my cup of tea, but I am still not convinced that this isn't a dream. Everything looks and feels so real. A whiff of wildflower fragrance floats through the air, and I know this can't be a dream. The meadow stretches out like a little knee-high ocean just beckoning us to wade in.

Josephine has her skirt hiked up to her knees in front as she bounces through the tall grass and flowers. The way she's kicking up her legs and feet remind me of the show-style marching bands back home. My band is more of a corps style, though. But I do love seeing the bands that high-step with energy across the field. It's pretty cool.

"Julietta!" she calls. "What are you waiting for?"

I grab a handful of my dress in each hand and stumble clumsily into the wildflower sea. I feel like I'm actually wading into the water at the beach. But it's just grass and flowers. With each step, I kick up a puff of pollen. Little translucent flying bugs buzz away noisily. I'm not sure what they are, but they remind me of a little grasshopper with see-through wings.

Josephine is about 30 yards away from me when she starts spinning with her arms stretched out to each side. Any minute now I'm expecting her to burst into the "The hills are alive with the sound of music..." It's one of my favorite old musicals. Actually, it's one of my favorite old movies, too. Julie Andrews kills it.

It kind of strikes me funny that, in a way, I'm in my own weird version of *The Sound of Music*. Except, instead of the Von Trapp family singers, I'm stuck here with the Brunswick family and the high-spirited, perky Josephine, who is now falling backward without a care into the grass. It's like that trust fall everyone does at summer camp, but without the mosquitos, sunburn, and, oh yeah, people actually catching you.

"Come over here, Julietta," she's out of breath. "Let's watch the clouds!"

I can't blame her, though. This life seems much more simple than mine. No television, no cell phones or computers. No interstate traffic or soft drinks.

Wait a minute, no soft drinks?

I chuckle to myself. I don't think I can live without Cherry Coke. It really is a different way of life here. I realize I'm zoning out, so I shake my head a little to clear my thoughts. I can hear Josephine humming. It's a familiar tune, but I can't place it.

I make my way over to her. She's on her back holding a little bouquet of tiny white flowers.

"Fall in!" she says excitedly.

I'm not sure about this. I turn slowly and face away from her. I peek over my shoulder one last time as I let gravity take over and I begin to fall backward.

"Aaah!" I scream and fall into the grass and flowers.

I'm expecting to hit the ground hard, but the thick green grass cushions my fall. I can't help but laugh. Josephine starts laughing, too.

"Julietta," she says. "You're so silly."

"Thanks." I retort with a sniff.

The clouds drift slowly by, all shapes and sizes. They are white and fluffy and seem close enough to reach out and squeeze. Although I'm not in my comfort zone lying here next to this perfect stranger, this exact moment feels like it's meant to be. Everything just seems so right.

Maybe I was born in the wrong era. Maybe I COULD be a Von Trapp Family Singer. Maybe I SHOULD be Lizzy Bennet. I think I could totally rock this life simple life.

Who am I kidding? How could I possibly ever live without my iPhone?

19

A HORSE WHINNIES from the direction of the forest. I sit up and look toward the shadowy woods. There is a solitary figure sitting on a black horse. Even from this distance, I can tell the horse is jittery. It seems on edge, its ears flicking rapidly from front to back. It is breathing heavy, snuffing air forcefully in and out of its nostrils.

The rider is dressed in all black clothing. Everything, from his hat to his boots, is black. He's facing our direction, but not moving this way. It's hard to see his face because of the shadow cast by his hat, but it's obvious he's looking directly at us.

"Josephine?" I whisper through my teeth. "Who is that guy on the horse?"

She sits up slowly from her grassy bed of flowers.

"I'm not quite sure." She bites her lip nervously. "We really ought to get back to the cottage."

The horse rears with a loud whinny that sounds more like a shriek. A deep rumble rolls down from the mountains. A dark bank of clouds is forming on the peaks in the distance. I feel the tiny hairs on the back of my neck stand up. This is creepy. I don't feel safe at all.

The rider spins the nervous horse back toward the forest. He looks back over his shoulder at us, staring in our direction for an eternity. The horse bounces anxiously, kicking up dirt with its jittery hooves.

The happy white clouds we had been watching the last hour are morphing into dark, angry clouds. The air feels ominous and threatening. The temperature is dropping quickly. It's not cold, but it's enough to make me wish I'd brought a jacket.

The rider kicks the horse causing it to spring forward. They gallop away into the cover of the trees and out of sight. We hear the horse's hooves pounding the dirt for a short while and then it's quiet again, except for the fast approaching rumble. It's a storm that is quickly heading our way.

A single raindrop lands on my cheek. I turn my face to the sky and a second drop hits me in the eye. I shake my head and rub the water out of my eye.

Um, yeah. Time to get back to the hacienda.

"That was odd. I'm sure of it." Josephine says. "Let's make our way back to the cottage."

Drop after drop begins to plop down on us. First slowly, then building in frequency. It's picking up. There's no avoiding it now. We're far from the cottage, and there's nowhere to hide out here in the meadow.

"Lead the way, chief." I say awkwardly as we stand.

I've got to work on my turn of the nineteenth-century vocabulary. I'm finding it easy to communicate, even with the weird English-to-German translation thing happening automatically, but I'm still thinking like a sixteen-year-old from Georgia from the twenty-first century.

More raindrops. Plop. Plop. They are not small, dainty

raindrops. They are big and heavy. The sky looks and sounds angry and is hurling a barrage at us.

Josephine starts back toward the road. With the rain coming down harder, getting out of this tall grass is a lot more challenging than when we first came in. I quickly fall in behind her as she trudges ahead. The rain is steady and coming down almost sideways now. Even if we make our way to the chestnut trees or the forest, the rain is coming down so hard that we'd still get soaked.

I'm not about to be abducted by some weird emo cowboy out here in the country, so there's no way I'm heading toward the forest.

We tramp through the grassy wildflower sea, which literally feels like a sloshy sea now. We're moving as fast as we can in these big dresses. Water droplets spray up from the grass and flowers. My feet are totally soaked through my shoes.

As we near the edge of the meadow and approach the dirt road, I can't get the rider in black out of my mind.

Who is he? Why was he staring at us? Why did he suddenly bolt away?

Wait a second...the RIDER from earlier.

It comes back to me in a flash. I'm pretty sure I saw the same rider galloping away from the house earlier when I peeked out the window. Of course, I can't be one hundred percent sure, but now I'm pretty much convinced it was the same person.

The dirt road is more like a mud road now. A light bulb

goes off in my head. The black car. The shiny black sedan from the parking lot. Was it the same one driving through my neighborhood?

There's NO way that this could be connected...is there?

20

THE RAIN FALLS in a torrent. It's hard to see ten feet in front of us. Thunder rumbles angrily, and lightning illuminates the dark sky every few seconds. The wind is pushing the rain sideways like it has a score to settle.

We tiptoe our way across puddles and little channels that are cutting their way through the dirt road. It requires big awkward steps to keep from walking directly into the little streams. They aren't huge but just big enough to keep us from running the half mile straight back to the house.

"Julietta," Josephine calls out. "This way. There is an old barn we can shelter in."

"Right behind you!" I'm doing my best to keep up with Josephine as she gracefully leaps over a large puddle before leaving the road.

The same puddle lies in front of me, like a tiny ocean, mocking me. I envision myself leaping nimbly over it like a gazelle, but in reality, I am about as athletic as a chubby baby elephant. Reality wins and just like a funny meme, I find myself face down in the mud.

"I'm ok!" I awkwardly slip and slide my way back to standing. "I'm ok."

Josephine, apparently oblivious to my fall, hasn't turned back. She's now about twenty yards ahead of me just past the chestnut tree line. I can barely make out her form in the downpour. For a dainty and proper countess living in the 1800s, she's definitely a lot more agile than I would have imagined.

Me, on the other hand, let's just say that I'm in band for a reason. Not the most athletic specimen here. I wipe the mud from my face as best I can. It's amazing that even in this new body I still find myself tripping over my own feet.

"Hurry, Julietta!" Josephine calls as she nears a small grove of short, stubby trees.

I can hardly breathe as I catch up to her. She's approaching the door of a barn at the edge of this grove. It's a small wooden building with a single door and no windows that I can see. She tugs on it a few times, and it creaks open.

"Come on!"

I follow Josephine out of the storm into the barn. It's dark except for a few slivers of dim light coming in through the planks of the wall. It smells like wet dirt and rotten apples in here.

My eyes begin to adjust. There is a pile of burlap sacks in the far left corner and a stack of wooden crates to the right. Directly to my left is a wooden table. Josephine plops down onto the burlap pile with a giggle but leaps up immediately with a shriek as a handful of mice scurry to the other side of the room.

"Oh, my!!" she exclaims sharply with her hands over her mouth.

I guess it really doesn't matter what century you find yourself in, nobody likes mice! She kicks the pile a few times to make sure there are no more critters. When no more rodents emerge, she declares it safe and sits down again. Though, this time, she seems more wary. I chuckle out loud.

"Come, sit," she orders politely with a smile.

I untie the scarf that is holding my sagging hat in place. The floppy hat kept the sun out of my eyes but did little to prevent the rain from drenching my hair. My dress is soaked, and I can feel my toes getting wrinkly in my waterlogged shoes.

Josephine is in the same condition. Soaked all the way through. I guess she was right about having an adventure in the countryside.

"Josephine..." I'm curious about her home in the city.

"Call me Josie," she interrupts with a grin. "Only Mama and old men call me Josephine."

"Ok," I smile. "Josie it is."

The rain hasn't let up. The wind comes in gusts and shakes the planks of the old barn. It's so dark that it feels like night, but it's early afternoon. The sound of the rain on the old roof is soothing and terrifying all at the same time. This is not a sweet, little country sprinkle - it's a dark, and massive thunderstorm. The lightning flashes and thunder claps come every few seconds. I'm hoping this old barn will remain standing.

"Josie, tell me more about your home in the city," I ask.

I'm curious to learn more about this world I woke up in. I'm beginning to accept that this dream, or whatever it might be, is something else.

Have I really been transported to a different time?

Is this real? Could the old cornet and metronome really have some sort of enchanted power, some mysterious capacity to give the owner the ability to travel through time and space?

Why here? Why THIS time?

"Vienna, as you know, is beautiful this time of year," she says like a tour guide. "It reminds me of my home in Budapest where I spent most of my childhood."

"So, your mother moved your whole family here for better opportunities in music?" I ask.

"Oh, yes," she says with bright eyes. "After Pa-pa died, Ma-ma became the provider and protector of our household. Though, she'd argue that she already was!"

"Your father died?"

"Unfortunately, yes," Josephine says with sad eyes. "I was only fourteen-years-old when he passed away."

She explains that he was a Hungarian Count, a noble with lots of wealth and power. When he married Ma-ma, they became an even more powerful family. They own several castles in Hungary and several family homes here in Austria.

Several castles? Geez.

"Life is good for us here, though," she says with determination. "Ma-ma knew what would be best for us and moved our family here to Vienna."

"Do you like it here?" I ask.

"I love the countryside!" she blurts. "Oh, but you mean in Vienna don't you?"

"Yes, Vienna." I chuckle.

"Vienna is a fascinating city." She shifts on the burlap pile. "It is a bastion of progress. The nobles are treated well, the city is growing, and it seems we are the center of the musical universe."

"How long have you been playing?"

"I began lessons when I was very young." Josephine mimes playing the piano. "As you well know, every young noble takes music lessons from an early age."

"Yes, yes." I backtrack. "How silly of me."

"Julietta," her hands stop moving, and she turns to face me with an inquisitive gaze. "Tell me what life is like in Italy? It must be very exciting!"

What is life like in Italy? Italy!? How should I know!

This might be the moment that I get busted. Revealed as a fraud. I'm not the real Julietta. I have no clue who she is and where she's from. Thunder rumbles loudly overhead, and I feel the room closing in on me.

Josephine is smiling at me, waiting for my answer.

"Umm, Italy..." It comes out more like a question.

"Oh, yes!!" She claps her hands excitedly. "Trieste must be so lovely! Down on the coast. Your family must have loved it there."

I honestly don't have a clue what she's talking about, but I do know about life on the coast. Before Mom died, my family regularly visited a little group of barrier islands off the coast of Southeast Georgia called the Golden Isles. St. Simons Island and Jekyll Island. We stayed for two weeks each summer either on St. Simons or Jekyll Island. Compared to the Atlanta area, the pace of the "Islands" is slow. And more importantly, the food is great.

"Umm, yes," I offer weakly. "The coast is amazing. The water is pleasant, and the air smells salty."

I gain a little more confidence as I fill in the details of my so-called life in Trieste with real details from the Golden Isles in Georgia.

"There is beautiful sand on the shore, and the sunrises are glorious." I'm on a roll now. "And the food...the food is superb, so many choices if you like seafood."

Josephine looks at me funny.

"You know, food that comes from the sea." I recover realizing that the word seafood might be foreign to her. "We have all kinds of fish to eat."

"Oh, that sounds divine," she bubbles.

The rain seems to be easing up as one last roll of thunder rumbles across the countryside like a timpani. We sit and chat for a while until the rain subsides to just a drop here and there.

I feel like I'm owning this scenario. I don't have to lie, but I can just fill in details here and there with what I *am* familiar with. The things that I *DO* know about my life can get me through this so that I can get back home.

"Julietta," Josephine interrupts my thoughts. "We should probably be heading back to the cottage."

We gather ourselves and peek out the door. The sun is peeking through the remaining clouds, and the orchard of stubby trees seems to be sparkling in the light. Water droplets are clinging to the leaves. Every few seconds one plops to the wet grass below it.

Waterlogged and shivering, but happy to have weathered the storm, we head back through the grove, back to the road. Happily splashing in the remaining puddles, we casually stroll the half mile back to the cottage, as the late afternoon sun emerges again.

21

I TRUDGE THROUGH the big iron gate into the courtyard in front of the cottage. I follow Josephine through the front door. We leave our shoes near the door in a wet pile.

In the room to the right, there is the somewhat noisy din of conversation and what sounds like fancy tea cups clinking on saucers.

"Josephine? Julietta?" Ma-ma calls out from the room.

"Yes, Ma-ma," Josephine answers. "You'll never believe what happened out..."

She suddenly stops with a gasp as she rounds the corner and steps through the doorway.

"Oh," she chirps embarrassingly. "Forgive me. We got caught in the storm. I must look a fright."

"My daughter, Josephine, whom you all know." Ma-ma reports in a matter of fact manner. "Her husband, the Count, is away on business. Where has your cousin gone off to? Did you lose her in the storm?"

"Julietta," Josephine calls. "Julietta, come in here."

I can hear the low, serious voice of a man, but I can't make out his words. I wonder if Franz, Josephine's brother, has come back from his business in the city. I peek apprehensively around the corner and begin to walk nervously into the room.

This sitting room reminds me of my grandma's front living room. It feels stuffy and proper. The furniture is ornate and colorful. There are elaborate oil paintings on the walls without windows. Across the room, Josephine dips in a short curtsy. At least thirty people are milling about, standing in small groups and speaking with one another quietly. These must be the "guests of honor" Josephine was talking about earlier.

I pad lightly across the cold hardwood floor until my wrinkly toes feel the comfortable cushion of a soft plush oriental rug.

"Distinguished guests," Ma-ma announces. "I present to you, the Lady Julietta of the Guicciardi family of Trieste, Italy and late of the Kingdom of Slovenia."

Ma-ma looks sternly in my direction and nods her head toward the center of the room in a not-so-subtle cue. I'm guessing she is directing me to curtsy. Her eyes are serious, and I know she means business. Josephine steps to the left. The man, who I assume was speaking earlier steps forward and bows ceremoniously, but quickly. Something about him seems so familiar.

I attempt to curtsy but step on the edge of my dress. I stumble toward the man. He steps forward and catches my arm. I regain my balance and raise my head to find him looking directly into my eyes. I'm now face to face with one of the most serious gazes I've ever seen in my life. His eyebrows are full and furrowed, and his hazel eyes are wild and deep. His hair is dark and swept back. He doesn't smile, but I can tell he is amused.

"My dear," he says. "You really must be careful."

I feel like I know this man, but I can't place his face. It's the eyes, definitely the eyes. They seem so familiar.

"Julietta," Ma-ma chirps loudly as she steps closer. "You are standing in the presence of Vienna's greatest musical mind. And I would venture to say, possibly the most brilliant mind in all of the world of music."

I step back in surprise. My hands are trembling, a shiver runs through my body, a combination of my cold, wet clothes and the sheer presence of this man standing before me. His countenance, the sharpness and seriousness of his features, is so confident. I don't believe I've ever met someone with such self-assurance. It's like he knows he's great, but not in an arrogant way. It's weird. He seems to effortlessly and fearlessly command the room.

And then there's me. Rigby Raines. I mean, Julietta Gicar... Giscard... Oh, whoever I'm supposed to be here in this...this whatever this is. I look like a sad, scared, waterlogged cat. You know, the one that accidentally falls into the bathtub and can't get out? My dress is soaked. My hair is wet and matted down around both sides of my face. I can feel my ears burning as the tingle of embarrassment rises up my neck.

Way to make a brilliant first impression, Rigs.

He tilts his head to the side and brings his finger to his lips as if he's in deep thought. He's studying me. He inspects me from the top of my head down to my wet toes. He takes a few steps and walks slowly around me. He mutters something under his breath. I can't make it out.

I feel like I know this guy, but I can't figure out how.

When he makes it all the way around, he takes my hands in his. His hands are warm and firm. Another chill runs through me, and I can't help but tremble. He leans in slowly until we're almost eye to eye. He's not a tall man, but he more than makes up for it with his demeanor.

"Yes," he whispers. "She will make a fine student."

"Julietta," Ma-ma proclaims, "this is your new piano teacher. I present to you the most distinguished, and certainly unrivaled, Ludwig van Beethoven."

22

*Ludwig van Beethoven? Ludwig van freaking Beethoven!?
THE BEETHOVEN? My favorite composer ever!?*

Now, I know this is a dream. It has to be. There's no way in the world that I could be meeting Ludwig van Beethoven. It's not possible. Not even remotely. This is the stuff you see in sci-fi movies.

But why can't I wake up? Why won't this dream end? It just keeps going and going.

If this is some sort of dream, it is the most elaborate and detailed dream I've ever experienced.

Experience?

Yes, that is the only way to describe this. I am having an out of body experience. And it is totally creeping me out.

"Julietta." His voice is almost a whisper.

I'm just about to really lose it here. The room is spinning. I can't tell if I'm just going crazy or is there some sort of actual hope inside of me that wants this to all be real. I can feel my heart racing. My palms are clammy. I'm getting lightheaded and dizzy. A distant rumble of thunder rolls in the background.

"Julietta." The voice is a bit louder.

Ok, ok. Even if this isn't real, it's the experience of a lifetime. Just go with it, Rigs.

I plant my feet firmly on the soft carpet. I need to find a steady place inside, something to center me. I need an anchor, something to keep me from spinning out of control. My best friend's face flashes through my mind.

Chewie.

His smile. His goofy antics. His attention to detail. His care for me. It works. I begin to grin a little as the room stops spinning around me.

"Julietta." Ludwig places his hand on my shoulder, and I come back from my momentary spiral.

"Oh, umm, I, uh..." I'm fumbling for words. "What? I'm sorry I was...um..."

"Julietta, dear," he says. "It would be my honor to have you as a student."

"Thank you." I can't contain my excitement, but I'm trying not to lose it like a pre-teen school girl at a One Direction concert.

Ludwig van flippin' Beethoven!!

"We'll get started tomorrow."

I literally can't believe it. Seriously, this is one of those situations where I might be ok with using the phrase *I can't even*. Because, honestly, I can't even...anything.

I'm standing here speechless in front of my favorite composer. I mean, how many people get the chance to travel back in time to meet one of their biggest influences?

Wait? Did I just say travel back in time?

Am I a time traveler? This *experience* IS happening in 1801, supposedly. It feels like 1801. But, then again, I'm from the twenty-first century. How would I know what it feels like in the early nineteenth-century? Everything here reminds me of a movie or a book I've read or my grandma's house. It *feels* so real, though!

Time.

It dawns on me that I should have known this whole time. It hits me like a freight train. I think my mind is officially blown.

Pops.

He totally set me up! He knew that this would happen. The last thing he said to me was totally related to this. What was it he said?

Time stops? Time starts? Something like that...

I *AM* a time traveler.

I can hear it now: "This just in, teen musician Rigby Raines discovers the secret to time travel and proceeds to thoroughly embarrass herself when she's introduced to her personal musical hero, Ludwig van Beethoven. It's not known at this time whether she'll make an absolute fool of herself like she usually does, but as we get the details, we'll pass them on to you. Over to you, Veronica."

When time stops, time starts.

I thought that was just crazy talk. You know, like a senile old man. I mean, I like Pops, but I really thought he had lost his mind. But interestingly enough, he wanted *ME* to have that old cornet, knowing that I'd find the metronome and...

The METRONOME!! That's it!

It's upstairs in the bedroom. If I can just get back up to the metronome, and figure out how to make it work, I can get back home. I tried winding it earlier, but I must've missed something. If I can figure it out, I can get out of this dream or experience or whatever it is and get back to my normal life.

My normal life? Wait a minute. What am I thinking?

This is actually happening. Right here and right now. I am experiencing the adventure of a lifetime. Something that you only see in the movies. *THIS* is something that most people would give anything to go through, and I'm already trying to figure out a way to get out of it.

What is wrong with me?

I think I need this adventure. Ludwig van Beethoven is literally standing in the same room as I am. I'm going to get the opportunity to take lessons from one of the greatest composers and pianists in the history of humankind. I can imagine Chewie pumping me up with one of his pep talks. In the background, there's a droning bass wobble and a thumping kick drum.

Dang it, Chew! I let you into my mind for a second, and your stupid dubstep music takes over!

I really miss Chewie. I wish he were here with me. But he's not. He would absolutely love all of this. Of course, he probably wouldn't be able to stop talking long enough to enjoy any of it.

But, this is *MY* adventure. Something that I am experiencing for me. I've made my mind up. Nothing's going to stop me from having the adventure of a lifetime. I decide that I, Rigby Raines, in the body of some stranger named Julietta, will become Vienna's greatest young piano player under the guidance of the world's best piano player, Ludwig van flippin' Beethoven.

Let's do this.

23

I STILL DON'T know what to do with myself, though. Even after hyping myself up I still feel like an outsider. I'm an outcast in the middle of all these powerful people. There are nobles, Counts, and Countesses here in this room. And then there's me, Rigby Raines. I'm a sixteen-year-old girl from Georgia who loves the Beetles and Beethoven.

Hold on...I love Beethoven. I LOVE BEETHOVEN!

This is so weird. Did my love for the music of Beethoven somehow bring me here to Vienna in 1801 to actually meet him? Nothing really makes sense, but if I ever make it home again, I'm going to have so many questions for Pops.

It all makes sense. Now that I know that I'm standing in the presence of Beethoven, it registers that the reason he seems so familiar is that he looks like a younger version of the portrait poster on my wall. He's got the same intense eyes. Same serious face. Same wild hair, except he's much younger here, so it's not gray like it is on the poster.

It's hard to describe what it's like to see someone who I've only seen in Google image search results and history books. The portraits that we have in the twenty-first century depict Ludwig as harsh, wild, and stern.

In person, he's all of those things, but he's literally ALIVE right here in front of me. He's not just a moment captured in time in an oil painting on canvas. He's REAL!

He's not just a snapshot in a book. He's breathing. He's thinking. He's here interacting with others in the room.

One thing that I can tell right off the bat is that he is extremely uncomfortable with the social aspect of this gathering. That seems to be a direct contradiction to the confidence which he exuded just minutes ago when he was introduced to me. He has retreated into the far left corner and is only speaking to people as they approach him.

You and me both Mr. Beethoven.

I can totally relate. There are people like Josephine that are like a sponge soaking up all the energy in the room through conversation. And then there are people like me. When I get in a room full of crowds like this, it feels like I'm being squeezed. My energy gets wrung out of me, and I feel an overwhelming desire to be alone.

I step backward toward the opposite corner just to watch him. It's an incredible feeling. People are excitedly chatting up Beethoven as if he's hung the moon. He is obviously humoring them, but I can tell he'd rather be somewhere else. I can spot an introvert from a mile away!

"I know who you are, Miss Rigby Raines..." An almost whispered voice comes from behind me.

It startles me. I didn't know someone was standing behind me there in the corner.

I turn around slowly wondering who in the world could possibly know that my name is Rigby Raines. I've not told anyone since I arrived here this morning.

"W-w-what did you say?" I ask apprehensively.

"I said, I know who you are, Miss Raines." The accent is clearly British.

Wait, is he actually speaking English?

The man in the corner is wearing all black. Everything from his boots up through his neck scarf is black. Black pants, black shirt, and black coat. Everything. He is tall. He towers over me.

The man in black!

His face is pale like he hasn't seen the sun in ages. His hair is jet black. A scar runs across his forehead from the left eyebrow down across his nose and then across his right cheek. His hard, narrow eyes are black and dark as midnight. Something about his stare betrays his intimidating stature, though. I don't know if I'm imagining this, but there are torment and hurt in his eyes.

If it weren't for the pale skin and scar running across his face, he'd be handsome, but something about him just looks off.

"Don't worry, young lady," he says through clenched teeth and thin lips. "I'm not going to hurt you."

"Who...who are you?" I stutter, casually looking for escape routes. "What do you want?"

"Who I am, well, that's unimportant at the moment," he says. "What matters is that I *am* here now to help you. Everything is going to be fine."

"But why?" I ask. "Are you following me?"

As if seeing him on the horse looking like a stalker earlier today wasn't creepy enough, seeing him right here in front of me, knowing my name, and telling me that everything is going to be fine is really wigging me out.

When people say that everything is going to be fine, it usually means something is really wrong.

"Wait...were you in the black car?" I think out loud, connecting some dots.

"Yes."

If he is here in this room with me AND was in the black car back in Georgia, then *HE* is a time traveler, too. So, this is getting weirder and weirder as the day goes on. I still don't understand why I am here. Throw into the mix a creeper wearing all black, following me around in two different time periods, and this is getting all kinds of strange, even scary.

I wish Josephine would come bail me out here.

Josephine is on the other side of the room engaged in a spirited conversation with another young woman who looks her age. Her hands are flailing. It appears as if she's describing our earlier adventure in the storm. She's too engaged to be any help.

"Ms. Raines..."

To be so intimidating in appearance, this man speaks with a somewhat pleasant, proper English lilt. His accent reminds me of a Sherlock Holmes movie.

I turn back to face him. I have to look up to see into his raven black eyes. His gaze is laser focused, but I see so much more than that in those eyes. Again, I see pain.

"I'm going to need you to hand over the relic."

24

"THE RELIC?"

I have no idea what he's talking about. The word makes me think of Indiana Jones trekking across the world to find a holy chalice or something. What would I be doing with a relic? The oldest thing I have is my mom's trumpet...

Dang it. Mom's trumpet.

Thinking about it stings. Taura destroyed it. I really, really want to punch her right in the face the next time I see her. But, then I see my mom's face. I can hear her saying, "My sweet little Rigs, fighting never solves anything. You be the better person."

If only she knew Taura.

"Yes," the man in black says. "The relic. We know that you have it."

I'm racking my brain trying to think of a religious item or treasure that I might have come across. Maybe there's something here in the house that the Brunswick family has stashed away? Or maybe it's something that the real Julietta has hidden somewhere. She IS a noble after all.

"I'm sorry...uh..." I don't know his name or even what to call him.

"Ms. Raines," he says. "You wouldn't be here if you had no knowledge of the relic."

I turn to walk away from him, but he grabs my wrist and pulls me back toward him.

"Quit being coy, Rigby," his words are measured. "We know you have the metronome."

The metronome? Gah! Why didn't you just say so, you emo freak.

"The metronome is this relic that you're talking about?" I ask incredulously. "What's so special about a metronome that doesn't work?"

I know it works, but at the moment, I'm telling the truth because, for the life of me, I can't figure out how to get it to tick again.

"Let me educate you on relics," He says as he lets go of my hand.

He goes on to explain to me that the word relic comes from the Latin for "to leave behind." A relic is anything that has been abandoned or that remains when the original possessors have gone. In a religious sense, it even refers to the remains of someone who is consecrated and special, like a saint.

"The metronome IS unique," he explains. "But, in YOUR hands, we believe that this relic is much too powerful to be left unchecked."

Wait, what?! MY hands?

The man in black leans in close, and his voice becomes even more serious and hushed.

"Ms. Raines, I'm afraid you've been caught up in something that is much bigger than yourself." His gaze softens briefly.

"What do you mean, unchecked?" My voice cracks.

"What's going on? Is this a dangerous..."

"Situation?" he finishes my sentence. "Yes. Your life is in danger, and if you don't hand over the relic now, you'll force my hand."

I can't believe this is happening. I thought I was getting to experience the adventure of a lifetime. Seems about right, though. Whenever something seems too good to be true, it usually is.

My mom is the best friend and music teacher a girl could have. She dies. I have an above average talent in music. I'm too scared to perform in front of people. I want to be drum major. Taura makes my life a living hell. I get to travel back in time and take piano lessons from *THE* Ludwig van Beethoven. A creepy time-traveling stalker shows up and ruins the fun.

Story of my life, bro.

"If you just hand over the relic, we'll return you to your time, and you'll carry on as if nothing ever happened."

A wave of sadness comes over me. I don't want to hand over the relic. I don't want to carry on as if nothing has happened. I *want* to be here. This experience is the best thing that's ever happened to me.

"I'm sorry, but I can't do that." I set my jaw like stone, and even though my insides are fluttering like a flock of spooked starlings, I'm not giving up.

"Rigby." His demeanor softens. "The future of the world depends on you giving me that relic. It's of tremendous import that you relinquish it to me."

Those eyes. Something dark and scary is driving him.

For a second, his face almost looks friendly. He almost smiles as I ponder my predicament. His eyes are distracted by something behind me, and his countenance suddenly becomes stern again.

"Oh, Julietta," a giddy Josephine grabs my shoulders, "Who, pray tell, is your handsome new friend?"

The man in black quickly steps back and looks at the floor. He fidgets with his hat in his hands.

"Hello, Countess." The fire disappears from his eyes as he bows slightly.

"Pleased to see you, Mr...?" Josie inquires curiously with a huge grin.

"Smith, Blake Smith," he barely looks up to speak. "From London."

"Oh, splendid!" Josephine claps her hands. "A guest all the way from England here in Vienna! What brings you to our party tonight?"

"I'm here for business." His eyes narrow.

Josephine cuts a glance at me. I know that look. In a simple, quick glance, a girl can ask her friend several questions without ever saying a word.

Are you ok?

Do you need to be rescued?

He's pretty cute, right?

Can you get his number for me?

I chuckle to myself. That one look carries so much meaning and can get you out of, or into, just about any troublesome situation. Here I am two hundred years before my time, and it's the same.

I nod my head so subtly that it would take an expert in body language to decipher my response.

HELP!

Josephine puts her arm through mine and pulls me away from Blake and the awkward conversation about relics and time travel. He tries to protest, but before he can say anything we're facing the opposite direction and walking across the room.

"We really should retire for the evening since you have lessons tomorrow at Mr. Beethoven's apartment in the city." She tugs me toward the door.

Ma-ma is rambling about something to Ludwig. She is waving her arms wildly like any minute she might take off in flight. Therese and Charlotte are standing close to Ma-ma. Everyone is leaning in to hear her story.

"Good evening, everyone!" Josephine bubbles.

The red-orange rays of the setting sun are filtering in through the windows. It will be dark soon. I can't wait to get out of these wet clothes. Dry clothes sound so nice right now. But then again, I'm not sure I really want to put that vintage granny gown back on.

25

HALF AN HOUR later we're in warm, comfy nightgowns and sitting by the fireplace in an upstairs sitting room. Candles and oil lamps fill the room with a warm almost yellow glow. It's so different than the harsh bluish fluorescent lights we have everywhere back home. And of course, I'm not staring at a phone screen every few minutes. I feel so much more relaxed now.

Josephine is curled up in a blanket sipping hot tea. I've got my old lady gown back on, but honestly, I don't mind. It's not that cold outside, but the storm has cooled everything off and getting rained on earlier definitely chilled us to the bone. It's nice just to sit and warm up by the crackling fire.

"Josie," I take a sip of my tea. "Do you know the man I was talking to earlier? Have you ever seen him before?"

"I don't believe that I have ever met him before," she squirms in her blanket to get more comfortable. "But he seemed to be enamored by you."

"Really?" I cross my legs Indian style as best I can in this gown. "I just thought he was creepy."

"Yes, he did seem to be very pensive and introspective."

I can't get his sad eyes out of my mind. He's on a mission to get the relic. He seems to be driven to get the relic, but there's also something about him that seems to be hiding just out of sight under the surface.

"He seemed sad, didn't he?" Josephine sighs.

"Yes, I was just thinking about that."

Blake's deep, black eyes betrayed his attempt to be menacing. He came across as a force to be reckoned with, but I sense a sadder, softer side.

There's more to him.

I'm not sure if I should tell Josephine about the time travel stuff. She'll probably just think that I'm crazy. I mean, what would you do if your cousin showed up and started talking about being a different person in this body and from the future? She'd probably call an exorcist.

If Chewie were here, he'd understand. I'd spill it all, every detail. We'd be time travel buddies, and go visit all the best places and times in music history. There are so many awesome places and times we could experience. I'd love to go see the earliest Beatles concerts. I'm sure he'd probably like to visit John Philip Sousa's marching bands to see the earliest versions of the Sousaphone.

I wonder how that would work, though. Would he have to take over another body, too? This is too weird.

Aww, Chew. I miss him.

Even though it's only been a day since I've seen him, it feels like a lifetime. My band bud feels are kicking in hard. It's funny how that works. When I'm around him every day, I don't think much about us. But here, in this encounter, I miss him. Something is tugging at my insides every time I think about Chew.

Is he more than a friend?

I shake my head. I push it to the back of my mind. I don't have time to be daydreaming about Chewie right now. There are more important things to figure out. For one, like getting back home. That is, after I meet with Beethoven tomorrow and learn everything there is to know about playing the piano and writing killer music.

This is going to be so awesome.

26

THE CARRIAGE RIDE is bumpy and uncomfortable, but it beats walking all the way into the city. I'm headed into Vienna to meet Ludwig for my first lesson. Josephine told me that it was an honor to be invited to his studio. Most of the time he meets his students at their homes.

I woke up this morning with a flutter of excitement and something else rumbling inside my chest. I didn't sleep well last night. I tossed and turned all night. I couldn't get my mind off of the introductions yesterday. Two guys who seem interested in me for two separate reasons. Ludwig will be my piano teacher and Blake is some sort of secret time travel agent out to get my metronome.

Ludwig seemed so disconnected and uninterested in even being there. I get it, though. He probably just wants to be sitting behind a piano making music. I would feel the same way if I were the world's greatest composer. He seems so cold and distant. I just hope he is a little warmer at my lesson.

Blake, although polite, has a very creepy vibe going on. Wearing all black and following me through time, trying to get the metronome from me. I sense a depth to him that betrays his calm demeanor on the outside. People like that scare me. I'm not really sure what to do if he shows up again. My escape plan is to flail my arms and scream like a baby. It's not perfect, but I'm still working out the details.

I actually have the metronome with me. I wrapped it up in a scarf and brought it with me. There's no way in the world I'm leaving it unattended. I don't know what Blake or the people he might work for are up to, but I don't have a good feeling about it.

Breakfast was almost a non-event, more like a snack. A cup of tea and a small pastry. Lunch and dinner are the biggest meals of the days. My stomach rumbles in protest. I'm not used to missing my favorite bowl of cereal. Chewie keeps trying to convince me that the paleo diet is better for me. He eats eggs and bacon every morning. I'd rather eat Lucky Charms.

Now, the straight-from-a-postcard countryside is bouncing by outside the carriage window. The friendly boy from the courtyard is driving the carriage. He's whistling and humming happily. Josephine sent him along with me and said he'd accompany me to the lesson "for propriety's sake." I'm not sure what that means, but I think she sent him to keep all the old ladies from gossiping about our midday lesson time.

Vineyards, pastures, and cottages stretch as far as the eye can see. The landscape is so green. It's so different than the Atlanta area with its four-lane roads and strip malls on every corner. You can't drive a mile without seeing fast food restaurants and storefronts. You have to drive way out of the sprawl to even find farms. But here, it's like every direction you turn there are beautiful groves of trees and mountains in the distance. The beautiful scenery reminds me of that old guy on t.v. with the fro painting happy bushes and trees.

After about an hour in the carriage, the landscape begins to change. Vineyards turn into fields of crops in rows. The young boy says in just a mile more we will soon pass through Leopoldstadt, a small suburb just to the northeast of Vienna.

Fields turn into houses that get closer and closer together. We cross a few small bridges over streams and then one large bridge over a wide river.

It's hard to tell the difference between Leopoldstadt and Vienna, but as we cross over one more bridge, it's clear that Vienna is ahead of us.

"The Danube is looking exceptionally beautiful today," the boy driver calls out.

The smells in the air change. The fresh, clean air of the countryside has been replaced by a fusion of all kinds of smells. The river and its fishiness, the stones of the streets and buildings, the piles of garbage every so often, and even the faint hint of a sewer system combine to make an odd odor buffet. It's an assault on the senses, but I guess folks who live here are used to it.

As we approach the city walls, the serene sounds of the countryside all but disappear and are replaced by the constant din of a noisy city. The streets become cobblestone, the horses clopping along rhythmically. Merchants are peddling their wares. People are busily scurrying along the streets.

The gates of the city are impressive. The walls look ancient. Vienna is an old center of settlement and population. I'm not sure how long it's been here, but I know every big city in Europe outdates just about every town in America by hundreds, if not thousands, of years.

"These walls are my favorite part of Vienna," the young boy calls out. "My mother told me that we don't really need them anymore in this modern age, but they sure are impressive are they not?"

"They sure are."

Most of these walls and buildings are older than my country. Well, they WILL be older than my country.

It's weird to think that the oldest buildings in America were not even a thought when these walls were built. My country wasn't even a thought. But here I am, entering into Vienna in one of the most exciting times in the history of the musical world.

Mozart. Haydn. Schubert. Beethoven. They're all connected to Vienna. In my history class, we learned that these four composers can be considered to be the most influential during the periods in which they worked. And what's amazing is that they all lived and worked in Vienna within a seventy-five year period.

And now, in just a few short minutes I'll be meeting Ludwig van Beethoven for a piano lesson. I'm excited, but nervous. The more I think about it, the more anxious I get.

What if I'm not good enough?

What if I make a fool of myself?

What if my fingers freeze up and I embarrass myself?
What if he hates me?

I really just want to sit and listen to him play. I want to look at his music scores, to see the notes on the original paper. I want to be in the same room while he's composing, like a fly on the wall. I just want to BE close to Ludwig while he's creating masterpieces. Maybe I'll learn a thing or two about playing in front of people so that whenever I make it back home I can play a solo without freaking out in front of the whole band.

27

THE APARTMENT IS on the second floor of a four-story building in a bustling section of downtown Vienna. The entire heart of the city is contained within huge walls that have been here since the Middle Ages. The city has a very stately and antique feel to it.

And here I am standing at the door of one of music's greatest figures. Everything is large in this building. The doorways are huge. The hallways are wide. The staircase to the second-floor apartment has a ton of steps.

"Are you ready, ma'am?" the young boy asks, raising his hands to knock on Ludwig van Beethoven's door.

"As ready as I'll ever be."

The door knocker is shaped like the head of a lion with angry eyes. The mouth holds a big brass ring. I think it's appropriate because the Beethoven I've read and learned about is said to have been intense and serious, at times even rebellious. The lion reminds me of the portrait of Beethoven back home. His windblown gray hair is like the mane of an aging, but still wild and dangerous lion.

My heart is racing, and my mind won't slow down. I turn my head to the side and strain to hear if there's any music coming from inside the apartment. I hear only silence. My palms are getting clammy.

Remember, Rigs, this is a GREAT opportunity. Don't mess this up.

After another three thumps of the door knocker and a brief period of silence, footsteps sound out behind the large white door. It swings opens slowly opens to reveal a stiff Ludwig van Beethoven.

My heart flutters again as he invites us in. The apartment is well furnished, but sparse. A small, wooden piano sits in the corner. Stacks of paper are scattered all over the top of the piano and on the shelves behind it. A fancy sofa with spindly legs sits on the opposite side of the sitting room. Next to it there is a tall wingback chair upholstered in the most colorful, busiest floral print I've ever seen. A large book sits in the chair.

I love a good book, too.

"Welcome to my home." He bows quickly.

"Thank you." I feel like a giggling school girl. "It's such an honor to..."

"Before we begin," Ludwig turns toward the sofa. "I would prefer to learn a bit about you, Miss Guicciardi."

"Umm. You can just call me Rig..." I catch myself mid-sentence and fake a cough. "Julietta, sir. Please call me Julietta."

"Indeed. Julietta it shall be then." He moves the book and sits in the tall floral chair. It strikes an interesting contrast. The stiff and serious piano teacher, and the busy, almost gaudy, floral print behind him.

"Please have a seat," he directs.

I sit down anxiously. I feel like Ricky Bobby. I don't know what to do with my hands.

Oh my gosh. I'm chatting with Ludwig van Beethoven! Like, literally shooting the breeze with Ludwig...right here...right now!

"Julietta." He pauses in thought. "Tell me a bit about yourself and your family."

Here we go...

"My family is from Trieste," I fudge my way through this part. "But originally from the Kingdom of Slovenia."

I'm not exactly sure how to tell Ludwig about myself when I really don't even know anything about the "self" that I'm in right now. I decide just to go for it, though.

"I come from a musical family. I love music. I play piano. I love listening to music. I even try to write my own music sometimes."

I'm looking at the floor. I'm not sure if he's impressed, or if he thinks I'm a fool. He probably thinks I'm just a young idiot. How could I possibly say anything about myself that could impress this man?

Maybe I should tell him about the time when I was seven that I played an entire recital piece with my goldfish, Bert, in his bowl on the bench next to me. I was convinced that Bert would bring me good luck. That was really before the anxiety over playing in front of people set in.

Or maybe I should tell him about the time that I got stuck to my seat when it was my turn to play at my ten-year-old recital. It was the first time that I think I had a legit panic attack. I couldn't move. I was frozen. Mom had to come and sit next to me so I could finish my piece.

Yeah, that should really impress him.

"My name is Ludwig van Beethoven." His announcement breaks my train of thought. "My family hails from Bonn, but I have made my residence in Vienna these last nine years."

I've got to figure out a way not to look like an idiot. All I can think of to ask him is what his favorite song is. Yeah, that'll do the trick. Ask the greatest composer of all time what his favorite song is.

C'mon, Rigs. You're better than this!

Instead, I sit here fidgeting nervously, trying not to lose it. Why is *he* just sitting there awkwardly? He's supposed to be the teacher, and yet here we are sitting in nerve-wracking silence.

I look up, and I'm taken back by Ludwig's gaze. He's staring intensely at me. The kind of stare that you know has purpose. I feel like he's looking into my soul.

"Umm." My introvert self is taking over, so I try to move the attention off of me. "Tell me a little more about your music, Mr. Beethoven."

"Call me Ludwig, Julietta," he says curtly.

He shifts in his seat and seems to relax a bit. I can tell that he is generally uncomfortable, though. He slowly opens up and tells me a bit about his childhood dreams and journey to Vienna.

He had dreamed of moving to Vienna and becoming a student of Mozart. But by the time he was able to actually move to Vienna, Mozart had died. I can tell that the death of Mozart impacted him. All these years later, and he speaks about it in an almost hushed, whispered tone.

Beethoven moved to Vienna and began lessons with Haydn in 1792, although he had met him some years earlier. Beethoven's tone changes when he speaks about Haydn. There's a slightly rebellious hint in his words as he talks about his former teacher. They didn't get on too well, and eventually they parted ways.

Ludwig goes on to tell me about his rise to prominence as a piano virtuoso over the years. He defeated all challengers in improvisation contests. Just last year was declared to be the greatest piano virtuoso in the city.

Seriously, this dude is at the top of his game.

I'm in the presence of greatness. It is an overwhelming feeling. I am speechless. I want to ask him question after question about music, but I can't think of anything. I want to tell him how much I love his music, but I'm afraid. I'm scared I'll just look like a big goob.

He hasn't stopped with the intense stare. I don't know exactly what to think. One thing is for sure, though. There's something about his eyes that draw me in. I see something of myself in them. The only difference is that I think he's a lot more confident. I have a hard time looking people in the eyes. He won't stop looking at me.

"Well, then." He claps his hands together softly, but loud enough to make a sound. He stands, signaling the end of our get-to-know-you chat. "Shall we move to the piano?"

28

I FOLLOW LUDWIG to the small, boxy piano.

"Have a seat." His manner is so aloof.

Am I so uninteresting? Am I just not worth his time?

I'm beginning to feel like, even though this could be the greatest opportunity of my life, Ludwig just doesn't want me here. It almost seems like I'm some sort of burden.

Does he feel this way about all his students?

I know that many of the greats throughout history taught music lessons to the upper crust of society. Part of me wonders if it was just for the money. It gave the composers an income, and it gave the hoity-toity rich class something to brag about. I imagine being able to claim that Bach or Mozart was your piano teacher would earn some uppity status points.

"Julietta." He taps the piano. "Shall we start at the beginning? Let's start with your scales."

Scales. I can actually do this.

There's a part of me that immediately goes into anxiety mode. I second guess myself. It's the old familiar voice. The part of me that knows I'll screw up everything and make a fool out of myself. It's the dark part of me that always seems to beat the part of me that knows I can do it.

I used to sit and play with Mom for hours, every note perfect. Put me in front of a small recital audience or even in front of just the band director and I fall to pieces. I don't understand why I can't just be me. The good me. The me that masters every musical piece I've ever attempted to play in private. The me that writes melodies and harmonies in my bedroom without a care in the world.

Where is THAT me?

I put my hands on the keys. They are cold to the touch. My fingers are trembling. I'm so nervous.

"Which scale should I start with?"

Ludwig walks up and stands almost directly behind me. I feel like a tiny mouse. He's a fearless lion, a ferocious predator about to swat me aside with his paw. I feel like an insignificant rodent, afraid of my own whiskers.

"C-major," he seems bored. "If you please."

With shaking hands I attempt to play a C-major scale. But, instead of a scale, it sounds more like a bad attempt at jazz improv. I hit two notes instead of one. My crossover is all wrong. I'm all thumbs.

What's wrong with me! I can't even play the easiest scale known to all of humankind.

I don't even want to turn my head to see his reaction. I've just embarrassed myself in front of one of history's greatest piano players. I hear him breathing behind me, but I'm too afraid to look.

Oh my god. Kill me now.

I hear muffled laughter. Seriously. I hear laughter coming from directly behind me.

Oh, please, no. Not laughter.

I turn my head around slowly to painfully discover that

Ludwig has his hand over his mouth. He's trying to keep himself from laughing.

ARE YOU KIDDING ME?

It's my worst nightmare. I want to run away and get into a hole somewhere. This is worse than any botched chair placement test or piano recital. This is terrible. A wave of embarrassment burns through my ears as I unsuccessfully try to hold back a sob.

"No, no, dear girl!" Ludwig places his hands on my shoulders. "Please do not mistake my laughter for malicious mockery."

I'm thoroughly confused now. Tears are escaping from the corners of my eyes, but the look on his face confirms that he's not making fun of me. He seems genuinely concerned that I'm about to lose it.

I feel so helpless.

"I don't understand." I sniff back tears.

"I have seen worse!" He chuckles. "Much worse!"

"But I can't even get through a C-major scale without really messing it up!"

"But, Julietta," he sits on the bench next to me so that we're face to face. "You *DID* play a C-major scale. It just happened to be a terribly shaky and awful C-major scale!"

He laughs at himself, and I can't figure out where this is coming from. The serious, dark and moody Beethoven has been replaced with this smiling, chuckling guy in front of me. He seems much younger now, and in a weird way, more handsome.

"Allow me to explain." He stands and paces the hardwood floor and rugs. "My goal for today is to ascertain whether your skill level is that of a virtuoso or a student."

Well, it's pretty obvious. I'm no virtuoso, eh?

"It's clear to me that you have a foundational bit of musical knowledge," he says. "You're just a tad jumpy, aren't you dear?"

"Well, yeah." I bite my lip. "You're Beethoven. Like, the greatest piano player in the world."

"You also speak in a very odd manner," he says with curious, smiling eyes.

Believe me, that's not the first time that I've heard that in the last few days.

"Let's try it again," he instructs calmly. "But this time, take a breath, set yourself firmly, and then just let the scale play itself, dear."

Easy for you to say.

"Listen to me, Julietta," he says sternly. "To play a wrong note is insignificant, to play without a shred of passion is inexcusable."

That kind of makes sense.

"Anyone can memorize the notes of a scale," he says.

He puts his right hand on the top of the piano as he leans in close to me. I feel his left hand in the small of my back. Ludwig applies a little pressure on my back, and I straighten up. His hand lingers for a moment, definitely longer than necessary.

Whoa.

"Young lady," he speaks in hushed tones. "I sense something within you that will someday move crowds to their feet. I can't put my finger on it, but it is in the air all around you. You strike me as a small, but fiercely passionate, storm with hands and feet."

A storm? With hands and feet? I have no clue what he's talking about.

"Passion, Julietta," he says. "You exude it. I can see it in your trembling hands. I can tell by even the simplest desire you have to play the right notes for me. I cannot help but see it. You truly *care* about the music."

I do care. I really do. But is it me just caring about not making a fool out of myself in front of people or is it something else? I don't know.

"Let's try the scale again."

I've got this. C'mon, Rigs, don't let me down.

I take a breath, sit up as tall as I can, and then play the second worse C-major scale I've ever played in my life. Ludwig chuckles again. And although I'm still mortified inside, I let myself smile. This lesson is a disaster.

But, it's a beautiful disaster. Ludwig's chuckles seem to be so out of character compared to everything I've seen so far. It's like he's actually got a living, breathing soul. Last night, when I met him face to face, he became more than just a recollection from a history book. Here and now, he seems to be even more than that, more than just a stuffy historical figure. He's a real person that could legitimately be my friend.

Beethoven has a sense of humor!

"BAMM!"

The doors burst open, and a tall masked figure wearing all black storms into the room and points an odd looking black device at us. I'm no weapons expert, but it's clearly a gun of some sort.

Third Movement: Minuet

29

LUDWIG STEPS FORWARD in protest.

"I wouldn't do that if I were you," the masked man in black says forcefully.

"Blake?" I stand up slowly. "What are you doing here?"

"After our little chat, it became painfully obvious that you're going to make this hard for everyone."

"You know this brigand?" Ludwig is confused.

"No, not really." I just want to go home now. "We met at the Brunswick's cottage last night."

Why won't this guy just leave me alone?

Ludwig takes a step closer to Blake.

"Ah, yes. The man in black sitting alone in the corner. What is this all about?"

Blake lowers his mask. I don't know why he's wearing a mask in the first place. I figure he must be a super-secret time traveling agent that has come back in time to take the metronome from me. What does it really matter if anyone sees his face?

"This is between the young lady and me, little piano man," Blake snarls.

"I beg your pardon, sir," Ludwig's eyes become narrow and stormy. "But if you don't leave my home at once, I will be forced to resort to violence."

"Mr. Beethoven," Blake says sternly. "Do yourself a favor and sit down."

Ludwig steps closer to Blake. He is clenching his fists. His breaths are deep. His jaw ripples from the clenching of his teeth.

Oh, no. No, no no.

"Wait a minute, guys." I can't believe this is happening. "Stop...please...stop."

Blake raises his gun and fires off what seems to be a some sort of laser blast. Ludwig ducks as a vase on a shelf behind him shatters and sends pieces of porcelain smashing to the ground.

"NO! NO!" I scream.

I charge Blake and hit him with all the strength I can muster. It's like running into a brick wall. He doesn't move. I do. I bounce off of him and tumble to the ground.

Well, that didn't work. What was it I said about my escape plan? Screaming and flailing my arms like a baby?

"The RELIC!" Blake demands. "Hand over the relic and all of this will end!"

Something has come over Blake. The calm and collected, almost handsome, guy I saw just last night has become a monster. The darkness that I saw in his eyes last night is now roaring out of him. It's like a switch has been flipped and he's losing control.

"BLAKE!" I yell. "It doesn't work. It's a dud. There's nothing special about it. I swear!"

"LIES!" He counters. "We have the technology to track relics like this. We knew that it would be activated from your time and location. Then you activated it, confirming our data. We also know that it will activate a second time from here, so we now know that it's somewhere here in the vicinity of Vienna."

"What is all this nonsensical talk about?" Ludwig inches closer, but this time he's more wary of the weapon Blake is waving around. "What is all this relic business?"

"It doesn't concern you." Blake points the gun at Ludwig who raises his hands in surrender and sits on the sofa. "Just tell your girl here to give up the relic and nobody has to be hurt."

A blaze of anger flashes across Ludwig's face. He is not happy and is hating the fact that he can't do anything about the present situation.

A blur of motion whips into my peripheral vision. A dull thud rings out, and Blake lets out an "oomph." His eyes roll back in his head, and he topples forward, crashing heavily to the ground.

Standing behind him with a scared, sheepish look on his face and a boot in his hands is the young boy. I'm not sure how he knocked Blake out with just a boot. It becomes clear when he pulls a horseshoe out of the boot. His left foot is bootless, revealing a big toe poking out of a hole in a red sock. His right boot is still on.

"I do not know this mean man," he says with an angry frown. "But he is not very nice to the good Fräulein and the Piano Teacher."

Blake is out cold. Ludwig is pacing. The young boy is putting his boot back on.

"What is your name?" I ask, embarrassed that I hadn't spoken much to him earlier.

"My name is Carl," he says proudly.

"Well, Carl." I pat him on the shoulder. "Thank you for that. You saved us."

"What is all this, Julietta?" Ludwig stands over Blake.

"I can't explain right now, Ludwig. But this guy, Blake, is not my friend. I have in my possession a very important relic that, for some reason, he wants to take from me."

"What relic?"

"A few days ago an old man gave me this relic," I reply. "I had no clue that there was anything special about it."

I'm trying to explain without revealing that I am, in fact, Rigby Raines, a sixteen-year-old time traveler from the twenty-first century.

"Is this all some dark sorcery or enchantment?" Ludwig asks as he warily eyes the weapon laying at Blake's feet.

"Ludwig, I have no idea." I'm trying to be as reassuring as possible without freaking him out. "But, I do know that the item I have does seem to be very, very powerful."

"This is all too odd," he says with a frown. "And this old man that you speak of, who is he?"

"His name is Pops McKenzie, but I really don't know much about him," I explain.

Blake suddenly rolls over onto his stomach and then leaps for his gun.

Oh, crap! Why didn't we tie him up or get the gun?! We're such amateurs.

Ludwig attempts to kick the gun out of the way, but Blake beats him to it. I turn back to the piano, grab a pile of sheet music and papers, and throw them at Blake. I hope that there are no masterpieces in that stack.

"RUN!" I shout. GO, GO GO!"

Ludwig, the young boy Carl, and I break for the door as a cascade of paper containing musical sketches and ideas that would later become masterpiece symphonies and concertos rains down on Blake. Out of the corner of my eye I see him swatting them aside. He fires a blast that hits the wall behind us and then stumbles groggily toward us as we scramble out the door.

30

CARL LEADS THE way down the stairs and out the wide front doors. Ludwig holds my hand as we skip down several steps behind. As we burst out onto the busy street, we are met with a throng of people scurrying in all directions like busy worker ants.

Carl has disappeared. I look left and right, and he's nowhere to be seen.

"He can take care of himself." Ludwig pulls me to the right, and we join the busy throng of people moving along the street. We head further into the heart of the city, weaving in and out of the street, dodging horse-drawn carriages and farmers' carts.

I glance quickly over my right shoulder to see Blake stumbling out of the doors we had just come through. He's dazed but somehow still pinpoints us in this bustling crowd. I see his dark eyes lock onto us. He sets his jaw, a look of firm determination on his face, and he moves purposefully toward us.

"He's seen us, Julietta," Ludwig swears. "This way!"

He clamps my hand with a grip like a tightened vise. If we weren't being pursued by an angry and somewhat scary time traveling secret spy, I'd feel pain. But now, in this moment, in this scary situation, I only feel safety. Ludwig is looking out for me.

I feel safe with Ludwig. In the midst of all this chaos

and uncertainty, I'm being rescued by Ludwig van Beethoven. I barely even know him, but right now I feel so connected to him. Part of me wonders if this is infatuation or if this is even love? Is it possible to love someone you don't yet know?

Maybe it's just these crazy circumstances and the fact that he's a historical rock star.

Ladies in big fancy dresses and feather hats stroll along escorted by men in long-tailed suits, top hats, and ornate canes. Merchants with wooden crates and burlap bags hurry onward. On the street, horse-drawn carts and carriages click and clack along noisily.

The heart of Vienna is like a huge maze of stone and brick. Streets and alleyways stretch out between buildings in every direction. The buildings are five and six stories high, each of them with lots of windows and balconies. The streets and sidewalks are cobblestone.

This block and slab maze is entirely free of grass or trees. The only plants are in the hundreds of flower boxes hanging on balcony railings and windowsills. If I weren't running for my life, this would be an almost picturesque scene. It looks like an oil painting from a museum.

There are shopfronts with colorful awnings over the first-floor windows and doors. We run by a glass shop. The mirrors inside reflect the sunlight back into the street. We pass a bakery, the air smells like flour and pastries. Across the street is a restaurant of some type. Diners are sitting stiffly, some laughing, some eating.

Blake is still behind us. His head is down, and he's approaching quickly. An old man pushing a wooden wheelbarrow filled with flower pots stumbles and tips his cargo right into Blake's path. Blake crashes into the unlucky man and tumbles to the street.

Ludwig leads the way down a side street. The alleyway is much narrower here. The smell of sewage is stronger here. Clotheslines are strung across the alley from the upper stories. All kinds of white linens and undergarments hang to dry. The sun peeks through the laundry, but it's mostly shaded down here in the alley.

I'm running out of breath, but I'm determined not to let Blake get his hands on the metronome. I can't figure out what is driving him. There has to be something bigger at play here. Blake seemed odd, but cordial when I first met him at the cottage. But as our conversation went on he appeared to turn desperate.

At Ludwig's apartment, he became downright violent. The vibe I'm getting is that this is not a good thing. The problem is, I can't ask anybody anything about what's going on. Blake seems to be controlled by an outside force. He seems to be pushed by something outside his control, but I can't put my finger on it.

Is he traveling through time to protect these relics he keeps mentioning? Is he the good guy or the bad guy? Is he an agent of some evil organization bent on world destruction? Is he from the past? Is he from the future? I know he's traveling through time, just like me, but why?

What is his goal in all this? World domination? Control? War? Power?

I shake my head because now I sound like a conspiracy nut. We take several turns down alleyways and across streets. I have no clue where we are, but Ludwig is leading us somewhere safe. We make our way deeper and deeper into this stone maze.

Get it together, Rigs.

That's the thing. I thought I was dreaming. But, hours passed, and I didn't wake up. Everything looks and feels so real. More hours passed. I could smell the rain coming in the air yesterday at the meadow. I could feel the rain drops hitting my face and the mud under my feet. Blake's hand on my wrist last night was real. The keys on Ludwig's piano were cool under my fingers.

Everything IS real. This experience is no dream.

Ludwig stops in front of a red door on what appears to be the back of a tall four-story building. I turn back to see an empty alley. No Blake. Maybe we lost him. Ludwig fumbles with keys and unlocks three bolt locks, one at the top, one in the middle and one at the bottom of the door. It creaks as he pushes it open.

He has a key? And ANOTHER red door?

"In there, Julietta!" Ludwig firmly escorts me into the doorway, and for the second time today, his hand on the small of my back.

I don't mind, though.

We dash through the doorway and into a dark room.

Darkness envelops the room when the door swings closed behind us. Evidently, Ludwig knows his way around this room because I hear him behind me locking the bolt.

This is a safe place.

Here in the darkness, my first instinct is to be creeped out, but I trust Ludwig. He shuffles around me, and I hear two more bolts unlocking then another door creaks open. He takes my hand in his. His grasp is much gentler now as he leads me through this door into another dark room. I can't see anything, but this room feels much larger.

Ludwig strikes a match, and a dim glow spills out into the space. He lights an oil lamp. As my eyes adjust, I catch my breath. It reminds me of old Pops MacKenzie's storage room. Instead of instruments and cases, though, there are trees and stones, huge animal faces, and what appears to be racks and racks of colorful clothing.

What is this place?

As Ludwig lights more and more lamps, the room brightens up, and I see that at one end there is a large black curtain. There are all kinds of colorful props and set pieces strewn all over the place. Above me there are wooden beams with ropes and pulleys hanging from almost every joint. Wooden plank walkways connect different areas high above in the rafters.

"What is this place, Ludwig?"

"This, my dear..." he sweeps his hand in a grand gesture. "This is The Burgtheater."

31

"HAVE YOU NOT heard of 'die Burg'?" Ludwig looks astonished. "The Burgtheater?"

Die Burg? The Palace?

Even with my auto-translation powers kicking in I'm still having trouble understanding what he means. I try to smile, but I'm afraid that I just look like an uninformed and uncultured goof.

"The Burg Theater is *the* place to see and to be seen." Ludwig begins to tell the story of this very theatre, the backstage in which we are now standing.

It reminds me of all the behind the curtain scenes in *Phantom of the Opera*. In every corner, and piled high to the ceiling are set pieces and props for operas and ballets.

"Maria Theresa, the Empress of Austria, desired a theatre next to her palace," Ludwig stretches his hands wide, "and so they converted this old banquet hall into a royal stage for opera and drama."

History comes alive as Ludwig continues his lesson. He tells me about the royal boxes where the nobles sit. I can't imagine all the magical things that must have happened here. Well, in light of what I'm experiencing now, magical is probably not the right word.

This is so amazing.

"Die Burg, as the people call it, is the National Theatre of Austria. It's the Royal Theatre." He looks toward the other side of the closed curtain.

Ludwig recounts the debut of Mozart's operas here. He goes on and on about *Le nozze di Figaro* and how groundbreaking the music was for 1786. I don't have a clue what the title means, but since the real Julietta is supposed to have just moved from Italy, I just play along. I do recognize the name Figaro, but I'm not sure if it's from Mozart or another opera. I love classical music, but I don't listen to a whole lot of opera.

He tells me about how when *Figaro* was first performed, the Emperor Joseph, Maria Theresa's son, thought that the subject matter was too heavy and controversial. But, even with the emperor urging him to reconsider the subject mater, Mozart wouldn't be deterred. He pressed on and eventually convinced Joseph that he would tell the story in such a way that it would be entertaining without stirring up class warfare among the nobles and "common" folk.

"Ah," he sighs. "What could have been."

There's sadness in his voice. The missed opportunity to apprentice under Mozart still weighs heavily on him. He was only able to experience all of these amazing performances by Mozart vicariously through what the newspapers said or through hearsay from people who had actually been here in person to experience them.

"How I wish I could have been here for the *Figaro*," he looks dejected.

It amazes me, though, because I know that some two

hundred odd years later this man standing in front of me will be considered to be as great as Mozart. And by some, he'll be considered even more significant in his own right. When you talk about the greats of orchestral music, you always mention Bach, Mozart, Beethoven and maybe a few others like Haydn or Schubert. But Beethoven is *ALWAYS* on the list. Always.

He doesn't even know.

But there is a part of me that thinks he *does* know. From the first time I met him, I could tell that he was complex and intriguing. You don't become one of the world's greatest composers by being an ordinary, run-of-the-mill person with nothing going on. It seems like most of the people I've learned about that make beautiful music and art have such rich and, at times even dark, life stories.

He talks about the divas. The big time vocalists. The star singers in the opera. I gather that they are like the rock stars of their day.

"Do you play here?" I interrupt him.

He stops, surprised. After an awkward pause, he steps toward me.

"Oh, my. I must have been rambling your pretty little ears off." He smiles.

"I don't mind." I can feel my cheeks turning red. "Really, I don't."

Honestly, I get him. This whole time, I'm seeing myself in him. The serious, dark introvert. I wouldn't consider myself "emo" or anything, but I think most people think

I'm unapproachable because I hate life or something.

Well, I do hate life sometimes lately...

But it's not like that all the time. I'm not trying to be distant and unapproachable. It's just who I am. It's how I'm wired. I can't deal with drama and unnecessary chaos. It drains me.

And now I see the exact same things in Ludwig. He's not mean. He's not unapproachable, well at least not intentionally. As soon as we spent a little time together, he opened right up and became a real, warm human being. It's like night and day, though. In a crowd of people, I just want to run and hide, but inside my comfort zone, with people I know and like, it's like I can just be myself.

He's a lot like me.

"I debuted my First Symphony here in The Burg," he says with a humble smile. "April of last year. It went well."

"I bet it was amazeballs!"

He looks at me with a curious expression.

"I mean, I'm sure it was fantastic!"

Amazeballs? A-maze-balls? What am I thinking? I can hear it now: "This just in: Local teen musician and time traveler, Rigby Raines, blows her cover by using a stupid phrase and ruins all chances of her becoming Mrs. Ludwig van Beethoven. Back to you, Ron."

Then I laugh to myself for thinking I could ever actually be Mrs. Beethoven.

"Yes, yes," he says. "I worked on it over the course of five years. Sketching and re-sketching. Then writing and re-writing until it was finished. It was my way of announcing to the musical world 'I am Beethoven, master composer, not just Beethoven the piano virtuoso.'"

He exudes a confidence that I wish I had. I'm no Beethoven, by any means, but why is that we could be so similar, yet so different? Both introverts, but one so full of confidence, so much so that people think it's full-on arrogance. And then, me. Shy, scared, and the least confident person I've ever heard of.

"Julietta." He takes my hand. "I do not know who this Blake character is or what he desires, but know this: he is going to have to go through me if he thinks for one second that he can harm you."

His eyes are so determined. There's no doubt that I "feel" safe here with Ludwig. But I know that Blake is a dangerous man with a dangerous laser blaster gun from the future. That means that he could easily go through Ludwig if he so chose to.

I still don't understand everything about the situation and what Blake wants, but I am determined to resist for as long as I can. If he's a time traveler who's been able to track me somehow, I'm not sure that I'm safe at all. Even here, with Ludwig, in this beautiful theatre.

"Thank you, Ludwig. But we probably should go. I don't know how long we'll be safe here."

"Before we go," his eyes twinkle in the dim lamp light, "I would ask of you a simple request."

With that smile and those eyes, I don't think I could

possibly resist any request.

"What is it?"

"Julietta," he says firmly. "I believe that you have greatness within you. I don't know how to explain it, but I feel a presence, and an authority about you that is betrayed by your outer nervous manner."

"I'm not sure what you mean." I look at my feet.

The truth is, I know exactly what he means, even if I don't understand it. Mom used to tell me the same thing.

I couldn't count the times that she wrapped her arms around me and told me that I was her "great little Beethoven on piano." In the moment, it made me feel like I could conquer the world. I would pretend I could bottle up that feeling and take it with me. I always hoped that I could use it to get over my fear of playing in front of people. Then when I got in front of other people, like I always do, I'd end up freaking out and screwing everything up.

"I sense a deep tempest of emotion just below the surface that is yearning to escape." Ludwig moves a wild stray curl of hair from my face to behind my ear.

Oh, man, is this the moment that I get kissed by Ludwig van Beethoven?!

I have to admit that I haven't really ever kissed a guy. Unless you count kindergarten. I've just been too shy to put myself out there like that. I thought I was close last Halloween when Chewie came over to cheer me up dressed as Superman.

It was the worst Superman costume I've ever seen

because he was also wearing a ski mask and huge puffy winter gloves. He said it was cold. He brought me a Lois Lane outfit to put on, complete with my own ski mask and gloves. And just before we went out, he moved in really close to me. I thought he was going to kiss me, but he was just putting oversized clown glasses on my face, because that's just how he rolls.

Way to read the room, Rigs!

I am eye to eye with Ludwig. But, instead of moving in for a kiss, he turns and pulls me toward the curtain.

And there ya have it, folks! She swings and misses!

A rush of cool air hits my warm face as he pulls aside the curtain. On the other side, there is nothing but darkness, but I can tell it is a large room.

He lights a small lamp to reveal an empty stage. Well, it's empty except for a lone piano sitting in the middle of the large stage.

"Now is your time to shine, Julietta," he says as he points to the piano.

THE PIANO OCCUPIES a small space on the big stage, but it seems to be larger than life. It's like a tiny baby grand piano, but fancier. The outside is a smooth polished brown wood with some ornate carvings and inlays. It kind of looks like something that should be in a museum. It probably will be one day.

This thing is totally going to be worth millions some day in the future!

I walk around the piano, letting my hand glide over the smooth, polished wood. It's a lot smaller than my piano back home. The keyboard is colored in reverse. The natural keys are wooden and stained black. The accidental keys are smooth white ivory. The distance between the lowest and highest keys is only five octaves. My piano at home covers seven whole octaves.

There's a part of me that really does want to sit down and play this instrument. But with Ludwig watching, I'm sure I'll just freeze up. I freaked out the last time I tried to play in front of him. He's the greatest piano player of his generation, and then there's me.

Rigby, the nervous noob with butter fingers.

Out of the corner of my eyes, I can see that Ludwig is quietly watching me. His gaze is unsettling, but at the same time, I like the way he follows my every move. He's analyzing every little thing about me. It's a little freaky, but flattering at the same time. It doesn't make any sense.

"It would do me great honor if you played for me, Julietta." The question jolts me out of my haze.

How could I possibly bring honor to Beethoven? I can't even play in front of a marching band or a room full of moms. There's no way that I could hold it together to play for *the* Ludwig van Beethoven. I just want to run and hide.

"Just play what you know, sweet girl." He steps down off the stage and takes a seat in the front row.

My heart might beat out of my chest. My mind is racing. So many thoughts, like a whirlwind, in my head. I have never been confident at this sort of thing. What if I mess this up? Why is he staring? What if I'm not good enough? Will he like it?

Ugh...

I know that I *can* play. Skill-wise, I'm just as good as anyone. But I always get so nervous. The anxiety hits me like a truck when I try to play in front of people. My hands shake and my mind goes blank. Every single time. The only time that I am really comfortable is when I'm playing and writing music at home, alone in my room. Although, I haven't really wanted to do either very much lately. It's been pretty easy for me just to hide in the trumpet section in marching band.

But here I am now.

I sit down on the small bench in front of the beautiful piano. There's nothing to hide behind. It's just me, this piano and him. This theatre has probably seen and heard hundreds of masterpieces. Some were probably played on this very instrument.

I can't calm my nerves. My fingers are tingling. My nerves are fluttering through every part of my body, radiating out like angry butterflies from my stomach. I can't seem to relax. I still feel like I'm sitting at a piano for the very first time. Even after all of the hours and hours of lessons I took as a kid. Mom taught me well, but I can't ever express what she taught me.

Mom.

The sting comes back. Every time I think about her, my heart feels like it's being squeezed. It hurts like hell to think about. It doesn't matter when or where. When the memories creep up, the pain follows.

Has it already been a year?

"Everything will be fine." Ludwig's voice snaps me from my painful memory. "Let the music move you."

He is eager to hear me play something. I don't know why he is so intrigued by me. I am thankful, though. I'm happy to try and put my mind on something else.

Anything else.

I smile timidly at him, trying not to let on that I am so afraid at this moment. I could never have imagined I'd be here, in this time and place, in this beautiful theatre, playing a song for one of my greatest musical influences.

What am I thinking? One of THE greatest musical influences of ALL time. Crap. What song should I play?

I begin to panic. What SHOULD I play?

Will my presence here in this time do something to interfere with time and history?

I'm afraid that just being here and interacting with Ludwig could change the course of history.

Oh my god, I'm freaking out!

I can't think straight. I take a breath to try and gain control. I know a lot of the classics, but I'm not really great on when they happen date-wise. I know I can't play anything by Ludwig because it might not even exist yet! I've seen enough sci-fi to know that I could really screw things up if I play a piece that hasn't even been written yet.

My hands tremble a little as I stumble through my thoughts. The weight of my decision is freaking me out. I don't think I can handle this pressure. I just want to scream and run away. But I'm also fighting the fear. If I could just figure out something to play, maybe I can stay here and learn more about *why* I'm here.

Think, Rigs, think!

A thought pops into my mind. It's a simple idea, but it just might work.

What if I play something from MY time?

Something from the "future" but that couldn't possibly get mixed up in all the sci-fi, time travel, history bending mess I might create. Modern rock and pop music are so different than this really complex classical music.

Ok, Rigs, I think we're on to something!

I have to play something that is simple, but not recognizable. Maybe even something that would be easily forgotten. I think that will work. My mind immediately lands on The Beatles.

The Beatles! The Beatles! I could do that. Why didn't I think of that before?

I decide I can probably get away with this, by playing a song that is familiar to me. I don't think a Beatles song will mess with the wibbly-wobbly timey-wimey stuff. I can play just about every Beatles song by memory! I could even do it blindfolded if I wanted!

She shoots, she scores!!

Yes. That's it! I scroll through a mental checklist of all the Beatles songs I could play

Eleanor Rigby?

It's such a special song to me. If there is any song that has set the course for my life, it's *Eleanor Rigby*. Heck, when you're named after a song, it kind of fills a special place in your life. But something about it just doesn't seem right for this situation.

What about Yesterday?

It's a great song with great melodies. So many good covers. Especially the one by Boyz II Men. That's my jam. But, no, I'm not really feeling that one either. It's just not quite right.

Hmmm, How about Hey Jude?

It could work. It is probably one of the greatest modern "pop" songs of all time. At least, the critics think so. The melodic phrase at the end is very catchy and just about everybody recognizes it. That may be *too* popular. I really want to impress Ludwig, but I don't want him to somehow accidentally work any "Nah nah nah nah nahs" into his next opera!

C'mon, Rigs, keep cool. There's got to be something...

A thought hits me like a lightning bolt. A simple, dark melody begins to form in the back of my mind. It only takes a few notes to realize it's a song that I memorized as a kid. I haven't played it in forever. The last time I heard it was at Mom's funeral. It was her favorite song, and it became our song over the years.

Because.

I think about it for what seems like ages, but is more like seconds. This is the one. It's not one of the most popular Beatles songs, but it is lovely. I think I can play it, but it will be bitter, it's gonna hurt to go there again. At the funeral, I did everything I could to be strong, to fight the tears. I chose to stuff the hurt and pain deep down into some place inside that I never want to revisit.

Because.

I can see Ludwig inching closer to the edge of his seat. His eyes are so intense. I know he sees my fear. He wouldn't have pushed me into this if I was confident. Why is he so intrigued by me? What will he do if I really botch this. That is totally a possibility. Especially since I haven't played it for a while.

I'm afraid that I might literally just lose it and become a scream-crying mess. But something inside of me wants that. I actually want to let go. For the first time in a long time, I actually think I want to let go and just feel that pain.

Because.

Yes, that's the one. It's settled. I'm going to play the song *Because.*

Why? I can't really say. I think it must be because it is the song that takes me closest to the pain of losing Mom.

She's not coming back.

I have to accept that fact. I'm playing this song even if I lose it and make a fool of myself. This is my moment. I have to do this. I can't hide from these emotions forever. I have to face them.

Now, Rigby. Just do it.

One last nervous flutter tickles my insides. I might just throw up. Before I woke up here in this place, and in this time, I don't think I could have ever imagined that I would be sitting in front of one of the world's most famous composers actually playing him a song. But, here I am, and I'm ready to embrace whatever happens, whether it's good, bad, and/or ugly.

Here we go. Because.

33

I INHALE SLOWLY through my nose to straighten my posture and to steel my nerves. I exhale through my mouth and imagine all the anxiety leaving my body. Of course, it doesn't really but it doesn't hurt to try. I lift my fingers for a split second and then I begin.

Time seems to slow down as I play the first note of a haunting arpeggio. The dark, moody C sharp minor chord fills the air with a foreboding melancholy. The sound of the hammer hitting the strings resonates from the piano like a storm rolling in from the ocean.

The notes come back to me with ease. The old familiar song gathers dark clouds within in my chest. Memory after memory falls into my mind like beautiful, sad little rain drops as I move into the verse. My heart aches a little more with each new measure. The rain drops become tears and find their way to my eyes.

A picture forms in my mind. I'm four years old. I'm sitting next to Mom on the piano bench. She's teaching me the basics of reading music.

"Every good boy does fine. Good boys do fine always."

Her hands are warm as she places them on top of mine to help me learn the scales. She hugs me after I play the scales up and back down. At least once, during every lesson, she would hug me. Kind of like a reward for trying my best. I loved those hugs.

I miss those hugs.

This memory hurts. The pain inside is growing. I see myself at seven, then ten, then thirteen. She is always there next to me. We're laughing. Sometimes so much so that we're both crying.

Why did it have to be MY mom?

I remember how sick she got. The chemo didn't seem to help. Seven months. That was all we had. She seemed so healthy and full of life and then she couldn't get out of bed. I was so confused during those months. I couldn't believe it was really happening to her.

Why, God? Why? What did she ever do to anyone?

Toward the end, I got really angry. We could see the end coming and knew she would be gone soon. I withdrew. I couldn't handle it. The pain. The sorrow. If I had been that sad just thinking about losing her, how would I be when she actually did die. I didn't want to think about it, so I hid farther inside myself.

Some days I took it out on her. It was like my whole world was collapsing. I would be without a mom. MY mom.

Why couldn't she fight this?

All she wanted to do was spend time with me. To hear me play music. But I pulled away. I built walls. I didn't want to feel the hurt.

The week that she died she asked me to play some of her favorite songs for her. I couldn't do it. I wouldn't do it. I was so mean. So selfish. I was so afraid.

What is wrong with me?

But in all that she still wanted to hug me. She was dying, her body racked with pain, and she still wanted to show me how special I was. Our special reward system.

As angry and scared as I was, I couldn't live without her hugs. As selfish as I was, I needed to feel her arms around me. As the days went on, they got weaker and weaker until one day she slipped into a coma. And then she just faded away and was gone.

She's gone.

The sorrow hits me like a ton of bricks. To keep from sobbing outright, I close my eyes. But I keep playing. I know this song, note for note. I embrace every deep, dark emotion that is flooding into me right now. All of this sadness and sorrow becomes a violent tempest. It rumbles out from my heart and soul, pouring out forcefully like a wild, angry thunderstorm.

The piano seems to become a living, breathing creature capable of grieving. The keys, hammers, and strings all work together to cry out in anguish with me. Of course, it isn't *really* alive. It's just a piano made of wood and metal - a well-crafted instrument that amplifies the emotions and desires of the person playing it. Every drop of emotion, every ounce of heartache that I've been storing up for the last year pours out through my hands and resonates out through the piano.

I am not just playing a simple song anymore. I'm not just trying to get by without screwing up. I don't even care if this impresses Ludwig or not. It's as if the actual music is coming from inside me. It's scary and exhilarating all at the same time. I'm facing my sorrow head on. I'm owning up to my fears and faults, and I'm letting go now.

Ludwig was right.

As the music continues to rise from the piano, I embrace the melancholy and allow this beautiful, dark storm to rage within me. Before this, I was so worried that Ludwig would think I was a fool. If I messed up would he laugh at me? Would he hate me? I was so worried that I wouldn't be able to bear it if he thought I was an idiot.

All of that doesn't matter now because I'm soaring. I'm flying. My heart has just erupted into a sorrowful storm, but by embracing it, I'm ascending and breaking through the clouds. In this dark room, I can feel the warmth of sunlight hitting my soul. The tears are flowing freely, but I don't care. I haven't cried like this in forever.

Mom. I love you. I miss you so much. I'm...so...sorry.

My body sways to the music. It feels like an eternity but only about two and a half minutes have passed. The end of the song is coming. Just around the corner. I don't want it to stop. I'm climbing Mount Everest and swimming across the Atlantic at the same time. I'm walking on clouds and drinking in the sunrise. Something inside me is different by the time I reach the final notes of the last measure.

A warm blanket of peace wraps around me as the last chord softly fades away to nothing, my hands still resting on the keys. My head is bowed. I let out a contented sigh.

What just happened?

I was broken before, but somehow the music fixed me. I had been a mess, but something about playing the song just pulled my shattered pieces back together. I can't explain it. Is it possible that music really does have the power to move someone so much?

I still can't open my eyes. I'm so at peace. I'm just lingering in this quiet triumph. I think it's more than just a song. I had to let go. I had to let the sorrow in. I needed to grieve, and the song was just the doorway.

"Mom," I whisper, "I know you're proud of me."

The room is quiet. The only sound in the vast hall is my breathing. I can actually feel my heartbeat in my chest. The world is frozen around me, so unimportant in this moment. I've been transported to a secret, safe place, where nobody can hurt me. Nothing can torment me here. No fear. No anxiety. No sadness. No guilt. No bully. No mysterious secret agent from the future. Nothing's going to change my world now.

An unfamiliar feeling swells up in my chest. It's confidence. I haven't felt much of that, maybe ever.

I'm safe.

It's like I'm gazing out across the universe. Stars, planets, and galaxies spin beautifully. They're right where they should be. Right here and now nothing's gonna change my world.

Everything is so big, and I am feeling so very small, but it's ALL so beautiful.

I know it's all going to be ok. Something bigger than all

this is embracing me right now. If there is a god, I wonder if this is the way they speak to people. I don't hear any words, but I *feel* like my heart is being spoken to. Even though I've always been just Rigby, just the shy girl that nobody noticed.

Here in this quiet moment I hear the reassuring words, "You are enough."

Why?

"Just because."

As wonderful as this encounter is, something isn't quite right. I feel it before I even open my eyes. I realize that I'm alone. It's too quiet here.

I finally turn around to look at the front row, not knowing what to expect from Ludwig. I really do hope he enjoyed my playing. I had poured all of my emotion and fear into it. I expect to see him smiling, but I don't see Ludwig at all.

He's gone.

There's nobody in this empty concert hall. It's just me, all alone on this stage.

Where is he?

"Ludwig?" I whisper sharply. "Ludwig?"

I'm suddenly full of doubt again, unsure what to do. I scan across the rows of empty wooden seats thinking maybe he moved to a different spot. He's not there.

"Ludwig? Are you there?"

Alone. Again.

34

"LUDWIG?" I'M TRYING to keep to a whisper, but my voice echoes off the empty seats. "Where are you?"

I have never felt as alive, as unafraid, as I do in this moment. I looked the storm of my sorrow square in the eye and stood my ground undaunted. I didn't flinch. I embraced my pain and sorrow, and although I know I'll still deal with those emotions again and again, I've discovered healing in just letting go.

I wasn't sure Ludwig would be impressed, but I know that something changed inside me. As far as the actual notes, I'm pretty sure I rocked the song perfectly, but that seems irrelevant right now. And for what it's worth, impressing Ludwig with my playing seems less important. He encouraged me to let go and I did.

There is an electric sensation coursing through my body. I'm soaring.

Mom would be so proud.

I stand up and peer out across the theater. I narrow my eyes in a squint trying to locate where Ludwig might have gone. The room seems less dark than when we first entered it. Rows of empty red seats stretch all the way to the back of the large room.

Where is he?

I step down from the stage hoping to see him. I creep slowly and nervously toward the side aisle. There are doors at the back of the room.

Maybe he's out there.

This theater is amazing. The room is long and narrow from front to back, but it's tall. The rows of balcony boxes seem to stretch to the sky. In the dim light, I can now make out four levels of boxes. The ceiling is a big dome with a bunch of fancy gold ornamentation. A large chandelier hangs from the middle of the ceiling. It is beautiful.

I run my hands over the backs of row after row of upholstered wooden chairs. From the stage, it seemed like there were thousands of seats, but as I walk by, it becomes clear that there are only about twenty rows in all.

At the last row, I look back towards the stage and imagine the greats like Mozart and Haydn performing their musical masterpieces here. Operas, concertos, and symphonies filled this room with musical magic. It would have been amazing to sit here in these seats last year and take in the debut of Beethoven's First Symphony.

Ludwig.

Before this weird dream of an adventure, he was just a figure on a page. A name on my Spotify playlist. Background music in movies. The soundtrack of my piano lessons with Mom. I mean, he *did* have a tremendous impact on me, but he was just a ghost, historical ink on the pages of a history book.

Until now.

I haven't known him very long. We just met, but I feel like there's something that connects us, and I can't put my finger on it. Of course, the obvious connection is our introverted natures.

He'd probably win the gold medal at the Introversion Olympics, though!

As I turn to face the back door, the sound of a muffled sniff comes from the other side. I push the door open slowly. The hinges whine softly. Ludwig is there in the entryway of the theater. He is nonchalantly leaning against the wall trying to appear as if nothing is happening, but it's obvious that he's been crying.

What in the world? Did I do something?

A few minute ago he seemed to be so serious and in control. Now, his red, bloodshot eyes are betraying that cool, calm, collected manner.

"Julietta." He clears his throat as he straightens up, smoothing down the front of his suit coat and fidgeting with the buttons.

"Ludwig, did I do something?" I blurt out. "Didn't you like what I played?"

I'm wracking my brain trying to figure out why the best piano player in the world would ask me to play something for him, and then leave the room. And then, on top of that, I find him out here in the foyer crying.

"I was so nervous, and I didn't know what to play." I want to run and hide. "Then I just picked a song. It was my mom's favorite."

What have I done? I've gone and freaked out THE Ludwig van Beethoven!

He just stares at me with watery eyes, clenching his teeth. He looks as if he might cry again. Even though I just experienced a major win in embracing my pain and letting it out through the music, there's a small part of me that is dying right now. I *really did* want to impress Ludwig.

"I just wanted to play something without botching it," my voice cracks.

Ludwig leans in close to me and grabs my arm firmly, but gently.

"My dear, pray pardon me! I had no intention of displeasing you with my hasty exit. I can imagine what you must think of me, and I cannot deny that you have good grounds for an unfavorable opinion."

His eyes.

I'm captivated by his wild, hazel eyes. There is a fiery sorrow in them. I've never really had a thing for older men, but I am open to exceptional circumstances! I think I'm ok with the possibility of being called *Mrs. Beethoven.*

"Julietta." He speaks quietly and his voice sounds like a song. "I began music in my fourth year and since then it has ever been my favorite pursuit. Thus early introduced to the sweet Muse, who attuned my soul to pure harmony, I loved her, and sometimes ventured to think that I was beloved by her in return."

The passion for music is evident in his face as he explains how his father had taught him lessons at an early age and pushed him hard to be the next child prodigy, the next Mozart.

"What was your father like?" I ask.

"Sadly," his eyes drop, "Father was an unyielding man. He was no stranger to wine. I loved him for his music, and yet hated him for the back of his hand."

Oh, no.

"On a near daily basis Father taught me music lessons in his draconian manner." Ludwig's eyes reflect a sense of shame. "Piano lessons were often accompanied by floggings and extended times locked in the cellar."

He seems to stare deeply into the floor, into a different time and place. I can't imagine anybody physically abusing someone as talented as Ludwig. A wave of sadness hits me as I envision a young, scared little boy trying as hard as he can to please his tormenter, his father.

"Music. She's everything to me." Ludwig shifts his weight as he sighs. "My dear Juliet, as you began to play, my heart was inexplicably moved. I sensed a deep, dark sorrow that I have not felt for these last fourteen years, since the day my sweet mother died."

A small tear forms in the corner of his eye. It's starting to make sense. The connection between us is real.

"I was in my seventeenth year," he whispers.

"Oh, Ludwig."

My heart catches in my throat. His serious demeanor, his introversion, his passion. They all come from a place of pain. A father who drove him to excel, a natural talent for music, and the loss of his mother.

"She was indeed a kind, loving mother to me, and my

best friend." Ludwig stops to reflect.

It makes sense now why I feel so drawn to Ludwig. It's not because I love music or even the history of music. It's not even because I like the sound of Beethoven's music. I'm not star stuck, even though this has been the greatest experience of my life. It's not even because he is so mysteriously handsome, standing vulnerably here in front of me, all broody and serious.

I know exactly what it feels like to lose a mother. I know what it feels like to be crushed by the news that your mom is dying and will soon be gone.

Ludwig tells me that in 1787 his mother was sick with Consumption. I learned in Health class that it's what we know as Tuberculosis, a terrible disease. He had just moved from his hometown of Bonn to Vienna where Mozart had agreed to take him on as a pupil. Just two weeks after settling in, he had to return to Bonn because his father urged him through letters to come back to be with his mother. She was dying.

"I did everything I could." Ludwig sighs. "My longing once more to see my dying mother overcame every obstacle, and assisted me in surmounting the greatest difficulties. Who was happier than I, when I could still utter the sweet name of mother, and it was heard? But to whom can I now say it?"

Ludwig's mother passed away shortly after. His father went off the deep end further into alcoholism. At seventeen, Beethoven had to take on the responsibility of caring for his two younger brothers. This is what kept him from coming to Vienna when he had the opportunity to apprentice with Mozart. He bravely set aside his personal ambition to stay and look out for his younger siblings until they could take care of themselves.

This is breaking my heart.

"She is gone." He hangs his head, and his shoulders shake as he cries.

"I know, Ludwig." I slide my arms under his arms and around his sides and rest my head on his chest.

I know.

It's an awkward hug, but he sighs as he lets me embrace him. After about ten long seconds, his arms tentatively wrap around me, and we just stand there, breathing in and out slowly, recharging in the way that only introverts can - away from large, busy crowds, in small, intimate, one-on-one interactions.

It feels like time has stopped again. I'm loving this moment. It is what I've needed, but I realize something as we stand here gaining strength from each other. I could easily fall for someone like Ludwig, but even in this sweet, vulnerable moment, I keep seeing another guy's face.

Chewie.

It doesn't surprise me. But somehow in all this, in the middle of what seems like a weird dream or romantic movie scene, I'm thinking of my best friend. Don't get me wrong, I'm enjoying this moment. But, all I really want is to be hugged by Chew.

35

THE DOORS I had come through minutes before slowly swing open with a quiet creak. The messy-haired head of a young boy pokes through first, followed by the anxious face of Carl. A smile crosses his face when he sees that he's found Ludwig and me here.

"Whew," he exhales. "Am I glad to see you!"

"Wait a minute, Carl," I ask perplexed, "how did you get in here? This place is locked up like a bank vault!"

"Oh, I know my way around die Burg," he says with a mischievous smirk. "Nobody ever checks the upper windows. What are you two doing?"

"Carl," Ludwig awkwardly ends our hug and changes the subject. "Are you hurt?"

"I'm fine and you?" He grins.

"We're ok." I step closer to double check that he is ok. "You really gave Blake a good knock, didn't you?"

"I did indeed! I never leave home without my lucky horseshoe," he beams with pride. "Why does he want to hurt you, Fräulein?"

"He wants to steal my metronome, Carl. It's a very precious gift that someone special gave to me, and it means a whole lot to me."

"A metronome?" Ludwig asks. "I believe you that it's precious, but what, pray tell, is so special about it?"

"You have to trust me, Ludwig." I sigh. "I can't explain

why this is all happening. All I know is that we have to keep the metronome safe."

"It makes no sense. The violence. The fire-breathing weapon this Blake character possesses. The metronome. I don't understand, but I do trust you, Julietta."

"Carl, is it safe?" I turn towards the young boy.

"Yes, Lady Julietta." He is proud of himself. "When you gave it to me in the carriage earlier, I didn't understand why, but when that bad man showed up, I knew I had to keep it safe."

He tells us how he scurried through the streets to a clock shop and hid inside. There were cuckoo clocks, and grandfather clocks, and small bedside clocks, and even a whole section of metronomes.

"I placed the metronome on a shelf filled with a bunch of other metronomes." He smiles innocently. He doesn't have a clue that by leaving it unguarded it could potentially fall into the wrong hands.

"YOU DID WHAT?" Ludwig grabs the boy by the arm.

"I thought it would be safe, and hard to find if I placed it on a shelf filled with other metronomes."

"Ludwig, it's ok," I put my arms around Carl. "He is only trying to help."

"Of course, you are right, Julietta." He shakes his head. "Please forgive my outburst."

"We've got to make our way to that shop and find my metronome," I'm already thinking about losing the metronome. "It's imperative."

I can't even begin to imagine being stuck here in this time permanently. If I can't get to the metronome and figure out how to work it, I may have to settle for being Mrs. Beethoven. This experience has definitely been one of the greatest adventures of my life. So much better than all my summer trips to Six Flags. I love being here in this time, in this adventure, but I don't want to be stranded here forever.

36

IF THERE'S A bright side to this situation, it's that there's no way Blake could know where Carl hid the metronome. It makes sense that he knew how to find me at Ludwig's apartment because Ma-ma kept going on about my "first piano lesson with the esteemed Mr. Beethoven" during the party last night.

I know young Carl had good intentions, but this adds a new layer of challenge to our current situation. We were able to lose Blake in the busy streets of Vienna by ducking into this theater, but sooner or later we're going to have to move, and that puts us out in the open. If he's really from the future, and I have no doubt that he is, he might have some sort of technology to figure out where we are, or even to communicate with whoever it is that's ordering him to do all this.

Either way, when Carl let the metronome out of his possession, he opened a new can of worms. The Ludwig that I have known the last few hours has been calm and collected, but when he grabbed Carl his eyes flashed anger in a way that surprised me. It makes me nervous.

I hope he doesn't turn out to be like his father.

Since Mom's diagnosis, I haven't really been a praying person. I guess I was too mad at God to want to talk to him, and even now, sometimes I wonder if there's even anybody up there. But if there *is* a God somewhere up there in the sky, I'm praying that he would somehow let Ludwig be a better man than his father was to him.

We cautiously make our way back into the streets, stopping at the intersections of alleys to scan all directions for any sign of Blake. It's probably an exercise in futility, though, there are so many people in the heart of the city today, that it should be impossible to find us.

The three of us make an odd group: a master composer and pianist, a happy-go-lucky young boy, and a time-traveling trumpet-playing wanna-be drum major from the twenty-first century.

"The clock shop is two blocks over in that direction." Carl points to his left.

"Right," Ludwig says. "Lead on."

As we approach the block the shop is on, we regroup to plan our strategy. Ludwig thinks Carl should just go back and retrieve the metronome. I don't want to put him or Ludwig in danger, so I think I should go. Carl is eager to help, so he thinks he should be the one to go.

We decide that Carl is probably the best choice since he can slip in and out without drawing much attention to himself. Ludwig gives him some coins to pay for the metronome in case he can't discreetly sneak it back out.

Ludwig and I slip into a quaint shop across the street to watch Carl through the window. It's a shoe repair shop. There are shiny, polished leather shoes on shelves behind the counter. Black ones with buckles. Brown ones with laces. In the corner is a metal shoe stretcher that looks like a medieval torture device.

"Excuse me, can I offer you assistance?" The cobbler, a short, round man, asks.

"We are just looking around," I answer politely, "but thank you, sir."

"Looking at what, ma'am? This is a shoe repair shop?" The man seems perplexed.

"Oh, sorry," I try to come up with an explanation awkwardly. "We are very interested in what it takes to... uh...repair shoes."

Ludwig cuts a sideways glance at me with half a smirk on his face.

"Yes, good sir," he says sweeping his hands toward the metal shoe stretcher. "As a matter of fact, would you mind taking the time to demonstrate how this fearsome looking contraption here works?"

Ludwig motions me to the window. I take up the lookout post, as he occupies the storekeeper.

Carl is cautiously making his way to the clock shop entrance. He stops every few steps and looks around in every direction. He reminds me of the nervous deer I sometimes see on the side of the highway back in Georgia.

No, it can't be...

Down the crowded street two stores down, a tall figure in black is weaving through the crowd. He's scanning the crowd in all directions. It's possible that it's not Blake, but there's no mistaking the all black outfit.

Oh, no! Carl!

Maybe he won't see him. Carl reaches out to open the door. I look back toward Blake. A look of recognition appears on his face, and he quickens his pace. He sees Carl.

"Ludwig!" I exclaim. "I don't know how, but Blake is right over there, and I think he's seen Carl. What should we do now?"

"We've got to get that metronome," he turns his back on the cobbler. "If it truly means as much as you say it does, we can't let it out of our grasp."

"But, sir!" The cobbler tugs on Ludwig's coat. "What about the shoe stretcher?!"

"I'm sorry, good man," Ludwig hands him a large silver coin. "This will have to wait for another time."

The cobbler smiles at Ludwig's generosity, calling to us to have a good day as we exit the shoe shop.

Across the street, Blake is entering the clock store. Through the windows, we can see Carl with the metronome at the counter. He must be attempting to pay for it. The clockmaker is wagging his finger furiously at the frightened boy. As I get closer to the window, I can hear the shopkeeper yelling something about stealing. Blake steps behind Carl and puts a hand on the boy's shoulder.

"I'm so sorry about this," Blake tells the clockmaker. "My son has a habit of coming into stores and trying to run off with things."

"The boy tried to offer me some money," the clockmaker explained, "but it was *after* I caught him trying to stuff this metronome into his pants."

Ludwig takes up a post on the left side of the shop's door, and I'm peeking around the right side corner trying not to get spotted by Blake. I can hear everything. This isn't going well for Carl. If we don't do something, it appears that Blake is going to walk out of the shop and into the streets with the metronome. I may never see it again. I have no clue what he'll do or where he'll go, but I cannot lose that metronome.

Think, Rigs, think!

Blake has a firm grasp on Carl as he apologizes once again, pays the clockmaker extra for his inconvenience, and then turns to leave the store. Ludwig signals me to back off and then retreats to the corner on the other side and disappears behind a large carriage. I pull my head back quickly and duck back around my corner.

There is now a lot of space between Ludwig and me. I'm not sure I want to come face to face with Blake without Ludwig close to help. I flatten myself against the wall of the building, hoping that Blake doesn't see me. We'll have to regroup after they pass by, and try and rescue Carl and retrieve the metronome. For now, though, I'm trying to blend into the alley. Blake's voice is getting louder.

He's coming your way, Rigs.

"I don't understand you people," Blake says. "I asked politely. This relic means nothing to you, and yet you all risked your own safety to keep it from me. Why?"

"Why are you such a bad man?" Carl asks in return.

"Listen, little lad. I am *not* a bad man. I am just doing

my job. This whole situation is way over your head. I couldn't possibly expect you to understand what we're trying to accomplish."

I try not to panic. Blake's voice is literally right around the corner. The alleyway is narrow and empty. It ends in a high pile of boxes and crates. I don't see a way around them. If he comes around the corner there is nothing to hide behind. I stumble backward over my own feet, hoping he won't round the corner.

He does.

37

CARL'S EYES ARE wide with fear. Blake has a firm death grip on his tiny shoulder. I'm sure an unexpected blow to the head from behind with a heavy horseshoe-loaded boot has something to do with that.

"Ah, we meet again," Blake mockingly emphasizes each syllable as he steps closer. "Ju-li-e-tta, is it?"

"Leave Carl out of this, Blake!"

"But, don't you see," he looks down at the frightened boy. "Carl is my secret weapon. I knew he'd be your driver today, so I put a tracker in his coat. Wherever he went, I knew. He led me on quite the wild goose hunt, but fortunately for me, he led me right to the relic."

Carl looks confused as Blake pulls a small metallic object from under the collar of his jacket. He rolls it around in his hand before putting it into his own pocket.

"Too easy." Blake's smugness is off-putting. It reminds me of Taura.

I backstep farther into the alley as he forces Carl to walk toward me. The walls of the buildings on either side are closing in. When we are halfway down the alley, where no one can see us, he stops.

From the inside chest pocket of his jacket, Blake pulls out a small leather wallet billfold. But it's not a billfold. It opens up to reveal some sort of electronic tablet on the inside. He taps on the screen, and a blueish 3D projection of the area pops up into that air right above the tablet.

Okaaaay, that's not an iPhone.

"This technology is way beyond your simplistic satellite-based GPS systems in the twenty-first century," he seems bored and uninterested.

A red blinking dot flashes in the middle of what looks to be a holographic projection of the exact spot we're standing. Blake was able to track Carl to the exact location. And when Carl started moving, he was able to head right to the area he'd be in. He snaps the billfold shut and puts it back in his chest pocket.

Kind of like my phone, but way better.

"Listen, Blake." I step toward him with my hands up. "There's no need for anybody to get hurt here."

"You've made your stand. There's no turning back now," he growls with an angry scowl that doesn't cover up a look of slight hesitation.

I HAVE made my stand.

What he doesn't know is that I'm a changed person. I'm not afraid anymore. Oh sure, I don't want to get shot with his laser gun, but that's not what I mean. Something broke inside me when I played the piano earlier, and out of that brokenness something new grew and grew. I feel like the Grinch whose heart grew three sizes in one day, but it's more than just that.

I am not "just Rigby" anymore. I am Rigby Raines, teen musician, and time traveler. THE Rigby Raines and this guy has picked the wrong girl to mess with.

I grit my teeth and take another step closer. I don't know how this is going to turn out, but I will not let this time-traveling bully push us around. Even if it means I don't make it out of this.

Heck, I'm not even sure if this won't actually cause me to wake up back home in my own bed. But still, there's something inside my head tingling like spider-sense. This is real danger.

"That's close enough, girl." Blake pulls out his future gun and aims it at me. He pushes Carl to the ground. "Get over there with her, little lad."

Carl scrambles to relative safety behind me.

Where the heck is Ludwig?!

Blake laughs an almost desperate laugh as he tries to open the metronome with one hand while pointing the gun at me. I'm not going to budge. If this is the end, I'm going out protecting Carl.

The metronome cover snaps open. Blake's eyes are wide as if he's expecting to experience some miraculous and powerful event. He pulls at the metal arm. Nothing happens. He turns the box over and winds the mechanism. Nothing happens.

"Well, this is unexpected." He looks at the bottom of the metronome.

"Blake, *why* is this so important?" I ask, my hands still raised. "What could possibly be going on in the future that needs people like you to travel back in time to torment people like us?"

"You wouldn't understand." He keeps the gun aimed at me. "It's for the *good* of people like *you* that I'm doing this. Every agent exists and acts for the benefit of the collective."

"But *WHY*, Blake?" I import. "What do you mean by 'the collective?'"

From what I can piece together, I understand that he's some kind of agent from the future sent back in time to round up so-called relics. From what he's said so far, he seems to think they are dangerous. He's definitely acting on orders, but in his eyes I see something beyond that. He is definitely hiding something. Something deeper and more personal than just following orders.

"I'm a soldier." He focuses his eyes on me, and for a split second I see the same sadness in them. "I do what I'm told. Like any good soldier would."

There it is! The sadness! He's holding back.

Back toward the busy street we just came from, people begin shouting and running. Something is causing a commotion in the street. From around the corner comes the fast rumble of clopping horse hooves and what sounds like a carriage that is moving too fast. Women are shrieking, and men are swearing.

A large carriage bounces into view with Ludwig at the reigns. He's pulling back with all his might and stops the carriage right in the intersection cutting off the street from the alley. This means that there is nowhere to run for Carl or me. But, it also means that Blake is boxed in with us. He turns to see what's causing all the ruckus behind him.

Now or never, Rigs.

In a split second, my life flashes before my eyes. Well, not really my whole life, but I think of everything *good* in my life. Finding the metronome has been a weird, but life changing discovery. I don't know why Pops picked me to get the old cornet and find the metronome. I don't know if it is destiny or some funny coincidence. But when it all comes down to it, I decide that I'm not going to let Blake take this from me. This is MY adventure. Ludwig is MY friend. Carl doesn't deserve to be bullied by Blake. This is MY experience of a lifetime. He is holding on to a very special relic that is *MY* metronome.

This is MY time.

38

IN ANOTHER SPLIT second, I remember all the pain and
sorrow that I experienced and tried to stuff over the last
year. I gather it into the center of my chest. I recall every
time that I've missed Mom. I think about every time I
messed up an audition or chair test, even when I was a kid.
I remember every anxiety attack, every stage fright filled
recital. I replay every time Taura made me feel like a fool
and every time that I worked myself up thinking that
everyone hated me.

It all stings. It hurts. It's pure pain.

But this time, instead of stuffing it down, I embrace it.
Instead of trying to run away from it and hide, I use it. I
roll it up and envision myself packing it tighter and tighter
into an electric ball of pain powerful enough to wreck a
person, but small enough to hold in my fist.

All this happens in the blink of an eye. I'm ready.

Because.

I see Chewie's face in my mind, and that settles it. I'm
getting back to my best friend and nobody's going to stop
me. Especially not this guy in front of me who is bent on
stealing *MY* metronome.

Blake swings his gun around toward Ludwig and fires
off a shot that hits the carriage ten inches below where he's
sitting. Ludwig ducks off to the other side.

"BLAKE!" I scream loudly, my hands balling into fists.

"STOP THIS! RIGHT NOW!"

He turns back toward me.

My right hand feels like it's on fire. All of that electricity, that ball of fiery pain, is buzzing in my fist. I look down at it. There aren't any actual sparks or sizzles. But I can definitely feel it.

Because.

For all the folks pushed around by people like Taura. For all the people who have lost the most important people in their lives. For Carl and for Ludwig, I spring into action.

In two steps, I close the distance between myself and Blake. He swings his occupied arms wildly at me, grabbing for me, catching nothing but air. His eyes go wide in surprise as I pivot right and leap off my left foot. I let all that pain drive my fist straight into his nose. His head snaps back from the force of the punch. I'm surprised at how hard I hit him. I don't know if it's adrenaline or what, but I don't feel any pain in my hand at all.

He falls to one knee dropping both the gun and the metronome. I kick the gun to the side, and it skitters across the alley until it comes to rest against the wall out of his reach. Carl crawls over quickly and takes possession of it.

Blake is holding his nose. His eyes are watering, and blood begins to stream down his chin onto his jacket. A small part of me feels sorry for him, but I'm not letting him get the upper hand like he did back at Ludwig's apartment.

He reaches blindly for either the gun or the metronome. I'm not sure which. He pats the ground in front of him first left, then right, then left again.

"You won't get away with this," he mumbles. "They can see everything."

I pick up the metronome before his hand gets to it.

"I believe this is mine." There are drops of his blood on it. I wipe them off with the corner of my dress.

Ludwig climbs down from the carriage.

"Julietta!" He is out of breath. "I am not sure what just happened, but I do believe you might take the first prize in a fisticuffs competition!"

Blake rolls over onto his back and groans. I take the gun from Carl. It would be pretty bad if he accidentally shoots someone. His little hands are shaking, but he is standing next to me bravely.

"Not so fun when someone else is holding the gun, eh, Blake?" I say.

"You don't understand, this..." he stutters through bloody lips. "This isn't me. I can't control..."

Suddenly, Blake grabs his chest as his his body starts convulsing. It looks like every part of him is cramping at once. He screams through his teeth in pain. And then just as suddenly as it started, the convulsion stops, and he lays there motionless.

I can't tell if he's breathing. He's just laying there with his eyes closed. Carl inches closer and reaches the toe of his boot out to tap Blake's shoe. Nothing.

"Carl," Ludwig snaps. "Stand back, at once."

"He's right, Carl." I keep the gun trained on him. "We

don't know if he's faking it."

"This isn't me"? What is that supposed to mean?

Ludwig kicks him softly in the leg. Nothing. He nudges him with a little more force this time. Still nothing.

"He is either unconscious or dead," Ludwig says as he leans closer to check and see if he is breathing.

"Be careful, Ludwig!" I circle around him so that Blake is still in my sights.

I wait for him to lean in and listen for Blake's breathing but he doesn't. Instead, he puts his hand on Blake's chest.

"That is quite strange." He pulls the leather billfold out of Blake's pocket.

It's crackles and sends a small shock up Ludwig's arm. He curses and throws it against the wall. The cover flops open, and I can see that the tablet screen is flickering with the electricity running through it. Blake grabbed his chest right before he seized up and passed out.

Wait a minute! This tablet thing knocked him out!?

I smash down on it as hard as I can with my foot again and again. It flickers a few last times and then the screen goes black.

Ludwig warily puts his hand back on Blake's chest again. I'm not sure why he doesn't just lean in and put his ear over Blake's face. I see it in the movies all the time, but then again, I'm not an EMT or anything, but it just strikes me as odd that he just doesn't lean down and listen.

Oh, my gosh. I can't believe I haven't thought about this before now! Ludwig is losing his hearing!

Everyone that knows anything about music history knows that Ludwig loses his hearing as he gets older. Some stories say that he even composed music for years without ever actually hearing the notes. There are accounts that tell of him banging out notes while he laid his head on the piano so he could "feel" the resonance through the wood of the instrument. One of the most circulated stories recalls that he couldn't actually hear anything when he composed the famous *Symphony No. 9* and that he only knew it was a success because when it was over, he saw people giving him a standing ovation.

But he's too young to be experiencing that now, right?

It becomes evident that he's not. Although, I know he can hear now, could it be that he's struggling with hearing loss even now at this young age?

"He's breathing." Ludwig holds his hand just above Blake's mouth. "I'm not sure if this is good or bad."

"Ludwig," I whisper softly.

He doesn't turn toward me, but Carl looks at me with a quizzical expression.

He didn't hear it.

"Ludwig." I let my whisper get a little louder.

He still doesn't hear me. People are beginning to gather on the other side of the carriage. There is a lot of background noise here.

Maybe he just doesn't hear me because of all the loud street noise in the background.

"What should we do, Fräulein?" Carl asks.

"He said 'this isn't me' before he went unconscious." I'm torn because from the beginning I felt that there was more than meets the eye with Blake. "I'm pretty sure Blake is the bad guy here, but something just doesn't add up."

"It does appear that he was trying to tell you something before he convulsed," Ludwig suggests. "Almost as if somehow a force from elsewhere triggered the convulsion so that he could not complete his statement."

Blake had said that he couldn't control something. But I'm not sure what the something is. Himself? The situation? The convulsion?

Then, that tablet lit him up. Whatever it did caused him to seize up and then lose consciousness.

It's not adding up, and although I'm glad I punched him in his face, I can't get his sad eyes out of my mind. I couldn't live with myself if somehow in all this, he's really not the bad guy that I think he is.

What if in all this he's just the messenger? An innocent pawn or something?

It seems ridiculous, though. He is obviously working for someone that wants to control these so-called relics. I'm not sure what is going on now, but it doesn't seem right to be traveling through time and stealing all these special items from people.

He couldn't be anything *but* the bad guy, right? Blake had obviously tried to shoot Ludwig. Not once, but twice.

Or had he?

A thought nags at the back of my brain. In the

apartment earlier he had fired at Ludwig but missed. When I play the scene back in my mind, I question if Blake had actually shot at Ludwig and missed or was it just a warning shot? As we ran from him out of the apartment, he missed then, too. And then just now, when Ludwig pulled up on the carriage, he had fired low. Was that intentional? Or is he just that bad a shot?

"Ludwig," I bite my lip. "I know this sounds strange right now, but I think Blake needs our help."

39

THE CARRIAGE IS bumping along the road outside of Vienna heading north back to the Brunswick's cottage. Ludwig and Carl are sitting in the driver's seat outside the cab. I'm sitting across from Blake, who is tied up inside the carriage. He's still unconscious, out cold.

After the confrontation in the street, we sent Carl to get the Brunswick's carriage. The owners of the coach that Ludwig commandeered and slammed into the alley weren't too thrilled about the damage and were threatening to take the matter to the city authorities. Ludwig calmed them down and discreetly offered them each lifetime admission to the Burg Theater.

I convinced Ludwig that I thought Blake was in trouble and that his part in all of this was not what it appeared to be. He resisted, but after talking through all of the previous events, it did seem like Blake's intention was only to get the metronome. He was also purposefully trying to hold back from hurting us. He seemed like he didn't want to be doing what he was doing.

Before he got knocked out, Blake had actually said, "This isn't me. I can't control..."

Ludwig reluctantly agreed that we should get him off the streets. I don't know why he believed me, but he did. I think he trusts me. Maybe the fact that I took matters into my own hands and punched Blake in the face has something to do with it.

I'm trying my best to walk a tightrope between getting to the bottom of this whole thing with the metronome and keeping Ludwig and Carl out of it. I believe I have to dig deeper with Blake because it might be my only way to get back home. But, I also feel like I shouldn't talk about much in front of Ludwig and Carl because they don't need to be involved in all this.

When Carl pulled up with the other carriage, Ludwig was doing his best not to be recognized. People were gathered around the other side of the carriage asking what happened and if they could offer assistance. Ludwig was wearing Blake's black hat, and he was speaking in a funny voice as he told people that our "friend" had been drinking a bit too early in the day and couldn't hold his spirits.

That explanation seemed to keep them at bay as we loaded Blake into the carriage. It was a struggle to load his unconscious mass into the cab. Between the three of us, we heaved and pushed, and tugged and lifted him as best we could until he was sprawled out across the seat. Ludwig tied his hands and feet.

Ludwig was about to protest again when I asked him to ride in the driver's seat outside the cab. But, I showed him Blake's weapon and told him in the most confident voice that I could muster that I could take care of myself. I could tell the chivalrous part of him, the part that wanted to protect the damsel in distress, revolted against the idea. He reluctantly agreed, but let me know he'd be right outside if

I needed him.

Blake begins to stir as he regains consciousness. It's been about twenty minutes since we crossed the Danube River on our way out of Vienna and Leopoldstadt. Ludwig has called back at least three times to check and make sure that I am ok.

"Wha..Where am I?" Blake tenses. "Why am I tied up?"

"Easy there, big fella." I've got the gun pointed at him. "Remember that time you fired this laser gun at all of us, took an innocent little boy hostage, and threatened to steal *my* metronome?"

He groans as he reaches his tied hands up to his nose. He's starting to get black eyes. It reminds me of Taura and the water bottle. In a weird way, I kind of miss Taura, but I know I really just miss home. I hand him a handkerchief.

"Thank you." Blake holds the cloth to his nose. "But I fear this situation just went from bad to worse."

"We're taking you back to the cottage for now." I lean closer. "Have you reported that location to anyone else?"

The last thing we need is for agent number two or some kind of time travel army to show up and terrorize everyone at the cottage.

"If so," I say, "We need to figure something else out before we get there."

Blake reaches for his jacket pocket. He pats his chest and winces.

"My device?" He asks through a pained grimace. "Where is it?"

"Smashed into a million pieces," I say. "We figured that it was what knocked you out."

"Then no, no one is in danger at your cottage." Blake shifts painfully in his seat. "At least not immediately."

I believe him. He's in pain. He's not the menacing Blake from the apartment or alley. This Blake seems afraid and out of control.

But out of control of what?

"I'm truly sorry." Blake's eyes begin to water, but not from the punch.

He's trying to keep his emotions under control, but he's clearly not the big bad wolf I thought he was earlier today. So, first, I meet Ludwig and he's serious and dark, but turns out to be a really great guy. Then, I meet young Carl who I don't really even notice, but he turns out to be a little hero with a boot. And now, here in this carriage across from me is a guy who I thought was the dark, evil villain, and it turns out that there may be more to his situation as well.

Is there a lesson to be learned here? Something about a book and its cover.

For whatever reason, Blake has not actually used my name in front of Ludwig or Carl. If there's something else going on, and he's not really the bad guy that I think he is, I think he may be trying to protect them as well.

I'm not taking any chances, though. Although, it does seem that Blake's deep, dark eyes are sorry. His actions the last two days contradict that. I don't know what's driving him. But, I *need* to get to the bottom of it.

I'm trying to connect all these dots, and it's blowing my mind. My trumpet gets smashed, and I get the replacement cornet that just happens to have a time traveling metronome in the case? Did Pops know all this would happen ahead of time?

If Blake was in the car driving around my neighborhood at night last week, then somehow *THEY* knew ahead of time, too.

But how?

I'm thinking of all the time travel movies I've ever seen. They're all just adventures written by some clever author or screenwriter, but this...

What is THIS?

It's not like Bill Murray in *Groundhog Day*. He just lives the same day over and over. This isn't like Crichton's *Timeline*, where scientists basically fax people to a different place in time using quantum technology.

This isn't at all like the Star Trek movie when Kirk, Spock, and the original crew slingshot dangerously around the sun to travel in time back to the San Francisco in the 1980s. I laugh every time I see Spock saying "They are not the hell your whales." It's probably my favorite Star Trek scene of all time.

It's not like Bill and Ted traveling through history in a phone booth or even like the *Terminator* movies with the cool technology-based time machines.

I can't figure it out. I traveled through time as me, but I

ended up landing in someone else's body. It's like I'm seeing history through Julietta Guicciardi's perspective, but as Rigby Raines. This is so weird. What is *MY* body doing now?

Am I dead? Asleep? Dreaming?

I can't help but think about the real Julietta. Where is she? Is she caught in limbo somewhere? Or even worse, what if she's in *MY* body living as me back in my time?

Well, if she is, I really hope that she's a firecracker that stands up to Taura!

I can hear it now: Tonight's top story features two young ladies who traded lives. But the really fascinating thing about this story, is that they both traveled through time and space...

What's that? We've got some live action happening right now as we speak. Brian, what's going on out there?

"Well, Ron, it's quite a mess out here. Rigby Raines is now Julietta Guicciardi and is knocking out men twice her size. Julietta is...well...we're not sure what's going on. It looks like she has band bully and trumpet section leader, Taura Jacobs, in a rear naked chokehold..."

"Rigby." Blake whispers as the carriage bounces along the road. "We need to talk."

"Ok, Blake." I run my hand over the weapon in my lap, just to remind him who is in control. "I don't trust you right now, but I need you to come clean. I want you to just cut straight to it."

"Rigby, first off, let me apologize for the mess I've

gotten you in." His eyes seem sincere. "It's just..."

His voice trails off, and he hangs his head in shame.

"I was forced into this." His voice is a defeated whisper. "All of this, this time travel, trying to steal the relic, it's not what I wanted."

"Help me understand what this is all about then, Blake." I want to find whatever it was that I saw in his eyes the first time we met. Last night at the party, something behind his official secret agent face let on that there was something deeper to him. I need to know what's hiding there under the surface.

"They made me do it."

"Who is they?" I ask.

"They are called..." He pauses as his dread-filled eyes meet mine. "The Consortium."

40

"You would know my time as the year 2127 on your timeline." He winces as he leans back in his seat.

Blake begins to explain the "new history" of the future. In 2127, I would be one hundred and twenty-seven years old. Long gone.

"About thirty years after the present you know," he says, "the world's largest retail corporation merged with a conglomerate that held the two most influential virtual social networking platforms."

"No way." It sounds like something you'd read in a young adult fiction novel.

"Later that same year," Blake continues. "This huge company stretched its reach to every single corner of the globe by acquiring two of the biggest pharmaceutical companies on the planet and the second most profitable media and entertainment company. Right after the new year, the world's leading producer of food products was also folded into this monster corporation."

"Does America still exist?" I ask.

"In a sense it does, but not as you would remember it." He sits up with a groan.

"What do you mean?" I ask.

"It's now called the United Federation of American States," he describes it as if thinking back to a time he only knows about through historical documents. He begins to explain how the world as I know it pretty much changed. In the 2050s, Europe descended into anarchy and chaos. The United States merged with Mexico and Central America.

I can't believe it.

"When?"

"The Global Wars began in the year 2051," he says. "Interestingly enough, as world oil supplies dwindled, it was China and Russia that invaded the Middle East for their fuel and energy resources."

He explains that many of the countries that were traditionally associated with the Middle East formed a coalition to repel the Russians and Chinese. It was a brutal war which brought out the worst in people and set off a chain reaction of conflicts that happened all over the globe.

"The U.S. opted to stay out of the conflict and in doing so lost much of the dwindling influence to which they were barely clinging to in global affairs. With the fuel and energy resources shifting hands from the Middle East countries to the Asian superpowers, the landscape of world governments changed dramatically.

This is sad. I hate the thought of war.

But this wasn't just minor conflict between small nations or people groups within a nation. It wasn't just politicians playing cat and mouse. If this really happened, these wars would mean a total shift in world power. My country, the one I know and kind of even love, would eventually become a non-player in the world.

"So, how does The Consortium fit into all this?" I ask.

"The Consortium is the largest and most powerful corporation the world has ever seen." He puts his hand on his chest as he continues. "In the 2070s, The Consortium took its first step onto the political stage by running elections all over the world as *The Consortium Party.* "By funding and fueling every movement, they eventually covered enough elections to win them all outright. By the end of the decade, The Consortium Party was in control of every major country's government and also became the sole gatekeeper and provider of every major consumable product in the world. Food, entertainment, energy, you name it, they controlled it."

"That's crazy," I shake my head. "But where did The Consortium even come from?"

He explains that The Consortium started as an offshoot of an ancient secret society that has been pulling the strings behind governments and corporations for thousands of years. They believed they were destined to protect humanity and go to great lengths to manipulate and control history from the shadows.

"In the wake of WWII, they began to aggressively pursue a one-world government." He shifts in his seat. "With each successive generation, the leaders of The Consortium became more and more power hungry, resenting staying in the shadows."

He recalls that in the 1970s, conspiracy theories began to circulate more widely, but were generally dismissed when The Consortium secretly funded documentaries that painted such an unbelievable picture of the secretive society that most people lost interest and wrote the organization off as fictitious.

"In the 1990s, many of the dot-com billionaires were actually initially secretly funded by The Consortium, opening the door for them to gobble up tech company after tech company."

"This is hard to believe, Blake." In any other set of circumstances, I wouldn't be able to rationalize all this information, but the fact that I'm riding in a carriage outside of Vienna in 1801 makes almost anything possible.

"By the time you know as the present, every corporation that you know and are influenced by on a daily basis is in some shape, form or fashion controlled by The Consortium's network." He gestures with his tied hands as best as he can. "They've been behind the scenes controlling everything for decades."

Computers. Movies. Food. Clothing. Everything. When the Wars ended The Consortium stepped up and provided all sorts of humanitarian aid. But nobody realized that behind the scenes they were also funding rebels all over the world and stirring up civil wars. They were padding the pockets and growing the offshore accounts of almost every major country's executive, judicial and representative leadership. Presidents. Dictators. Prime Ministers. Parliaments. Politicians. Judges.

He goes on to explain that in the 2030s, the militarization of the police force was completed in the U.S.

Everyone knew that the police had become a for-profit entity, but no one realized it was secretly owned and manipulated by The Consortium. Their goal was population control, and total compliance. So, what used to be only isolated incidents of police brutality in previous decades, became daily occurrences. At the same time, The Consortium was secretly funding and fueling anti-police and military movements.

They were everywhere. If there was a protest, they were funding it. But, they were also providing support to the anti-protest protesters.

And now, if I understand this correctly, they ARE everywhere. Geez.

They have been keeping an eye on me back in my time. That seems stalkerish. And, they are able to reach all the way back here into 1801, too.

But why? How do I fit into all this?

"Ok, so they're basically running the world in the future." I'm stumped. "But what does time travel have to do with any of this?"

"In 2081, a young, zealous leader rose to the forefront, and won in the world's first multinational election," Blake answers. "He won in a landslide and was elected the world's first GP."

"GP?" I ask.

"*Global Prime* is the official title," Blake answers. "Nobody knows who he was or where he came from, but he went by the name *Superus Augustus* after winning the election. He vowed to protect and defend humanity at all costs. And after the turmoil the world had seen for the previous thirty years, no one thought twice about handing global control to The Consortium Party because of how they basically united the world under a common banner."

Blake explains that the next three decades Superus Augustus became more and more dictatorial. His goal was to follow in the footsteps of the empires of Antiquity. He based his governing style on the conquests of the Greek and Roman Empires. Although the political atmosphere was strict, it continued to move the world closer to a truly global society without nations or borders. Countries were merged into large regional unions, and new names were given to these newly created geographic areas.

Entertainment was censored and controlled by the state. Superus believed that unlike the empires of old, there was a need to clamp down on free expression. Classics in literature, movies, and music were labeled as divisive and inflammatory. Libraries were destroyed. Food became more functional and less pleasurable. Many of the world's larger countries became exporters of grain and corn to produce "food bars" that would replace meals, as other types of food became more and more scarce. All of this was done in the name of peace. Limit people's expression and choices and you're left with a bland, but functional society.

"After thirty years of rule, in 2102 the GP fell mysteriously ill and disappeared, only to replaced by his son, *Superus the Second*," Blake expounds. He reminds me of my history teacher as he delivers all these facts.

"Superus the Second is even more iron-fisted and zealous in his pursuit of forcing everything into a sterile and rigid order than his father was."

"Ok, that's all interesting, but still, where does traveling through space and time come in?"

"I'm getting there, Rigby," he scolds. "Patience is really quite the virtue."

41

I ROLL MY eyes as Blake explains that in 2103, driven by an obsession with history and time travel, the new Global Prime, Superus the Second, initiated a program that directs billions of dollars and resources into unlocking the key to time travel.

"On the surface it seemed to be an obsessive appreciation of the archaeology of Antiquity that drove the GP," he says, "but as an agent, I know the purposes are darker and more sinister. There are literally hundreds of powerful items of power scattered all throughout time. Superus II was driven by his desire to acquire and archive as many of these items as possible. We call them relics."

"Are you serious?" I should have known the most obvious and simple "I'm-obsessed-with-power-I-need-to-take-over-the-world" answer was the most obvious and probable reason for all this.

"Yes," he says. "And within ten years of starting the program, the technology became functional, and The Consortium is now able to track what we call 'Subversive Event Ripples' that lead us to the general area and point in time where a relic of power shows up on the timeline."

"So that's how you found me?"

"Rigby, it's hard to explain, but I'll try to simplify it." Blake rubs his temples. "This is actually what happens: whenever a relic activates and displays some sort of power, it triggers ripples that radiate out in both directions, backward and forward, into the past and out into the future. It's not one-hundred percent accurate because they are faint ripples, but we're able to get within several weeks of an event. We began to get ripples from what we believed to be a relic coming from your time and location. We also pinpointed several other ripple sources, but the waves radiating from your relic happened to be the closest to what I know as the present."

I'm thoroughly confused.

"We knew that your relic would be activated," he continues, "because of the ripples that alerted our tracking system. All I had to do was jump to your time, using the ripples as a target, and I knew I would be in the neighborhood, figuratively speaking."

"Literally speaking, too," I say with a hint of snark. "You were literally driving around my neighborhood spying on me, weren't you?"

"Well, yes and no." He says scratching his chin. "Believe it or not, tracking this particular relic is actually the first live jump that we've attempted. I'm the first person from my time to travel back to attempt to retrieve a relic. I'm a test subject, so to speak. For some reason, the ripples that triggered on the first live run of our program were larger than any that our physicists predicted or modeled. Something about *your* metronome is making it the biggest item of power that we've ever seen. Of course, there are other relics pinging our system, as well."

"So, you weren't spying on me?" I ask.

"Technically, no," he says. "We have no way of connecting a person to the relic. We just have a vague idea of where and when. Your house was the location and I knew that at some point the relic would power up and be activated because of the ripples we saw in the future. Unfortunately, since this is still in the alpha-stages and not yet one-hundred percent, we're basically guessing at the actual trigger time."

"You missed it, didn't you?"

"Yes." He looks embarrassed. "We're still working out the kinks of pinpointing the actual trigger moment. I was staking out your location trying to gather intelligence. I needed to determine whether or not the relic was actually there. I was unable to determine if the item was in your possession or somewhere else, even though I knew that it would be activated here. Or worse, it had already been activated, and I just missed it. That would mean I would have to jump back to my time and re-jump after we pinpointed the relic's reactivation."

"I didn't actually have it when you drove by that first night." I remember thinking how odd it was to see the shiny black sedan creeping through the neighborhood, but it makes sense now.

"Yes, but I did see you on your roof that night." He smiles. "It was a lovely night for star gazing."

"Yeah, it was."

"My mission was to jump back in time and to stay as

incognito as possible." He stares out the window. "I'm constrained by a strict set of limitations, that force me to interact with people from the timeline as little as possible."

"You don't want to mess with history?" I ask.

"Superus II is insanely obsessed with history and as odd as it sounds, he wants to house all of these items of power in his personal collection, all without disrupting the timeline of history. It really doesn't make much sense, but it is what it is."

"Yeah, sounds crazy to me," I chuckle. "Dictator wants to travel back in time and steal relics for his personal trophy case, but doesn't want to leave any traces? Crazy."

"Now that you mention it," he says. "It does seem a little batty."

"A little?"

"Okay," he surrenders. "A lot batty."

"So, I get it, now. You're not after me, you're after my metronome. But I'm not letting it go. It's special and for some reason, I believe it's my destiny to have it."

"I have a theory, that I can't really prove," he says, "but I think destiny might actually be the reason the ripples from the metronome were so large. What I mean is that *YOU* are the reason why the metronome is so powerful."

"I'm not sure I follow."

"I can't be sure," he ponders aloud, "but I believe that your experience here in 1801, whatever it is, has actually been destined to happen from the beginning of time."

"That sounds just as crazy as your Supes wanting to

start a power-up item museum in his basement." I laugh.

"Like I said, I can't prove it," he says, "but in seeing you from a distance, I've learned so much about you that points me to that conclusion."

"What do you mean?" I ask.

"I can't get over how much music is a part of your daily life." His eyebrows furrow in genuine confusion. "Playing in a band. Listening to music in your automobile. Songs on your communications device. The musical instruments in the house."

"Why is that so odd to you?" I ask.

"In the future, music is reserved for only the elite and influential. It's so powerful."

He pauses and stares into nowhere for what seems like forever. I'm not sure where he goes when he does that. He continues to explain how The Consortium outlawed what they call "Common Dispersal." Basically, in the future, it's against the law to enjoy music like this. He adds that books and art are also not allowed for regular people. The super wealthy and powerful are the only ones who can freely enjoy these things.

"Are you kidding me?" I ask, my eyes wide with disbelief. "Why would anyone want to outlaw music?"

"Rigby," he says under his breath. "You know as well as anyone that music has the power to move people. This Beethoven character that is sitting here not ten feet from us is a prime example."

"I don't understand." My eyebrows furrow.

"His music is rebellious. He moves people to emotional outbursts and displays of reckless passion. His music is the catalyst for revolution and that is not to be tolerated. Our leader has created a perfect society that runs on the utmost order and predictability."

"Do you really believe that about Ludwig?" My eyes narrow with distrust.

"I beginning to think I don't know what I believe." He pauses again.

Blake shifts uncomfortably on the seat and begins to share his story. In his eyes, I see the pain that I saw when I met him at the cottage what seems like ages ago. He isn't hiding it anymore.

"I was conscripted into the agent program at an early age, but I don't believe I'm actually *from* that time period. I don't think I'm from what you know as the future."

"What do you mean you're 'not from the future?!'" I blurt anxiously.

42

"Please, Rigby," he shushes. "Keep your voice down. I believe that I am from England from some time in the eighteenth century."

"What makes you think you're from eighteenth-century England?" I ask.

"Two reasons. First, I speak English, and my accent is reflective of what you would know as the United Kingdom. Second, and I think most important, I keep hearing the same tune in my head over and over. I believe it's a memory from my childhood, and if I'm correct, it can only be from eighteenth-century England."

It's not much to go on, and a wild guess at best, but I can't offer any alternatives to his theory. He believes that he is actually from even farther back in time than we are now. But, he's lived most of his life in a future where art and music are outlawed.

"So, if music is so bad in the future," I ask, "why are you here now? Why didn't you just kill us and take the metronome when you had the chance?"

"I...I'm not sure." He stutters awkwardly. "There has been something tugging at the back of my mind since the day that I jumped into your time period. I can't put my finger on it, but I think it has something to do with who I was before all this."

"You can't remember?"

"Like I said, the details of my childhood are hazy." He shifts uneasily in his seat. "I remember that one tune but not much else."

"But what about when you were taken to the future? How did they teach you that music was not acceptable?"

He stops and stares out the window of the carriage. He has a far-off look in his eyes as he tries to dig deep into memories that just aren't there.

"I can't be sure what they did with me individually," he whispers intently. "But, I know that we have and use technology that removes the memories and identities of each agent. I've seen them do it to others."

"That means that they did it to you, too, Blake."

His eyes seem to be lighting up as he digs deeper, reaching way back into the corners and crevices of his mind where things are hidden away.

"I know that we basically scrub the memories from the soldiers and agents of The Consortium, but I just accepted it as my reality until I began dreaming about a past that wasn't supposed to be in my mind."

"What happens in the dream?" I ask.

He explains that he keeps having a recurring dream about singing Handel's *Hallelujah Chorus* from *The Messiah*. He can't recall the details, but he is always in the choir singing. Hundreds of happy people in the concert hall join in. But then, one by one, all throughout the audience, people morph into agents wearing all black until only the last two, a man and a woman in the front row, remain.

"Every time I dream this, they are struggling to resist the change, and the woman reaches out for me." Blake seems disturbed, but confused, as he recalls this dream. "Then I wake up."

"Who are those people? Do you know them?" I ask.

"I feel like I should, but I honestly have no idea who they are. They seem to be connected to one another, and in some way, to me."

"What about your parents? Do you remember them?" I lean in closer.

"According to my files, I didn't have parents," he answers. "At least not that I'd remember. My records state that I was enlisted into the care of the Consortium at the age of three. It's the only life that I can remember."

That makes sense. But I still don't understand the need to travel back in time to kidnap a kid. This whole Consortium thing seems way outside my ability to comprehend. But if I'm going to be here in this timeline in the past, I want to do my best to figure out a way to get to the bottom of this, and maybe find my way back home.

The metronome still doesn't work. The winding mechanism appears to operate fine, it winds and winds, but as soon as I let it go...nothing. No ticks, no tempo, no anything. It just won't work.

For the time being, I guess I'm stuck here. Pops? Can you hear my thoughts? A little help would be nice!

We pull into the drive of the old barn. I can't believe all that I've learned in the last hour. The Consortium, Blake's past, and maybe somehow I'm destined to be some sort of time traveler hero? I still don't understand why I was *chosen* by Pops.

Or did the metronome choose me? This is all still too weird to comprehend.

"Blake, one last thing before we get to the barn." I still can't figure this out. "You said that coming back in time to try and take my metronome was The Consortium's first jump, right?"

"Yes."

"If that's the case, how did they jump back in time to kidnap you?" I'm so confused.

"It's a bit mind-boggling, I know." He pauses to gather his thoughts. "It's the way that time travel works. It can be hard to keep track of when things are happening. I was too young to remember anything when I was jumped to the future, but I know that I was actually kidnapped after I jumped here from the future. Does that make sense?"

Don't nobody understand the words that are coming' out of your mouth, man! Oh, wait, not the time to be quoting movies now...

"Honestly, Blake," I answer, "I feel like my brain is turning to mush just listening to you talk."

"It's ok. Here's the simple version." He slows down to make sure I understand. "Because your jump is literally the first, I can only assume that it has to be after this. It's the only logical way I can explain it. Someone from a future of *my* future jumped back in time, abducted me, and then jumped me back to what I've known for the majority of my life. Your future, my present, is when I grow up in the agent training program. I'm sent back here as the first time traveler from that period. It boggles the brain, but it's the only logical explanation."

"So you're saying that somebody *OUTSIDE* of The Consortium's time travel program jumped you through time?" I ask, trying to put the pieces together.

"That's all that I can figure out," he says, "Unless there's just something about me that the folks from *my* future were able to determine would be helpful to have in their past. It's bloody confusing. And I don't even know if I'm right."

The carriage stops in front of the old barn. I can't take Blake to the Brunswick's cottage. I still won't risk getting the Brunswick family involved. After our long conversation the last hour, I'm almost entirely convinced that he's not the bad guy after all.

My plan is to stash Blake in the barn for the time being. Ludwig still doesn't trust him, but there's nothing he can do about it now.

"Blake, I have to get back to *MY* home." I want to figure out if he knows anything else, anything that would help me jump back home. "If I don't get back soon, though, the Brunswicks will begin to worry and come looking for me. I'll come back later tonight with something to eat."

"I understand, Rigby." He whispers as he eyes Ludwig warily. "Can you untie me at least?"

"You should stay far away from Julietta," Ludwig steps in to stand in between Blake and me. "Julietta, let me escort you back to the cottage. It's not safe out here with all these brigands running loose."

"Now, Ludwig," Blake closes the distance and looks down at an indignant Ludwig, who is at least a head shorter than him, "you probably should run along and write some more music."

Ludwig balls his hands into fists as if he's about to throw a punch.

"BOYS!" I say firmly. "Enough."

I step between them, although I do enjoy being the object of their...affection? Not sure what that is, actually. I'm the target of Blake's mission, and I'm one of Ludwig's piano student fascinations.

They both kind of have to pay attention to me. It makes me think of Chewie. How I miss him. Out of all the guys in my life and in this adventure right now, he's truly the only one that I want to be with at this very moment. Of course, he'd probably be the first one to get knocked out in a fight between all these silly boys. That is unless he hit them with his sousaphone.

"Ok, Ludwig." I motion to the carriage. "Let's get back to the cottage."

Ludwig backs away, eyeing Blake with distrust.

"Blake, I'll be back to check on you," I whisper.

He steps back through the barn door and holds up a single hand to wave before the shadows close in on him.

43

THE RIDE BACK to the cottage is awkward. Ludwig and I are in the carriage cab. Carl is driving. If I lived in this time, I could totally imagine this being my life. Ludwig is a bit older than me, but in this time, it would be totally acceptable for me to be his wife.

What am I thinking!?

I have to get back home. Ludwig needs to focus on his music, not some young fangirl like me.

"Julietta."

Ludwig is sitting across from me, his back facing the direction the carriage is going. He is staring at me. I must look silly sitting there staring at him and daydreaming about a life with him that I couldn't possibly have.

"I just want to say that although I don't understand this roguish character, Blake..." He leans closer. "I am committed to trusting your judgment."

"Thank you, Ludwig," I say. "There are a bunch of factors at play here that wouldn't make sense to you, and I don't want you to be overly concerned."

"Oh, that I could make you see my ever deepening AFFECTION for you, Julietta." He has that look on his face. "I do believe that I have come to love you."

That look.

This is not what I was hoping would go down. It's very flattering and what almost every girl would *want* to happen, but I can't *let* it happen.

"Ludwig, I'm so flattered." I'm searching for ways to explain this. "I really believe that my focus should be on my music lessons at this time."

"So, you do not share my sentiments toward you?" He asks defensively?

"Here's the thing, Ludwig. You are one of the most amazing guys I've ever met. You're talented, and passionate, and your music, wow."

"But, all that is foolishness!" he interrupts. "Compared to the inevitable nature of love, my music pales."

"But we only just met yesterday, Ludwig!"

"I cannot alter the fact that I desire to be wholly yours." He reaches out and takes my hand in his. "Could it be that the gods have ordained what is further to be and shall be? Your love would make me the most happy of men."

"Ludwig. Please listen to me." I squeeze his hands. "Nothing else would make me happier than falling in love with you and living the rest of my life with you."

He leans in eagerly.

"But I can't." My eyes fill with tears. "I couldn't live with myself if I distracted you from your true passion, composing great music. You have such greatness within you that I fear that being tied to someone like me would stifle your creativity."

I know enough about Beethoven to know that much of his passionate work comes out of the tumultuous nature of his romantic relationships. He was never tied down to one woman for long.

Oh, but it would be amazing to be loved by Ludwig, wouldn't it?

"I can't." I sigh. "I just can't."

"Very well, my angel," he sighs as he leans back into his seat. "But know this, love demands all that I can offer, and thus it is I feel towards you. Should you change your heart towards me, I will be ever your true and only love."

"That means the world to me, Ludwig." I want to cry. "I will always remember this day. Because of you, I was able to play like I've never played before."

"And did you ever, my dear." He smiles. "I could not even hope to begin to describe the depths of emotion that you moved my spirit to experience with that simple...song. Such sorrow and such passion contained in so few notes. I do not know why, but I am so stirred to produce a piece of my own, something inspired by your lovely performance, yet to be wholly unique."

"Really?" I ask.

"The notes are even now beginning to haunt my soul." He stares out the window in silence as if he's hearing the notes and working out the melodies inside his head. "I fear I might lose them if I don't put them to quill and parchment with haste."

The sun is beginning to set over the distant mountains as we near the cottage. The wisps of red and purple clouds hover over the far away hills as if they're dancing. It's a beautiful sight. For one last time, I let my mind linger on the possibilities and what-ifs of a relationship with Ludwig. I imagine us dancing in a magnificent ballroom, moving here and there, surrounded by gentlemen and ladies dressed in their best attire.

"Julietta." Ludwig's voice cuts in, and my imaginary dance vanishes. "We are here."

He exits the carriage first and then holds my hand as step down from the cab. His eyes are filled with a puppy-like admiration for me. It causes a million butterflies to tickle my insides. It might even be infatuation, but whatever it is, he is clearly feeling it very deeply.

"Ludwig, I don't want to keep you. I want you to get back and write whatever it is that you're hearing inside." I put my hands on his chest. "Let it come from here."

"Oh, that I could fly into your arms again." He steps back and bows. "Will I see you again?"

Will you see me again? Oh, wow. Uhh. I haven't even thought of that.

"Um, I'd love to continue our lessons." I offer weakly.

"Anything for you, my dear." He kisses my hand.

I'm not sure if this is the last time that I'll see him. I need to get inside and let Josephine and the rest of the family know that I am alright. Later tonight, I plan to sneak out to the barn and check on Blake and hopefully we'll figure out a way to get me back home.

As amazing as this adventure has been the last two days, I'm so ready to get back home to my marching band, the drum major tryouts, to Chewie's dubstep, and maybe even to Taura's trumpet section.

From the driver's seat on the carriage, Carl offers to drive Ludwig back home to the city in Vienna.

"I don't mind," Carl says with a smile, "If Mr. Beethoven doesn't mind me sleeping on his couch?"

Ludwig steps slowly back into the carriage. He seems reluctant to leave. But, I smile and wave, and he appears to be content. The last I see of him as the coach bounces away, he's conducting at the air, as if there's some invisible orchestra in front of him. That quickly he's already lost in the new idea for his next masterpiece.

I smile. It makes me happy. I imagine him back at his apartment in Vienna, quill in hand, scratching furiously at staff paper and pounding out parts on the piano. And that's where he should be, at his piano, birthing wonderful works of art, totally consumed with his music.

Fourth Movement: Rondo

44

I'M AMAZED AT how much has happened since the first time Josephine and I left this cottage for our little excursion. I can't believe it has been only just over a day since we got caught in the thunderstorm out in the meadow. It seems like a week has gone by.

Josephine squeals with glee as I enter the cottage den. The family is sitting beside the fireplace. The yellow-orange light of the fire and several candles bathes the room in a warm glow. Ma-ma is reading, and the girls are engaged in a game of cards.

Josephine jumps up and grabs me by the hand. There's no getting around this. She wants to go upstairs to my room and hear all the juicy details of my day with Beethoven. I greet the family as Josephine tugs me out of the room and up the stairs.

"I'm beside myself!" she giggles. "Tell me everything!"

Of course, I leave out all the details about Blake and the metronome and time travel, but there is still plenty to talk about. We talk until after midnight about my piano lesson and trip to the palace theater. When I tell her about playing piano on the stage there, she giddily asks me to retell it three more times.

"I can't believe it!" she exclaims. "Oh, please, tell me just one more time!"

I finally have to make her leave. I'm getting anxious

about getting back to Blake at the barn. If there is any possibility of me understanding the metronome and time travel, I figure it has to be something he knows. It may be the only way I can get back home.

After about two hours, I decide it's time to head back to the barn. The house is quiet. I've got to do this in super stealth mode, because I want to get to the barn without anybody knowing. Josephine would definitely beg to come along and I can't deal with her right now.

I wrap up the metronome in a long scarf and use the long ends to create a makeshift fanny pack. It reminds me of my pack from back home. I tug tightly on each end to make sure it's secure. It's not going anywhere.

After peeking to the left and right outside of my door, I make my way out of my room and to the stairs. When I'm two steps down, the wood creaks. It's not loud but it's enough to wake a light sleeper.

I freeze.

Oh, no. I hope no one heard that. I need to sneak out of here without waking anyone.

After several slow and intentionally placed steps, I make it to the bottom floor. I creep slowly through the darkness and make my way to the front door. The door lock clicks quietly as I slowly turn the handle. I pull the door open just wide enough to slip outside.

Success!

The front courtyard is illuminated by an almost full moon. The metronome is wrapped in a scarf. I'm hesitant to bring it anywhere near Blake again, but without his device he can't jump back to his future. I already know he doesn't know how to activate it, but there has to be something in his story that can help me figure it out.

The night air is chilly. The chestnut-lined driveway is especially eerie in the light of the moon. Everything has a gray-blue tint. The shadows stretch out across the drive and on the other side into the grass fields and vineyards on either side of the road.

I make my way anxiously to a small break in the chestnut trees where the driveway to the old barn splits from the main driveway. If you didn't know the barn was back there behind the chestnut trees, you'd miss it. During yesterday's storm the road cut channels and little streams into the dirt road. I'm stepping with great care over tiny ravines and canyons. It's dry now, but I am almost tip-toeing every step because I don't want to roll my ankle.

I know I'm nearing the barn when I get near the grove of bushy trees. A sudden flutter of wings explodes from the trees, as a small army of pigeons takes flight. My heart leaps into my throat.

Seriously, birds. Come on! I'm pretty sure, I'm more scared of you than you are of me.

I approach the barn even more cautiously. I don't want a herd of rabbits with vicious streaks a mile wide to stampede me. Ok, that's a little extreme, but out here in the gray-blue moonlit landscape, my imagination is running wild. Even after the conversation with Blake today, and my unexplainable gut feeling that Blake is not a bad guy, the hairs on my neck are still standing on end.

My shoes are wet. Again. The overgrown grass around the barn is soaked with night time dew. The barn door is closed. The moon is higher in the sky, but it is on the far side of the barn. The front of the barn, the side I'm on, is in the shadows.

It's too dark.

"Blake?" I whisper through closed teeth.

I approach the door in darkness. There is no sound from inside the barn.

"Blake? Are you here?"

The heavy wooden door creaks as I push it open. I've watched too many scary movies to be doing this.

"Blake?"

Where is he? And why didn't I bring a lamp?

The barn is silent. I don't hear anything except the nighttime noises of the surrounding countryside.

Slivers of moonlight pierce the darkness inside the barn. As my eyes adjust, it becomes clear that there's no one here. The barn is empty. There is nothing but piles of burlap bags and wooden crates in the corners. It looks exactly like it did yesterday when we ran here to get out of the rain. It's creepy. All I can imagine are a bunch of beady-eyed rodents of unusual size staring at me from their hiding places.

"Blake?" I whisper one last time.

Nothing. No response. He's gone.

Gone? Why?

I sit down on a dusty pile of sacks. It doesn't make sense. I told him I was coming back later to check on him. He knew that we had more to talk about. Couldn't he tell it was important to me? Why would he just leave?

I have so many questions.

Could we fix his device?

Would it jump us both back home?

Does he know anything about how the relics work?

Why did it activate for me just one time and then not work again?

Will I ever make it back home?

I'm stuck here. I don't know what to do. I'm ready to go home. I know that I'm ready to get back to my real life. I'm ready to walk right up to Taura and tell her to leave me alone. I'm ready to solo in band and play scales for chair auditions. I'm ready to try out for drum major. I think I may even be ready to talk to Chewie about whatever it is that we are.

I'm just so ready to be home.

There's no sign of Blake. No note. Not a trace. There is not even a hint indicating where he might have gone.

Where could he have gone?

I guess this means I'm stuck here now. I don't have the energy to deal with the Brunswick family. I don't want to put on airs to impress Ma-ma and all the upper crust nobles here in Vienna. Josephine is wearing me out. My introverted self can't take much more. I really don't want to be this Julietta Guicciardi anymore. I'm tired. I'm exhausted from pretending to be this person that I'm not.

I just want to go home.

45

I SINK LOWER into the burlap bags. I just want to close my eyes and escape from this...nightmare. What started out as a crazy adventure has now become something that has trapped me. I can't figure out how to get back home. I tried to make the best of it, but I'm done with it. I'm ready to time travel back to my own bed.

I'm so over this.

I lean back. Through the beams and rafters of the old barn, I can see an opening. The sky and its twinkling stars are peeking in. I hear a faint hissing sound as a shooting star streaks across the opening.

The last time I saw a shooting star was on my roof.

I bolt upright and then scramble to my feet.

THE ROOF!

It may be nothing at all, but it's a connection to home. My favorite spot. On the roof. Watching the stars. The last time I was stargazing, I was listening to *The Moonlight Sonata* by Ludwig.

Wow. He's Ludwig to me now. Not just stuffy, old music history Beethoven.

I lean to the left to try and see up into the barn's wooden ceiling. Another star sizzles across the sky. I don't see this one through the hole in the roof, but I would recognize the sound anywhere.

Across the room, on the other side of the barn is a small

door. It seems to be the only part of the inside of the barn that is fully lit up. There are slivers of light here and there, but the moonlight is shining through the hole directly onto the rough wooden door.

I find myself excitedly bounding toward the door. Three steps later and I've closed the distance. My heart is racing. My hands are shaking. The last time I went through a door into the unknown, it started this whole adventure. Is it possible that this door could lead me home somehow?

I turn the handle. It's jammed.

NO! Not now!

I ram my shoulder into the door. I bounce off the wooden door and end up on the floor.

Oh, no you don't.

I stand up with renewed determination. I will not be denied. I am going through that door if it takes me tearing this whole barn apart. I grab and shake the handle again. This time, I put all of my desire to make it back home into it. The door begins to rattle. I pull harder. I grab with both hands and let all of my frustration fuel me.

"WHY WON'T YOU JUST OPEN!?" I scream at the door with one last yank on the handle.

A loud metallic snap rings out, and the handle falls to the floor. The door seems to sigh as it slowly swings open. I'm slightly baffled. Did I really just use my willpower to open that door? Or is it just a coincidence that the door handle broke?

Who cares? Let's do this.

I step through the doorway. There's a part of me hoping it's some sort of mysterious wormhole that takes me back home. I half-expect to fall into a shimmering pool of time travel or to walk into a sparkly portal of light on the other side of the door. And then, by some fantastic magic or weird technological sci-fi process, be carried back home to Georgia to my time.

My hopes are dashed. It's nothing like that. It's just a small room that runs the length of the barn. Almost like a tool closet. But there are clearly no tools. This small room is eerily empty.

There's nothing here except for a dancing shimmer of light on the far wall. I'm now thankful for the moonlight. Without it, I'd be groping around in the dark. The light is hitting an old wooden ladder. I look up into the ceiling. The rafters are open here. Just like in the other room. How did I not see this before?

I imagine Pops' face and, almost predictably, I envision him saying some vague riddle about light and darkness.

Pops. I've got an earful for you when I get back home!

I test the lower rungs of the ladder with my hands. It seems solid. I slide the makeshift pouch tied around my waist to my backside. I don't want the metronome to get caught on a rung and bring us both crashing down.

I reach up and grab hold of the highest rungs I can reach. I want to test and see if the upper steps can support my weight. I don't know how old this ladder is. I must look foolish hanging by my hands from a ladder as my feet dangle an inch off the ground. I'm not taking any chances, though. The last thing I want to do is fall.

Rung by rung I slowly make my way up the ladder. I'm not sure where I'm climbing. Dark shadows obscure the upper part of the ladder. As I get closer to the top, I make out a few planks balanced across the rafters.

Great. I don't know who is pulling the strings behind all this, but I hope you're enjoying yourself.

The planks are bouncy and not secured by any nails or screws. It's obvious someone put them up here as a temporary walkway to move across the rafters. I stretch my hands out to each side. I look like a tightrope walker. Every so often I bounce a little which causes me to flail about, grabbing anxiously for any rafter close enough to keep me from falling. The path of planks leads across the ceiling of the barn to the far wall.

There is a window. No wonder I didn't see it until now. It's boarded up, so no light is coming through. But, that's where I'm headed. I need to get out on the roof.

Another hiss from the other side of the roof. The meteors are out in full force tonight. I'm hearing them every minute or so now.

The old window is boarded up tightly. I squat down and tug at the closest board with my hands. It doesn't budge.

There's no way I can ram the boards like I did the door. I don't want to lose my balance and fall down into the barn. I can't really see what's below me now. I push on another board. It doesn't move. Then I try a third, and it wiggles a bit. I pry the edges up and get my fingers underneath it. It shimmies loose.

A little sliver of light shoots through the window as I remove the board. There on the rafter next to me is an old hammer. It's covered in dust. There is no telling how long that's been here.

Huh? Figures.

I use the hammer to pry the other boards loose, clinging carefully to a solid beam with my other hand. My legs are beginning to hurt from squatting so long. But finally, after a few minutes of wiggling the hammer and prying the boards loose, the window opening is big enough for me to squeeze through.

I crawl through the window out onto the roof of the barn. The night air hits my face and sends a chill through my body. It reminds me of my spot on my roof back home.

I'm disappointed, though. There is no magic time travel. No portal. Nothing really, other than a beautiful night sky. The mountains stand guard in the distance. The stars are twinkling all across the sky and occasionally a meteor streaks by. I had hoped I'd find some kind of answer. My way back home. Instead, it's just a roof. It's just a cool night. And I'm still here in 1801 trapped in this body with no way home.

I slowly lower myself to a sitting position on the roof. I'm moving very slowly. I don't want to lose my footing and fall off. I reach around behind me to double check that my precious cargo is still with me. The metronome is still there, wrapped safely in my makeshift fanny pack.

I pull it out and lay back. As the clear night sky looms above me, I apprehensively turn the metronome's winding mechanism. All that is within me hopes that something will happen. Anything.

Nothing happens. I wind it again and again and again as tears begin to form in my eyes.

Why would I go through all this just to get stuck here? Why would I meet one of the greatest musical minds ever and experience this one-of-a-kind adventure only to be trapped here? What kind of nightmare is this?

A sob slips out, spilling from my heart and into the cool air. The tears begin to stream steadily down my cheeks. I try to wipe them away with the corner of my sleeve. There's a part of me that is exhausted. There's another part of me that's frustrated. Then there's this part of me that's sitting here in the moonlight that simply wants to go home. I miss *my* life, and I want to get back to it.

It's not that this experience hasn't been good. It has been amazing. But, I don't know what to make of it all. I need to talk to Pops. He has to have answers. I have to stand up to Taura and make things right between us. I have to talk to Chewie about whatever it is that we are. He's my best friend and maybe something more. It's just *time* for me to be home.

The last thing I remember is a rumble of thunder in the distance. Lightning flashes across the valley in a bank of clouds hovering over the mountains. The meteors are still streaking across the starry sky every minute or so. It's so beautiful here on the roof, but after all that's happened today, I can't keep my eyes open.

46

I'M SNUGGLED FACEDOWN into a soft pillow trying to squeeze out every last drop of sleep from the night before I have to wake up. The dreadful sound of a cheery marimba melody starts chiming in the distance. It sounds far away, but at the same time, it feels like it is bouncing off the walls of the inside of my head. It's a happy enough sound, but for some reason I hate it.

Who the heck is playing a dang marimba when I'm trying to sleep in?!

The melody ricochets back and forth from behind my eyes to the top of my skull, bouncing angrily like a murderous ping pong ball. The notes are familiar, but I can't place the tune. It is closing in, getting closer and closer. I cover my head with the pillow.

Guh! Would somebody please shoot that blasted marimba player!!

I freeze. It hits me. There are no marimba players anywhere near the cottage outside Vienna in the year 1801. Although it's been around a long time, the marimba, an African instrument, isn't used in classical music in Europe. At least, I don't think it is.

OK, so where is it coming from and why is it ticking me off so much?

The marimba is now in the room with me. It sounds like it's right next to my head. I scrunch my eyes and nose in frustration. It is getting louder and louder, but it dawns on me that the marimba is not the only sound I hear.

Tick. Tick. Tick.

I pull the pillow away from my face. I roll over and struggle to open my eyes. Sunlight blasts my pupils. I only see blurry shapes and shadows. I reach out with my right hand to try and determine where the sound is coming from. My eyes are slowly adjust to the morning light.

Why is it so bright in here and why does my head hurt so much?

Everything's coming into focus now. That blasted cheery marimba song is coming from an iPhone, which is buzzing and chiming relentlessly on my nightstand. Next to it, a metronome is ticking a steady cadence. The arm clicks back and forth.

Tick. Tick. Tick.

WAIT A MINUTE! That's my nightstand! That's my phone! And the ticking...

The metronome! THE METRONOME IS TICKING!

That means...

I'm home.

Hallelujah! I'm home! "This just in: We bring you this live breaking story...oh you know the rest...I'm home!!

I reach over clumsily to stop the alarm. The annoying marimba is my alarm. On *MY* phone. I'm in *MY* bed. I'm in *MY* house back in Georgia.

YAAASSSSS!!

I can't contain my excitement. I throw off the covers

and bounce off the bed onto the floor. It's MY floor! I wiggle my toes. The feet below me are MY feet, chipped black toenail polish and all! Those legs and arms are mine! I'm not wearing granny pjs! Just some short shorts and a Braves tank top! I'm back!!

I fling open the door to the bathroom and double-check that my face is actually *my* face. Frizzy red hair? Check! This morning I'm rocking some epic bedhead. Green eyes? Check! I stick out my tongue for effect, you know, just to be sure. It's mine.

Yep! That's me! Welcome back, Rigs!

I raise my fists above my head in triumph. I've made it home. I feel like Rocky Balboa when he runs up the all those stairs and jumps around at the top. I don't really know why he runs up all those stairs, but it meant a lot to him. Of course, if I tried to run up that many stairs, I'd either trip halfway up and roll all the way back down or I'd get through about twenty steps and feel like that was a big enough accomplishment for someone who isn't really into running at all.

Home.

A tinge of sadness comes with the realization that I'm back. Knowing that I've left behind Josephine and Carl makes my eyes watery. And then there's Ludwig. My heart drops as I think about the connection we had and how much he helped me in such a short time. Although I know that we could never seriously be together, there is a small part of me that would have been totally cool with a life as

"Mrs. Beethoven."

But as intriguing as that would have been, I can't help but feel like there is something deeper and more real waiting for me back home. I can't help but wonder if Chewie has something to do with that. Over the years, I always just thought we'd be ride or die best friends. But now, after all this time away from him, it seems like we could be more. At the very least, I want to talk to him about whatever it is between us.

There may not actually be an us, and the last thing I want to do is ruin our friendship, because it *IS* the best thing I've got going in my life right now.

I should text him and see what he's up to.

I go back over to the nightstand and pick up the phone. There are no new message notifications. That's not surprising since I really only have a few friends, but I wonder how it's possible that I've been away for several days and not a single message.

Wait...

I click over to my calendar app. What I see stuns me.

Tuesday, August 8...

That's two days ago. I'm so disoriented. I sit down on the edge of my bed to try and wrap my brain around all of this. I know that I traveled back in time to Vienna in the year 1801. I then spent what I thought was all day Tuesday and Wednesday there. That means that this morning should be Thursday.

Something's not adding up. I wake up today, which I

think is Thursday, but it's actually still Tuesday. That means, that I went to bed on Monday night, had this crazy experience that seemed to last for the next two days, and then I wake back up here as if none of those days happened. Was all this just a dream? I have another brief moment of sadness as I realize that my adventure might not have been real at all.

Was it all just a figment of my imagination? What did I eat last night?

Even if that's true, if it was just a dream, I *know* that I am a different person. The experiences all felt very real. I could smell the burlap bags in the old barn. I could taste the tea and biscuits at breakfast with Josephine. The old granny nightgown, although not very stylish, was warm and comfortable. The Danube River smelled like fish and mud. The cobblestone streets of Vienna were so authentic, down to the last detail. Ludwig's embrace was so real.

I don't care if it was only a dream. It changed me.

If it's August 8, the second day of the second week of band camp, that means that yesterday was when Taura demolished my trumpet. It means that Mr. Z just made the drum major tryout announcement yesterday. I've still got three more days until the tryout on Friday.

Three days. I can do this.

I had hoped that I would make it back in time to try out for drum major. And here I am, waking up as if nothing took place, as if the last two crazy days in Vienna didn't happen. But my heart is different. My mind is different. I know that inside I'm a different person. I'm going to stand up for myself. I'm ready to do my best at this tryout. I don't know what the outcome will bring, but I do know that I am not anxious or afraid anymore.

I'm not JUST Rigby anymore.

47

I BRUSH MY teeth and tame my hair as best as I can. The humidity here in Georgia makes for some great after shower hair. The moment that I realized where I was and *when* I was, I knew I had to get ready in a hurry. I've got things to do and people to see.

Nothing's gonna stop me now.

I pull on my jean shorts and an old, black Panic tank top. I've heard about some bands who have to wear white shirts every day during practice, but we can pretty much wear whatever we want. Chewie says that the bands that do that use it as a way to dress their forms better. The drum major or band director can see the drill and forms better if the band is wearing a single color. It makes sense.

Where did I put my shoes?

I look all over my room for my Chucks, but I can't find them anywhere. I settle for an old pair of J's that I haven't worn in a while. They're red and black throwbacks. My dad thinks it's hilarious that all the kids today are wearing shoes that he wore when he was our age. He says that one day, when I'm his age, I'll look back and think it's funny, too, when my kids are wearing some of the same stuff I used to wear.

I think I've got everything. Keys? Where in the world did I put my car keys?

My keys are usually on my desk under the Beatles

poster, but this morning they are not there. I tear my room apart looking for my them. A pillow goes this way, and a stack of papers goes that way, as I search frantically through everything.

Of all mornings to lose my keys, why THIS morning!?

"Dad!?" I call out my door, "Hey, Dad? Have you seen my car keys?"

No response. It hits me. He's not here. He already left for work.

Dang it.

I grab the old cornet and quickly place it back in its case. The metronome is sitting on the table by the bed. There's no way I'm leaving that sitting out. I find an old shoe box, wrap it in some towels and place it carefully in the box. I put it in the farthest corner of my closet under a stack of winter sweaters that I won't wear for months.

Gah! I've got to leave if I'm going to catch her before anyone else.

I check the bathroom for my keys one last time, before heading out of my room and down the stairs. No luck. At the bottom of the stairs, I enter the kitchen. I don't see my keys anywhere.

As I'm walking through the dining room, a quick glimmer of light catches my eye from the piano. I turn my head slowly.

MY KEYS!

They are sitting on the music rack, the part of the piano above the keyboard where you put your music. I don't remember leaving them there. I reach out to grab them, and I realize the piece of music on the rack is not one I've ever seen before.

The scribbled notes and text on the music are all handwritten. It looks like something you could find in an antique store. There are scribbles all over the music. It looks more like a rough draft of something than an actual published piece.

Wait a minute...

My heart flutters for a second, I recognize the initials scribbled in the upper right corner.

"L.V.B., Your Eternal Friend"

There's no way!

I sit down on the piano bench. The paper the music is scribbled on is old. It's not like any paper I have here in the house. It's thick and a little rough under my fingers. It feels rough and gritty.

At the top of the page is scribbled something. It's not a title, as much as it is a description.

"A Sketch For J"

I turn the page over in my hands, in awe, as I read the note scratched on the back of the page.

"After hearing you play, I was haunted by this new melody, unique, but inspired by the sound and passion of what you played for me in the Theater. I couldn't sleep until I sketched this out. It is by no means complete, but one day I will dedicate the work to you, my dear, Julietta Guicciardi."

This piece of music is from Ludwig. And it's to me. But how did he...

I don't understand how it got here. But I do know this: If this sheet of music is here, and I'm holding it in my hands right now, then all of what I experienced was *REAL*. It wasn't just a dream.

I can't help but smile.

I place the piece of music back on the rack. Although the page is a mess of scribbles and scratches, I will cherish it forever. I place my hands on the keyboard. A sense of recognition washes over me in a wave as I begin to play the first notes.

Before I get to the third note, I know exactly what this piece is. Or, more specifically, what this piece will become.

It's the *Sonata quasi una fantasia*. The *Piano Sonata Number 14 in C-Sharp Minor, Opus 27, Movement Number 2*. One of his most famous pieces.

The Moonlight Sonata.

A chill runs through my body as it dawns on me that I might have inspired one of Beethoven's most famous pieces. And all I did was play a simple Beatles song called *Because*. I can't explain it, but in that moment, I understand everything. Ludwig didn't care about my skill or whether I could play scales correctly. He was interested in what I had inside. It becomes clear that his intrigue with me wasn't about teaching me piano technique. He was fascinated by something he sensed within me.

I don't know how he knew it was there, but sitting here

with this sketch, I see it clearly. Ludwig knew that music is a window into the head and heart of the composer. A musician can play scales and exercises all day, but if she doesn't *FEEL* the music, if she doesn't dig down deep within herself, she's just making noise.

When I sat there at the piano, in the theater, braving my fears and tapping into the depths of my own emotions, Ludwig sensed something that I didn't even know how to express. I'm honestly not even sure he *heard* what I was playing as much as he *SAW* and *FELT* the passion I played with as it rumbled up and spilled out of me like a dark, unexpected thunderstorm.

It all makes sense now.

Finding this little token from my time in Vienna is just what I need this morning. Without knowing it, Ludwig has inspired me yet again. I fire off a quick email to Mr. Z to let him know that I will definitely be trying out for drum major. I have a date with destiny and nothing's going to stop me now.

Let's do this.

48

THIS MORNING I'M sure not to be late. I head out the door to camp earlier than I normally would. I have a newfound confidence and much to do.

You're ready for this, Rigs.

I need to find Pops and get to the bottom of this. I have so many questions. Getting answers is on my list of things to check off today. That is, after I take care of the first thing on my to-do list. Taura.

My faithful carriage awaits. I open the door to my old Camry making sure not to yank the replacement handle too hard. It's 8:07. If I make good time, I'll be at the school almost forty-five minutes sooner than anyone else. Well, everyone except Taura. She's usually there before everyone.

I'm convinced that today is the day to walk right up to Taura and tell her how everything is going to be from now on. She will no longer pick on me. She will no longer single me out. She will no longer attempt to make me look like a fool in front of the section and band. She will no longer yell at the section like we're beneath her.

Today is the day.

Every traffic light is green. Every intersection is clear all the way to school. I've been listening to the second movement of Ludwig's *Symphony No. 7* on repeat all morning. There is something so calming, but motivational about the repeating motifs that grow and grow in intensity over the whole eight minutes.

I am pumped. I've never felt so alive in my life. There's a slight tinge of nervous energy coursing through my veins as I turn into the parking lot.

It's on like Donkey Kong...

Taura won't know what hit her. Of course, there's still a little part of me that just wants to literally hit her in that smug face, but that's not the road I'm choosing to go down.

It still would be nice, though. Right?

I pull into a parking spot on the far end of the parking lot. I want enough space between my car and the field so that I have time to compose myself. I'm ready for this, but I'm still a little anxious.

The parking lot is empty except for one car. Just as I expected, Taura is standing on the practice field all by herself. There couldn't be a more dedicated band geek than Taura. Why does she also have to be so mean?

I've always wondered what Mr. Z sees in her. It never made sense to me why he never picks up on her evil side, but I think this is the Taura that he sees. And I'll be honest, this Taura, the one out there giving her all to becoming the best trumpet player in the band, the best section leader, and possibly even the next drum major, is impressive. She's out here early every day working on her parts and going through the drill. She's literally the perfect band kid.

It's the interpersonal skills which she seems to lack. She's not a good communicator, at least not with the people that she's supposed to lead. The desire to lead them is there. She just doesn't get the relational part. Of course, I'm not really one to talk. My whole band career, I've had a hard time making friends. That is, except for Chew.

I'm okay with that, I guess. It's really the way that I'm wired, but I need to try at least. Being introverted is one thing. But, shutting myself off from the rest of the world because I'm too wrapped up in my own pain and loss is a completely different thing.

I need to come out into the light more.

And that's what I'm doing today.

Rigby, meet the light. Light, meet Rigby.

I step out of my car into the morning sun. It does feel good. Today is going to be another hot and sticky day here in Georgia. Band camp will be like it always is, lots of run-throughs and repeats. We'll reset a hundred times and love to hate every minute of it. Of course, there will be those who groan and complain, but in a few weeks when we're out on the football field doing our thing, we'll have so much love for and pride in the work we've put in here.

Now or never, Rigby.

I pause for a short moment to collect myself. Eyes closed, I inhale slowly and then as I exhale, I imagine all my fear leaving my body. I lift my chin and open my eyes. I set my jaw as I take the first step.

It feels like I'm walking through molasses, but I'm determined. My mind starts playing tricks on me.

What if I can't think of the words to say?

What if she laughs in my face?

What if she body slams me?

I step onto the grass of the practice field. Year after year, rookies have taken their first steps onto this field. Vets have come back for more. The thick grass is damp with dew from the night before. These chalked sidelines and hash marks have seen seniors crying as they marched their last rehearsal run-throughs.

Today, this field will see ME stand up for myself.

Ten yards from where I'm standing, Taura is marking time in silence. She has her back to me. Her perfect ponytail barely sways in time. She has headphones on.

No wonder she didn't hear me coming. She's probably not expecting anyone to be here for a while.

Taura raises her trumpet in four counts and begins to play. I immediately recognize the notes from the song *Eleanor Rigby*. A smile forms on my lips and I can't help but see this as a sign. It's time.

That's MY song.

"Taura," I call out trying to hide the little bit of nervousness that is trying to take over.

She doesn't hear at first, so I walk up closer. I'm five yards behind her. My heart is pounding. My hands get a little clammy.

Go away nerves!

"Taura," I call again, but instead of stopping to turn and respond, she takes off to the left, marching one of the best 8-to-5 steps I've ever seen.

Ugh. Why does she have to be so perfect?

I stand there watching her slide to the left across the yard lines. Her feet seem to float over the grass as she glides effortlessly down the field. I wasn't expecting her to be marching the show, but it becomes evident to me, that she's going through her own parts.

Dang. I can't fault her for that.

I decide to walk down the field after her. The funny thing is, I step off with my left foot. I'm not even marching, I'm just walking. I've noticed that I can be walking down the hall at school or just getting up from the couch to get a snack, and I always step off with my left foot.

Thank you, marching band!

She stops her left slide and snaps back toward the back sideline, still facing away from me. I know this part of the show. She'll mark time in place for sixteen counts, but with each step, she'll rotate just slightly to the right until she's completed a 180-degree turn and end up facing the front sideline. Which means in sixteen counts she'll be facing me. I count silently as she turns.

One, two, three, four...

She's a quarter of the way there. My mind goes blank. My mouth feels a little dry.

Two, two, three, four...

Halfway through the turn, I notice that she 's doing all of this with her eyes closed.

You have GOT to be kidding me!

If her being out here early making us all look bad with her amazing work ethic and almost inhuman commitment to being the best isn't bad enough, now she's doing it with her eyes closed? I chuckle out loud.

Three, two, three, four...

Three-quarters of the way there and she's almost facing me directly. I take two steps closer. I don't want to freak her out. Ok, maybe I do want to give her a little scare. I stop about two yards from her.

Four, two, three, four...

Taura's nose scrunches up, and her eyebrows furrow as she feels that something is not quite right. Instead of moving to the next part of the drill she freezes. Her eyes pop open, and she screams as she stumbles backward.

"RIGBY!" She's not thrilled. "WHAT THE HECK ARE YOU DOING?"

49

Taura rips out her earbuds and closes the distance between us quickly. In a second, we're face to face. The look on her face is priceless. She's furious. I can't say that I'm not a little satisfied with myself, as she gets ready to unleash her fury and let me have it.

She takes a deep breath. She looks like she's about to huff and puff and blow my house down. Except, now I'm not the first little piggy in a flimsy straw house, I'm the last little piggy in a strong brick house and this big, bad wolf standing in front of me doesn't scare me anymore.

Well, at least not as much as she used to.

There's something about Taura that deserves respect. No, not respect for the way she's treated me, but respect for her love of band. Her attention to detail. Her constant drive to be the best. If only she'd just ease up on the icy, cold-hearted, supreme leader angle, she'd be fine.

Before she can say anything, I put my hands up. My palms are out. My body is tense, and I'm standing firm.

"No, Taura." I look her square in the eye. "Not today."

She moves back half a step, surprise on her face. Her eyes are wide, her eyebrows raised. Her mouth is slightly open as if she is about to say something.

"Enough." My smile is almost imperceptible.

"Enough what?" Taura sneers.

"Today all of this ends." My chin is high, and my smile

is pinched. "All of this between us, it ends today."

"What are you talking about?" She purses her lips. Her right eyebrow raises, and she squints her eyes like she's trying to see through me.

"Taura," I say confidently. "Listen, Everyone knows that you've had it out for me since the sixth grade. You know it. I know it. I want it to stop now."

"Rigby," her voice wavers. "I'm your section leader, and soon to be drum major. If you can't respect that, then maybe you should just quit band."

The thought of leaving this big crazy family knifes through me. Even though I'm the weird, quiet one, I would never seriously consider it. But just the thought of it pierces me to the core.

Leave the music? Leave Chewie? Leave this field? Leave the band?

"I don't think so, Taura."

She doesn't seem to be getting it. This isn't about my lack of respect for her as a section leader. It isn't about whether or not I can follow orders or be a good section member. This is all about her desire, for whatever reason, to make herself look and feel better by walking all over other people.

And the main other "people" is me.

"No, I won't be quitting band." I step closer to her, forcing her to take a few steps back. "In fact, here's exactly what's going to happen."

"Rigby," she's confused and doesn't know what to do.

"No, you're going to listen to me. I want you to stop this. You know exactly what I'm talking about. You may not like to hear this, but you are a bully. You've always been a bully to me. And if you don't stop you're going to drive away everyone that cares about you."

"What are you even talking about?" she says in denial. "I don't know what you're..."

"ENOUGH!" I raise my voice just enough to let her know I mean business. "You listen to me, Taura. Your words have hurt me for too long. Your hateful attitude is not acceptable, and it needs to stop. I have wanted to punch you right in your pretty little mouth for as long as I've known you. I've daydreamed about dropkicking you in your head more times than I can count. You've made me feel like crap for years, and I've never said anything. But I want you to know this: I've wanted to hurt you in the same way that you've hurt me. Even right now, there's a part of me that wants to throw down..."

"Let's go then..." her body language is stiff, but her eyes are sad and confused.

"No, Taura." I smile at her, my hands up in confident surrender. "I'm not here to get revenge. I'm standing here on this field to let you know that I'm not going to take it anymore. You're not going to embarrass me in front of the section anymore. And you're not going to single me out when I'm trying just as hard as everyone else to be my best for this band."

"Whatever, Rigby," her eyes drop. "I don't single you

out, you just need..."

"I need, I NEED?" All the pain from the last year plays like a movie in my mind. "How the hell would you even begin to come close to knowing what I need? You've never taken the time to get to know me, Taura."

"But, but..."

"No, I'm serious. You're too busy being the best whatever it is that you are. You never come down off your high horse to really get to know us in the section."

Taura's shoulders drop as she seems to soften. Her eyes water. Her lip quivers.

"Look, Taura," I say. "I could easily hate you right now. I'm trying really hard not to. I lost my mom just last year. I've been through the worst year of my life. For some reason, I can't play my trumpet by myself in front of people. It's always been that way. I guess it's some sort of legit stage fright. If you took the time to get to know me, you'd see that I'm actually a decent musician. In fact, I love music. It's my life."

"Rigby," she says, but I'm not finished.

"Taura, let me finish, please." I sit down in the grass. She sits down in front of me. Her hard exterior is beginning to crack.

"I can't explain it to you, but I'm a different person now. I will not tolerate your selfish attitude anymore. If you come at me with that stuff again, I *will* defend myself, but I want to give you the benefit of the doubt."

"Ok?" she seems to be taken back by my confidence.

"I really respect who you are when it comes to this band. You're a great trumpet player. You are committed to making our section the best, and I'm pretty sure you have the technical skills to be a great drum major. But, you lack basic relational skills. You need to work on that."

"I'm not sure I agree, but I'm willing to think about what you're saying." Taura sniffs in defiance, but I can tell she's thinking about what I've said.

My goal isn't to embarrass her or tear her down in front of everyone else. I truly want her to change like I've changed. If I can be a better person and come out of my shell, then so can she. It's just that her shell is a different kind. I don't know why she's so harsh, but I'm willing to give her a second chance.

"Taura," I begin to stand. "Do you understand what I'm saying? I won't be bullied anymore. You get that?"

"Uh, yeah, I guess." She's not quite ready to apologize. "Just keep doing your best and I'll, uh, I'll try and treat you like everyone else."

"Good." I offer my hand to help her stand. "I'm not saying we have to be friends, I just want you to know where I stand. I'm drawing this line in the sand today, and I don't want you to cross it."

"Ok, I get it," she stands without my help and begins to put her earbuds back in. "Just pull your weight and we should be good."

As she walks away, I feel a swell of pride. I feel good about this conversation. She didn't actually accept full responsibility or apologize, but the most important thing is that *I* made myself known. I drew my line, and I let her know that enough is enough.

Over on the sidelines, an alto saxophone player is warming up. Honestly, I don't understand why he's over there playing so loudly. I think it's a question for the ages, a timeless conundrum.

Why do saxes feel like they have to warm up so the whole world can hear them?

The sound of several car doors shutting jolts me out of my thoughts. The day is about to start, folks are arriving, and making their way across the parking lot. I'm not sure what to expect, but I'm excited about the day.

I'm totally doing this.

50

THE NOTES OF the recorded band version of Eleanor Rigby are blaring through my dad's sound system in the living room. The speakers are in those old wooden boxes with the black screen on the front. He won't get rid of them. He says that when he and Mom were in college, they used to listen to all their favorite music through those speakers.

I smile when I think about Mom and dad together when they were younger. It occurs to me that I was trapped by the deep sorrow of her loss for much too long. It's time to start letting the light of her memories brighten my life. No more hiding in the shadows of sadness. Of course, I'll always hurt thinking about her being gone, but I'm going to try and live in the best parts, which span across almost sixteen years of my life, instead of the handful of bad months right before she left.

I imagine her looking down on me. She's somewhere beautiful. It's a place filled with laughter and a lot of music. She's smiling, her eyes lit up with pride.

For me. I know if she were here now she'd be pretty proud of me.

I'm literally standing on a dining room chair in the corner of the room, waving my arms in time. I've never really conducted before, so this is new to me. I've got to get this down, though, if I want to have any chance at beating Taura at the tryout. I'm not the best at directing, but if I could just transfer the "new" me into this task, I think I could do this.

No, I know I can do this.

Even louder than the almost cheesy, canned studio recording of Eleanor Rigby coming from the speakers is the loud honking of a sousaphone. Chewie insists on "being my band" as I practice my conducting. We moved the coffee table out of the living room so that he could march around playing his parts, and so that I could practice cueing the low brass.

He's hilarious. I don't know what I'd do without him. He's smiling at me as he plays. It's that same goofy smile as always, but it's partially obscured by his big mouthpiece. His eyes are locked on to me. I can't tell if he's intently watching me because I'm playing the drum major or because he's seeing something in *ME* and what I might be feeling for him.

It's hard to tell.

Ellis is standing in the opposite corner watching me like a hawk. Every so often he calls out tips and pointers.

"Keep your focal point the same!"

"Don't let your ictus drift!"

"You're doing great," he encourages with a smile, "but stay focused!"

This whole situation has to be bittersweet for him. This is his last big give to our band program. He knows what Taura did to me and to my trumpet. He still can't understand why Mr. Z didn't do more to remedy the situation. I convinced him to just let it go, but he still seems aggravated. I'm thankful, though, because he can't stand the thought of her being the next drum major. He is doing all he can to help me win.

I cue the imaginary cymbal line. Then the trumpets, then the low brass. Chewie spins wildly and kicks one leg out in front of him in true Michael Jackson fashion.

"CHEW!" I call out over the music. "Stick to the drill!"

I can't help but smile, though. He's one of a kind.

We practice for hours it seems. I can't tell you how many times I've heard Eleanor Rigby tonight. Of course, I'll always love that song, but I'm convinced that I'll be just fine if I don't hear it again for a while after all this is over.

"Back here again tomorrow night?" Ellis asks.

"More?" I think I've got this down pretty good.

"Oh, yeah." He smiles deviously. "You're nowhere near ready. We've got LOTS of work to do. Mwuhahaha."

That kind of stings a little, because I'm feeling pretty good about it. But I trust Ellis. He wouldn't be drum major if he didn't go through this same process himself. They had weeks to get ready for their tryouts in the spring.

I have days.

51

I CAN HARDLY sleep tonight. The last two days seemed to fly by. Tomorrow is the last day of practice before the tryout. I feel ready. I'm so thankful for Chewie and Ellis. They've been such a big help, each in their own way. I put in my earbuds and try to sleep, the soothing sounds of *Fur Elise* are not really counteracting my nervousness.

I don't think anyone actually knows who Elise is, but this tune is one of the most recognizable melodies in the world. Beethoven was almost completely deaf when he wrote it. I can't even imagine not being able to hear the very notes and sounds around which your whole life revolves. So many people labeled Ludwig as a hostile and anti-social person, but in reality, he was just struggling to cope with his deafness. He was humiliated by the fact that the great composer and piano virtuoso, the one whose claim to fame was crafting incredible melodies and harmonies, couldn't hear a single note.

That had to be devastating.

The last two days of camp have been uneventful as far as Taura goes. She's been keeping her distance. For the most part, it seems like she's sticking to our agreement.

Well, if you can call that an agreement.

I would still love to hear her actually say the words "I'm sorry" but the fact that she's eased off of singling me out is good enough for now.

There's a part of me that just doesn't understand how a band director like Mr. Z could miss seeing the part of Taura that is so evil. I can't figure out how she's been able to keep her mean, bossy side on the down low all these years. It's like she's a super villain to me, but everyone else only sees her mild-mannered little-miss-perfect alter-ego.

I don't want to be a tattle or a snitch either, but there's a part of me that wishes I had worn a hidden camera to capture all the times she was cruel to me. Even if it was just to show *HER* how badly she treated others. But, that doesn't matter now. It's all about moving forward.

Speaking of moving forward, Taura seems to be cautiously testing the waters of her new self. It's very awkward to watch because there is a certain level of witchiness that I've grown accustomed to with her. I expect her to be a jerk. I even think that the trumpet section is waiting for the moment she blows up on me and dishes out hundreds of push-ups. But, fortunately, that never comes.

She is still Taura, the hard-driving dedicated band queen, but she seems a little less tyrannical with each day that goes by. In fact, earlier today she actually complimented the third trumpets.

Guess who's a third trumpet? This girl!

I haven't had a chance to talk to Chew about *us* yet, it just doesn't feel right. I need him in my corner. This tryout is one of the toughest challenges I've ever faced, and although I'm ready to tackle it head on, I need my best friend. I don't want to derail our friendship.

I'm lying here in the dark trying to keep my legs from twitching. I'm so restless. The poster of Ludwig catches my eye. The moonlight accentuates his features. The Ludwig I left is much younger than this one, but I feel connected to him in a way I never did before. I can't get over how simple, yet hauntingly beautiful, his music is.

I'll never forget our embrace and hopefully, something in that moment inspired him as much as it inspired me. A sense of peace washes over me as I drift off to sleep with *Fur Elise* on repeat.

52

THE HALLWAY OUTSIDE the band room is quiet. No sousas are honking out the theme from the underground world in Super Mario Brothers. No color guard selfie sessions. No trumpet players are enlightening anyone that will listen to why they are the greatest. Usually, it's just the other trumpet players that agree. Most everyone has gone home.

Although the last two days of camp flew by, today's rehearsal seemed to drag on forever. Even with an early knock off time for the audition. Everyone is anticipating the results of this afternoon's tryout. It's a closed audition. Just the candidate and the "judges" in a closed room. Mr. Z and Ellis are the panel of judges who will ultimately decide who the next drum major will be.

I don't think I've ever been as excited for something in my life. I'm nervous, for sure, but not the "oh my god, I'm freaking out" kind of nervous that usually paralyzes me.

I'm ready.

The new and improved Rigby Raines is supercharged and ready to rumble. I've had the most amazing experience of my life, an adventure I'll always remember. I'm different. Taura doesn't scare me anymore. Even if she doesn't change and stays as mean as she's always been, it doesn't matter. I'm not going to let her have any power over me.

I'm ready.

Taura is on the other side of the hall pacing. Her face is a mask of false confidence, but she's fidgeting. I recognize that sign of nervousness. She's scared. She keeps looking back at me. Her eyes betray her anxiousness. She quickly looks away, when it's clear that I won't be intimidated.

I feel like I've already beaten her. In fact, I think she's doing a great job of psyching herself out now. All I have to do is just take my past, my experiences, my hopes and dreams, my fears and loss, and everything inside and use it. Just like I did when I played for Ludwig, when I punched Blake, and when I stood up to Taura. This is the easy part.

I'm ready.

This week there's been a buzz around the practice field and the band room. Everyone still thinks Taura will be the anointed one. Given my history of flubbing chair tests and recitals, they could be right. On sheer surface ability and the way Taura has always been driven to be the best at everything she does, she's the shoo-in candidate.

This is definitely an uphill battle for me. I know I'm prepared for this, but there's still that little part of me that wants to run and hide. I suspect that I'll be battling the "bad Rigby" for the rest of my life. The dark side of me that doubts myself at every turn. The little voice inside my head that tries to convince me that I don't have what it takes, that I'm not good enough.

Just be yourself, Rigs.

I *am* good enough, though. I played for Ludwig van

Beethoven. And he loved it! I stumbled and pretty much made a fool of myself when I tried to play a scale for him, but I did it! And then I did it again, and it got a little better. Well, not really, but I did it! Then in the middle of a crazy run-for-your-life chase through the streets of Vienna, I played a song for Ludwig, the greatest piano player and composer of his time.

Did I mention he loved it?

I *do* have what it takes, and I am so ready to do this.

"Taura," Mr. Z calls from inside the band room. "Come on in and shut the door behind you, please."

Taura straightens up and smooths her shirt down her torso to her shorts. I don't know why, though, because she looks perfect the way she is, like she should be on the cover of a marching band magazine or something. Well, except for her purple and blue black eyes she's still sporting from last week's water bottle incident.

I had kind of hoped that I would be the first to audition to get it over with, but I'm kind of glad it's Taura instead of me. It gives me a few more minutes to get set and go over everything in my mind again.

Taura takes a deep breath and takes a few steps toward the door, but hesitates just past me. She turns slowly, and her usual scowl softens. I'm not sure what's happening, but she almost looks like she's about to cry.

"Rigby." She stiffens up a little as she realizes that she might let on that she's not in control. "I, uh, just wanted to say. Well, uh, I'm, um. Just, uh, good luck, ok?"

I'm pretty sure this is her way of apologizing. I don't know what to do with it. For a split second, the old Rigby imagines my hand flying out of nowhere and smacking her across the face. Doesn't she realize that a weak apology like that couldn't possibly make up for all the times she made me feel like crap? Doesn't she realize that people like her are the reason why people like me cry themselves to sleep at night? Isn't she aware that she doesn't deserve my acceptance of her apology?

Blake didn't deserve your acceptance either, and he shot at and chased you, Carl and Ludwig all over Vienna.

Sometimes I wish I could put my inner voice on mute. It's speaking truth, though. If I can forgive a super secret time traveling agent from the future sent to steal my metronome for some tyrannical corporation's world domination schemes, surely I can forgive Taura, right?

"You, too, Taura." I nod confidently at her, my eyes are locked onto hers.

She walks slowly into the band room and closes the door quietly behind her. For the next few minutes, I hear muffled voices through the door. I can't make out words, but I know she's going through the interview portion of the tryout. Mr. Z will be asking a lot of questions to get us to share the "why" behind our desire to tryout.

In our regular tryouts, sometimes this weeds out people who are just in it for a popularity boost, or even folks who are just too self-centered. It's a great way for Mr. Z to make sure that the candidates are really in it to help the band with leadership and not driven by selfish *I, me,* and *my* type ambition.

Earlier today Mr. Z conducted a silent student vote. Each band member writes their choice for drum major on a slip of paper and puts it in Mr. Z's upside down shako that he's had since college. He uses it to collect these votes every year. This gives the judges a different perspective and sometimes provides insight into the pulse of the band. Most years, it usually lines up with what the judges decide, but every now and then a student vote will be split down the middle or even lean the opposite direction of what the judges decide. I'm sure that makes it tough for the panel to make a decision.

The muffled voices stop for a few minutes. It's quiet except for Taura's voice counting out numbers. I imagine her on the podium demonstrating her skills through each required meter. First 4/4, then 3/4, then 2/4, then 6/8. Each meter has its own pattern that you follow with your hands. The band can follow the drum major and know where each beat falls.

A flutter hits my stomach. The corners of my lips turn up into a smile. I'm so pumped for this. With all the help from Chewie and Ellis, I'm literally chomping at the bit to get in there and show them what I can do.

Music. Through the walls comes the muffled, but familiar, sound of the arrangement of Eleanor Rigby that we're marching on the field in our show this coming Fall. Now Taura is showing the panel she can cue different sections. I'm sure she's doing fine. Knowing her, she's just as prepared as I am.

This will come down to who Mr. Z thinks is the best candidate. I have a lot to overcome. All he's seen of me is the shy, quiet, and last chair Rigby. But, I'm ready to show him the confident and ready-to-lead Rigby.

Two minutes later and the music stops. She's done. Another minute of muffled voices goes by and then the door opens. Taura walks out with her head up. She doesn't look at me as she walks a little further down the hallway and sinks down the wall as if she's glad to have gotten that over with.

I'm not sure what to make of that. She didn't smile. She wasn't smug. She wasn't crying or excited. I wonder how it went. There's no way she could have messed up, right? She's been waiting for this moment ever since she got to high school.

Doesn't matter now, Rigs. You're up! Let's do this!

Out of the corner of my eye, movement down at the opposite end of the hallway catches my attention. It's dark on that end of the hall, but I can make out Pops in his maintenance uniform. His toothy grin is unmistakable. Even in the shadows, I can see that he's smiling. For a brief second, we lock eyes, and although I have a million questions for him, I know that now is not the time.

Soon, I'll ask him about his part in this whole time traveling adventure. Did he know where I was going? Was he in control? How did he get the metronome? Why me?

He nods his head as if he knows exactly what I'm thinking. He tips his hat in my direction, and as he disappears into the shadows, I have this feeling that everything is going to be okay.

"Miss Raines," Mr. Z peeks his head out the door. "You're up, kiddo. Let's see what you've got."

"I'm ready."

53

THE LONG WALK to the door seems to take an eternity. I feel like I'm moving in slow motion. I step through the doorway. The whole scene makes me feel like I'm walking into a royal throne room to be knighted. Ellis is sitting at a small table in the back corner of the room. Mr. Z joins him.

There is a single chair opposite the table.

"Please, have a seat," Ellis smiles.

Here we go...

The interview portion begins. The little flutter is there, but I let it work itself from my stomach into my words. I'm not going to try and beat it back, I'm going to embrace it and let it fuel my passion.

I don't know why, but this whole tryout seems to float by like the pivotal scene in an action movie. I hear the notes of the Moonlight Sonata played by a massive orchestra inside my head. It's like my tryout has an amazing soundtrack in the background while everything happens. With each question, I imagine the music crescendoing and becoming more and more epic.

"Why are you trying out for drum major, Rigby?" Mr. Z has a serious, but calming look on his face.

I answer honestly and to the best of my ability. I explain that I love music, that it's the best part of my life. I'm passionate to share that with others.

"I really want to honor my mother by following in her

footsteps as drum major," I explain. "I want to help the band be the best that it can be. I am willing to learn to be a leader. I know that I'm not as experienced as some others, but I do have a very strong musical background and I'm eager to accept the responsibility. I'm not expecting to be everyone's friend, but I do feel like the drum major should enjoy their role. They should take it seriously, but also allow their passion for music and the band to overflow into great leadership."

"Ok, thank you, Rigby," Ellis says. "Let's move on to the conducting part of the tryout. You can take your place up on the podium."

I stand and crack my knuckles. I feel like a mad scientist about to mix up a concoction of awesomeness.

"Let's start with some meters and patterns," Mr. Z says. "If you don't mind let me see you go through your different conducting patterns."

In my mind, for a split second, I recall and rehearse all the things Ellis worked with me on the last few days.

Solid poise.

I own this podium. I'm here to lead the band. They need to know that I know what I'm doing.

Body carriage.

I am confident. I'm going to use as much movement in my arms as I need to convey the beat, but I'm not going to over do it. I'm not here to win awards for being an over-dramatic and sensational hand-waver. I'm here to simply lead the band.

Focal point.

My conducting is steady and easy to follow. My patterns are constant.

Consistent Ictus.

Each beat that I conduct will hold the band together. I am a human metronome. I can feel time. *My* hands will help others see and feel the beat. Especially the downbeat. I am the only thing that will hold our band together on the field in the middle of a show.

I'm focused. Ready to start.

Ok, Rigs. You're ready for this now. Let's show 'em what you got.

I move through each meter as close to perfect as I can be. Well, at least in my mind I'm doing a great job.

4/4 then 3/4.

I'm confident, cool as a cucumber. I actually smile a little as I quickly settle into my groove.

Then comes 2/4 and finally 6/8.

I feel like this is what *I* was born for. I'm right at home.

As I finish up my counting and conducting portion, an image flashes through my mind. I'm conducting the marching band. Over my shoulder I see my mom and dad are sitting in the bleachers, front row at the fifty-yard line.

Mom?

The scene trips me up because I know I'll never actually have that experience. She'll never see me on the field. But I know wherever she is, it would make her proud. My heart catches in my throat. I want to sob right here and now. But

I can't, I've got to finish strong. I finish my last pattern and slowly bring my arms to my side.

Ellis catches my eye. He knows something is bothering me. I'm sure I didn't mess anything up, but a sliver of doubt nags at my mind.

"Thank you, Rigby," Mr. Z says. "Everything ok?"

"Was it not right?" I ask.

Now I'm getting worried that I might have drifted too far into that mental image and lost track of where I should have been in that last pattern. Is it possible that I just totally zoned out and stood there like a lifeless scarecrow for a few measures?

Oh, no. Please, God, no.

"Oh, no," he assures. "It was pretty close to perfect. You just seemed a little distracted right there at the end."

"I'm ok, Mr. Z," I'm fighting back tears. "It just really hit me that whether I get drum major or not, I'm making my mom proud, by doing this."

"I'm sure she'd be very proud, Rigby." Mr. Z grins awkwardly trying to find the words to say.

"I'm ready for the next portion, if you are," I offer. I figure it's better to just move on past the awkwardness. People just really don't know what to say when the death of a loved one comes up.

"Rigby, are you ready to conduct your prepared piece?" Ellis asks.

He smiles because he knows I am. We worked on it for hours. Scenes from the last few evenings of Chewie bouncing around my living room wearing his sousa make me smile. Most of the time I was laughing because Chew is such a goof, but I worked hard.

I'm ready.

Before I start, I bring back the image of my parents in the stand. Mom may not ever be able to be there again, but I wrap myself in that scene. It makes me sad, but it also fuels my desire to win this tryout. I'm going to make her proud by giving it my all.

"Band, TEN-HUT!" I call out from the podium.

The invisible band waits silently for my next command. I imagine a football field full of band members who are standing like statues.

"Band, HORNS UP!"

Every band member in this imaginary band snaps their horns up, ready to play. I close my eyes, take a deep breath, and wait to hear the count off. Ellis hits play on the mp3 player attached to the band room's sound system and *my* song, Eleanor Rigby, blares steadily through the big speakers up in the corners.

The next two minutes seem to fly by. I conduct like a girl on a mission. This *IS* my song. This is an incredible moment, and I am living in it fully. I feel the same way that I felt when I gathered all of my past, my pain, and my fear to punch Blake back in Vienna. The fact that Mom will never see this does make me sad, but it also drives me. I let it fuel my performance.

The invisible band moves through their shapes and

formations. In my mind the drill is perfect. Every instrument is in tune, even the piccolos, all horn angles are perfect, and everyone is in step. But more importantly, on the fifty-yard line, in the front row, I imagine my mom smiling and proudly cheering on *my* band.

54

THE LAST TIME I was sitting in Mr. Z's office I was in a daze. I was holding a demolished trumpet, and I was struggling to piece together why. Since then, I met Pops, found the metronome, traveled in time, met Beethoven, faced my fears, came back home, and even stood up to Taura.

She's sitting across from me trying not to look worried. I don't think she expected me to do well in the tryout. In fact, I'm pretty sure she didn't think I'd even show up.

But I did.

I did show up. And I came in with all my guns blazing. My game face was fierce, my confidence level at an all-time high. I'm feeling really good about myself.

I don't know if Mom was there with me during the tryout. I'm not sure if I had some sort of leftover fairy dust or magic residue from the theater in Vienna. I can't explain what really happened, but I do know this: the new Rigby Raines is bold as...

Well, you get the picture. If I had a fire-breathing T-rex to ride into the tryout, I totally would have. That's how fearless I felt.

I kind of imagine myself coming into the room riding a wrecking ball. But with my clothes on of course. I chuckle to myself, not able to contain my amusement.

"What's so funny, Rigby?" Taura's annoyed voice is dry and monotone.

She's trying to conceal her worry, but she can't hide the concern on her face. Her countenance looks like she's already beaten. She sets her jaw, and looks down her nose, but her eyes are sad. Taura is at war within herself. I think our confrontation the other day really jarred her reality. I don't think she knows what to do with someone going against her expectations.

"Nothing, Taura." I look directly into her eyes. "I was just thinking how funny it would have been to crash through the walls into the tryout riding a wrecking ball."

"Seriously?" Her eyebrows furrow in confusion. "You are so weird, Rigby."

"Yeah, I get that a lot."

She fights back half a smile as she looks at her bouncing feet. She's nervous. Mr. Z and Ellis have been deliberating for a while. It seems like we've been waiting forever, but the ticking clock on the wall confirms that it's only been about ten minutes.

Tick. Tick. Tick.

My lips curl into a little smile as a wave of contentment washes over me. I realize confidently that I'm satisfied no matter the outcome.

It doesn't matter if I win or not.

I sucked it up. I let go. I embraced the pain and confronted my dark self and I lived to tell the tale. It was truly the hardest thing I've ever done. Instead of being beat down and crippled by that selfish fear of living life without my mom, I'm going to live every moment like she would want me to.

I showed up. I grabbed life by the horns, and I went along for the ride. I traveled back in time. I played for Ludwig van Beethoven. I punched a bad guy. I prepared for this tryout and then actually walked into this building and tried out. I actually did it!

I stood up. I walked right up to Taura. I looked her in the eye and drew a line in the sand. I told her that I will not let her single me out and pick on me. But, I refuse to turn it back around on her. I've decided to forgive her. Although I'm sure I'll still be tempted to see her as the old Taura, I will not treat her badly just because she bullied me. I have to let go and move on even if she did repeatedly try to make me look like a fool.

Of course, I wouldn't mind if SHE made a fool of herself in some way.

Oh, behave, Riys!

When you live an adventure and see as much as I've seen the last few days, your worldview expands. Life is too short to be holding grudges. Taura and I may never see eye to eye, but I do hope that she learns to be kind. She actually has some pretty great qualities, and if she'd just ease up, I'm sure people wouldn't mind getting a little closer to her.

The door swings open as Mr. Z and Ellis come into the band office. Mr. Z takes a seat behind his desk, and Ellis stands at his side. I can't read his face. I thought for sure he'd give me a hint, but he's expressionless.

"Ladies," Mr. Z starts. "Let me first start by saying that

I am very proud of both of you. Your preparation is evident and you both came ready to get the job done. I appreciate and respect the hard work you've both put in."

Taura shifts nervously in her seat. She doesn't know what to do with her hands. I almost expect her to hold them up awkwardly like Ricky Bobby. She's fidgeting again.

I'm excited, maybe even a little nervous, but I'm not anxious. I feel like I proved to myself, and to Mr. Z, and even to my mom that I have what it takes.

"You both demonstrated confidence and poise on the podium. Ellis and I were both very impressed by your commitment to preparing well."

Ellis is still not giving any hints. I understand, though. It's not his job to spill the beans.

"We both feel like you each would make a great drum major for the band..."

Here it comes...

"With that in mind, please understand that this is a tough decision. In fact, it's one of the closest auditions I've ever judged."

JUST SAY IT, MAN!

"Rigby, I am so proud of you for stepping out of your comfort zone. Taura, as usual, your commitment to excellence shows. You both deserve this."

Aaaannnnddd?

Taura looks like she's about to faint in anticipation. Mr. Z pauses as he gathers steam to make the announcement. Ellis is staring down at his papers.

"Congratulations, Taura," Mr. Z says. "You're the next drum major of our band."

55

MY HEART DROPS for a moment. I said I'd be ok with whatever, but this still stings. There was a part of me that thought for sure, that I'd won this audition.

Taura is elated. She's keeping it together, though. The anticipation and nervousness melt off her face and are replaced by a giddy happiness. Honestly, even though the drum major position is what I've always wanted, I'm happy for her. It's what she has always wanted.

I'd be lying if I said that the little part of me that secretly wanted to see Taura trip over her perfect ponytail and get stuck in a sousaphone didn't want to rear its head. Who wouldn't have to fight jealousy in this moment? But I'm better than that.

"Rigby," Mr. Z's voice breaks into my thoughts, "you should be very proud of yourself. You exhibited so much of what we're looking for. I honestly couldn't believe I was looking at the same person."

"Thanks." That makes me feel a little better. "I really tried to do my best."

"And your best exceeded my expectations!" Mr. Z stands. "I want you to know that there was no real loser here today. You both brought it. Traditionally, we have always had one drum major, so I had to make a tough decision. I'd be happy to have either of you in this position, but I had to choose one. It all came down to experience."

He pulls out his papers and scans his notes.

"Taura just has a little more experience as a section leader. She's just a bit more ready to take the podium."

Ellis reaches over to shake Taura's hand. He's not happy with the decision, but he tries not to show it. I follow his lead and extend my hand toward Taura.

"Congratulations, Taura." A week ago I would have had to force it out, but I genuinely mean it. "I'm happy for you."

"Thanks, Rigby." She can't contain her happiness.

"Rigby, there's one more thing." Mr. Z seems to be trying hard to make sure my feelings aren't hurt.

"Okay?" It comes out more like a question.

"If it's okay with you, I want you to be my new trumpet section leader." He smiles.

"Really?" I ask. "But, I'm last chair."

"Really," he says. "Ellis and I both agree that you should be the leader of the trumpets. You've got what it takes. We can work on your playing later, but your leadership is what we believe you can offer to make the trumpet section better."

Taura initially seems shocked, appears to be too happy to care for long.

"Oh, ok," I say. "If you think I can do it, then I'm willing to give it a shot."

"You'll rock it," Ellis says.

"Well, ladies," Mr. Z cuts in, "this has been an interesting week for sure. Ellis, thank you so much for being a part of this transition. I know I can speak for the girls here when I say that you will be missed. Goodbyes are never easy. We wish you the best. Please keep in touch."

He shakes Ellis' hand and pulls him into a sincere hug. Mr. Z is the best. I know Ellis has loved his years in the band here under Mr. Z.

"Thanks, Mr. Z." He seems sad. "I'll definitely miss everyone here for sure."

Taura says her goodbyes to Ellis and then bounces out of the office, gathers her things, and exits the band room. When the doors close behind her, we all hear her let out a jubilant scream in the hallway.

Ellis lingers in the band room. Today is his last day here. I can see the sadness in his eyes as he knows that he'll have to move across the country and try to join a whole new band family. I know I'd hate to do that. Even though I don't have a lot of friends in band, or anywhere for that matter, I still feel a special bond with all the hooligans that converge on this special place.

"Ellis," I say. "Thank you so much for your help. It means the world to me."

"No problem, Rigs." He smiles with watery eyes. "I just wish I could have gotten to know you a little sooner. You're an amazing person. For the record, I think you'd make a great drum major."

That means a lot coming from him. Neither one of us wants to leave the band room. Mr. Z turns the lights off in his office and joins us.

"Well, kiddos," he says, "it's time to shut it down for the

night. Big day coming on Monday with the big first day of school and everything."

Ellis hugs me and says one last goodbye to Mr. Z, and then we head for our cars in the parking lot. Ellis waves as he drives away from this band room and practice field for the last time. A wave of sadness hits me, and I fumble with my keys. They fall to the ground.

"Oh, wait, Rigby!" Mr. Z calls out from the double doors. He jogs over.

"One more thing!" he says excitedly. "I wanted you to know that the student vote was totally in your favor. Every single person except one voted for you as their choice for drum major. That says a lot about you. I know it might cause a little stir going forward with Taura, but I wanted you to know that you are more influential than you know. People really like you."

People like ME?

I'm not sure if that makes me popular or what, but it does make feel good. A whole band, all of those people wanted *ME* to be their leader. That does mean a lot.

"Thank you, so much, Mr. Z." I don't know what to say really. "Thank you."

56

I DON'T REALLY feel like going home just yet. I climb up on the hood of my car. The sun is setting over the practice field. The scene is perfect. The clouds are red and orange. From behind the tops of the scrubby Georgia pine trees, the sky fades up into a beautiful deep blue. The field's green grass and white chalk contrast with each other in this golden hour. It reminds me of the beautiful scenery in Vienna, half a world and two centuries away.

The parking lot is empty except for one other car.

"Hey, Rigs." Chewie's voice startles me a little. "Can I have some of your water? I lost my canteen."

"CHEW! Were you waiting for me this whole time?"

"Yeah, I've been sitting in my car waiting for y'all to come out." He joins me on the hood. "I saw Taura come skipping out of the band room a few minutes ago. I guess she got it?"

"She did."

"Aww, man!" He puffs up. "Do you want me to take her out for you? I've been practicing my wrestling moves."

"Yeah," I chuckle. "I'd bet you'd like to wrestle with Taura, wouldn't you!?"

"Hey, wait a minute," he says defensively. "I saw that going differently in my head. Seriously, though, Rigs, are you alright?"

"Chew, I don't know how to explain it," I pause. "But, I

think for the first time in a long time, I'm actually happy. Sure, I would have liked to have won that tryout, but I'm actually happy for Taura."

"I'm proud of you, Rigs. It takes a mature person to let go like you did." For a second, he seems so much more grown up than he is. Then he ruins it by crossing his eyes and saying, "It's a good thing I'm so mature, too."

"Chew!" I punch him in the arm.

"Hey, want me to take your mind off of all this drum major stuff?" he asks.

"Sure, Chew," I smile. "Whatcha thinking?"

"I think I found a music story that will stump you!" His voice cracks a little.

"What?" I'm curious. "What kind of music story?"

For years, we've both tried to one-up the other with obscure music facts and trivia. I'm pretty good at it. Any time Chew is over at my house during *Jeopardy*, he calls out the most obviously incorrect answers. The funny thing is he's actually sincerely trying to guess. He's just aways wrong. I've always been better at factoids and trivia, so he tries really hard to stump me.

"It's about your favorite composer, Beethoven."

Beethoven!?

"How do *you* know he's my favorite composer?" I ask.

"Well, there's that big poster in your room," he counts his fingers individually as he ticks off a checklist. "You used to play his music all the time on the piano, you're always talking about him, and you basically only listen to

Beethoven's music on your phone!"

He does have a point...I guess.

"Ok, so, I guess you're right."

He knows me well. But what could he possibly know about Ludwig that I don't? I mean I'm not an expert on his life or anything, but I did get to meet him in person and even take a lesson from him. I feel like I know everything there is to know about him.

"Did you know that the Beatles song *Because* was inspired by Beethoven's *Moonlight Sonata*?" he asks.

"Of course, everybody knows..." I pause. "Wait, what?"

I didn't know that.

"Yeah, I read an article about how John Lennon said that he was inspired by the *Moonlight Sonata* to write the song *Because*. He was chilling at his place with Yoko one day, and she was playing the piano. Apparently, John must've been a little out of it, because he asked Yoko what she was playing. Do you know what she was playing?"

"Well," I roll my eyes. "Obviously it has to be the *Moonlight Sonata*, right?"

"YEAH!" He is overly excited. "But that's not the cool part. John asked her to play it backwards!"

"Are you trying to tell me that the song *Because* is the *Moonlight Sonata* played in reverse?!"

There's absolutely no way that can be true. I would have heard about it.

"No, no, Rigs." He slows his words down. "It was the *sound* of the *Moonlight Sonata* being played backwards, the passion that Yoko was playing with that inspired him to write *Because*. If you listen to it, you can hear it. Lennon was inspired to write *Because* by the passion, emotion, and *SOUND* of Beethoven's music when Yoko played it backwards. At least that's how the story goes."

I can't believe what I'm hearing.

"You're telling me that Yoko was playing that song, John was inspired by the way it sounded backwards, and then wrote *Because*?"

"Yep!" Chewie looks smug. "And, I think I should get some sort of trophy because I know something about music that *you* don't!"

If only Chew knew what he was telling me!

I can't say anything, though. Nothing about my time travel, my adventure in Vienna, or meeting Ludwig van Beethoven in person.

At least, not yet.

And *THIS*, this fact can't be real, can it? *Because* inspired by the *Moonlight Sonata*?

What would Chewie think if I told him that in the year 1801, a shy, scared, depressed, and sad sixteen-year-old time traveler named Rigby Raines landed in the body of a countess named Julietta Guicciardi, and played a Beatles song called *Because* that inspired Ludwig van Beethoven to write the piece that would eventually become known as the *Moonlight Sonata*?

He would think I was crazy!

I smile, though, because it completes the circle. It's like

destiny or something. I played the song that means the most to me for Ludwig, and it sparked something in him that became the *Moonlight Sonata*. Then hundreds of years later, Ludwig's song inspires Lennon to write the song that means the most to me.

"Ok, Chew," I surrender with a huge grin. "You win."

I'm genuinely happy to be back here, sitting on the hood of my old, beat up Camry, with Chew, talking about music and watching this glorious sunset. Although it seems like ages have gone by since the water bottle incident, it's only been a little over a week.

I am content right now. I lean back against the windshield as the ebbing sunlight paints a dazzling display in the clouds. Chewie leans back, and we just lie here, side by side, the best of friends, taking it all in.

I don't know what Monday will bring, but the first day of school is always exciting. We have a whole marching season ahead of us, but there's something about the end of the last day of band camp that is also a little sad. No more full days of band rehearsal until next year. For some folks like Ellis, and all the other seniors, this was the last band camp of their high school career.

But enough of that sadness. I can't complain.

For some people, it's a new beginning. Taura gets to start over as drum major. We'll probably never be BFFs, but I think we'll work well together this year. That is as long as she doesn't act like the old Taura.

It's a new beginning for me, too. I'm the brand new

section leader of the trumpet line. I get to contribute to the leadership of our band. I don't know exactly how, but I imagine I'll just be the me that a few others have seen long before I did. Ludwig saw it in me. My mom saw it in me. Chewie sees it in me. I just need to be me.

I have an awesome cornet that plays better than anything I've ever played before. I've made some new friends and experienced an amazing adventure.

The band overwhelmingly voted for me as drum major, even though I didn't win the tryout. That means that they don't hate me. It means that we really are one big family. And although our family will go through ups and downs over the months and years, one thing will stay true:

Band family is forever.

And the best thing of all, after all my adventures and experiences, I'm back home, here in my time, lying on the hood of my faithful old chariot next to my best friend. We watch in silence as the first twinkling star appears in the twilight sky.

It doesn't get any better than this.

•••

Epilogue

"Focus, Miss Rigby," the old, toothy grin of Pops McKenzie is the last thing I see as I hear his voice fade into oblivion. "Focus on the time."

I close my eyes tightly, but I can still see. Pops' storage room with all the instrument cases is not what I see, though. In front of me, the most vividly colored clouds begin to materialize. Reds, yellows, greens, and blues seem to bubble up from nowhere, forming giant puffs of vibrant hues. Brilliant purples, pinks, and oranges explode into my field of view.

Am I dead? Is this Heaven?

Dazzling pinpoints of light flicker from behind the rolling rainbow clouds. They must be stars or distant planets, blinking through the forming storm of color.

For a brief second, I'm afraid. With me, anxiety always seems to accompany thunderstorms. But these are unlike any thunder clouds that I've ever seen. They are giant pillars of dazzling color. This is a moving painting. It's too exquisite to be real.

The giant bubbly fingers of color are undulating slowly, growing toward what appears to be up. It could be down. I can't tell which direction is which. I could literally be floating upside down and not realize it.

Whoa. This is insane.

"Rigby," Pops' voice echoes from a distant place, yet

fills my entire consciousness. "What do you see in front of you? Where are you?"

The clouds ripple and the lights continue to flicker, almost as if they are blinking in morse code, calling out to me to join them. Something pulls me toward them, almost as if they have their own gravity. I began to drift closer to the pillars. My hands and arms are sparkling, shimmering as the light dances all around me. I look as if I've just completed an elementary school project, but used way too much Elmer's and glitter.

Not that I ever actually did that...

Something is drawing me to the lights. There is something inside my chest that seems to be initiating the pull. I float toward the middle of the colorful storm. I feel like a small spaceship that's been captured by a tractor beam. The clouds and the stars are like a massive mothership pulling me in. I am not afraid. This gravity, this attraction, is familiar. I don't know why, but I think I've been here before. I can't put my finger on it, but it feels more real the longer I'm here.

"Focus on the time," Pops says again.

I look in every direction, all around, but I can't see him. The only thing behind me is a tiny, round speck of light in a massive expanse of darkness. A small, lonely star, probably. Or maybe even someone holding a dim flashlight. To my left and right is nothing but empty blackness. I only want to look forward.

It's so beautiful.

"...the time," Pops' voice reverberates through space again, but it's more like an enormous whisper. "...the time."

It dawns on me that I've been floating here in this beautiful oblivion for a really long time.

Or has it been seconds?

I'm thoroughly confused now. Nothing makes sense. I'm extremely disoriented. I don't know if I should proceed into the mysterious storm of color and light, letting it draw me into whatever it is. I can't remember anything.

What am I doing here?

The tiny lights begin to flicker rapidly, but more brilliantly. The dazzling display is almost too much for my eyes to take in. I squint, attempting to keep from blinking my eyes closed. I don't want to miss anything.

"...the time."

What time?

In an instant, the pillars of color move toward the center of the storm and I begin to move faster and faster toward them. I feel like my hair should be waving behind me in the wind, but there is no wind. In fact, there is no air.

How am I even breathing?

The clouds pull me toward the center. Curls of colorful mist swirl around my arms and legs as I whisk through the outer fringes of the storm. The haze gets thicker and thicker. The light gets brighter and brighter, and as I get closer to the center, I move even faster.

No turning back now.

"Focus...time," Pops' single words echo through the

storm, layering over one another so that it sounds like there is a choir filled with hundreds of the cheery old man. "...The...focus...time...the time...focus."

My training.

It hits me. I need to remember my training. Pops has been working with me for weeks. We've been preparing for this moment tirelessly in my spare time after band rehearsals and on the weekends. I feel like the Karate Kid when he finally understands what Mr. Miyagi has been teaching him all that time. I am like young Luke Skywalker with Yoda on his back, training to focus my powers, and learning to master the Force.

Pops has been teaching me how to use the metronome. To actually harness its power and use it to jump through time and space to wherever I choose. So far, it has been a bust. I keep ending up on the floor of the storage room, opening my eyes to find Pops staring at me with what I've come to know as one of his best features. His smile.

There's almost no situation in which Pops isn't smiling.

Focus, Rigs, focus.

The colors blaze by me as I begin to tumble head over feet. The spinning begins to take its toll. I am right on the edge of motion sickness now. I don't know which way is up, and there's nothing to ground me. I just might throw up.

2000. 2000. 2000. Take me to the year 2000.

I always center my jump attempts around this year. Pops said to pick a good round even number to start with. So I chose the year 2000. It's not too far back. I can't even remember how many times I've tried to jump, but the result is the same. Each time I fail.

But, this time, it seems different. I don't think I've been in the jump this long. I always come out of it, and no actual time has passed. That's pretty freaky, but it makes sense. I'm just stepping out of my timeline and into a stream where time as I know it doesn't exist. Pops says that all I have to do is learn how to step out of my present and then back into a different time.

Easier said than done, Pops.

"Focus." The repeated word is beginning to annoy me.

I press my hands to my head and close my eyes, shutting out the brilliant, flashing light as I spin rapidly out of control toward the core of the converging color storm.

2000.

BOOM! An explosion rattles my insides. It's the loudest noise I've ever heard, but surprisingly, it doesn't hurt my ears. A sound that loud should have burst my eardrums. But they seem to be fine. I still hear Pops' voice echoing all over the place.

"The time..."

And then, suddenly, I am enveloped by an eery and total silence. I'm not tumbling anymore. I hesitate to open my eyes. Is it possible that I'm not hearing or feeling anything because I've just been blown to smithereens? I shudder at the potentially gruesome sight I might see if I open my eyes.

It's so quiet.

I cover my eyes with my hands and then apprehensively crack my left eye to take a peek. I spread my middle and ring fingers apart, ever so slightly, not knowing what I might see through the small opening.

There is no more shimmering color, no blinding lights. I see only a blur of figures moving in front of me in what appears to be a small, dark space. There is a steady beeping sound, like the sound of a heart monitor in a hospital room. People are speaking, but I can't make out any of their muffled words. I hear the garbled and distorted notes of a familiar song. It sounds far away, but I recognize the tune. It's by the Beatles.

Eleanor Rigby.

A woman is breathing heavy as if she's in pain. A man with a soothing voice sounds like he's trying to keep her calm, but I can't decipher any of his words.

Why is everything so muffled? I can't hear anything. Maybe that explosion DID mess with my hearing.

Another voice, calm and in-control, seems to be giving instructions. The words are just indistinct noises, but I clearly make out the syllables when he begins to count down from three to one.

The woman screams. It's a bone-chilling, guttural sound that seems to come from deep within her. And just as quickly as I was transported to the edge of this scene, silence surrounds me again as it begins to fade from my field of vision. The little bit of light that is illuminating this room starts to close in on itself like the circle of a spotlight dimming at the end of a show. But, it's in slow motion.

Wait, what's happening to the lady? Who is she? I can't see anything.

The circle of dim light gets smaller and smaller, and the blurs are less recognizable as people. There is no beeping, only silence.

The instant before I begin to lose all hope of figuring out where I am and what I am struggling to comprehend before me, the tiny, helpless sound of an infant gasping its first breath pierces the silence. The cries of the baby seem so quiet and small. The scene before me has gone almost completely dark, but as I squint to make out the last dimming details, I recognize the screaming woman's voice, and I hear every single word that she utters very clearly.

"Welcome to the world, my sweet little angel," she says with what can only be the love of a mother for her newborn child. "I am so very glad to meet you. Your name, little one, is Rigby Juliet Raines."

BECAUSE

Acknowledgements

Many thanks to my fellow band kids, young and old, the majority of whom self-identify as band geeks, who are an important part of the Marching Band Is Awesome communities on our social networking platforms. I'm so appreciative of everyone who has followed, liked and commented on MBIA content. Thank you to my friends who encouraged me to keep posting funny marching band and music memes. To those who are proudly wearing an MBIA tee or tank top, thank you! Without this huge family of tens and thousands of band kids, this novel wouldn't have happened.

Thank you to my college roommates and buddies who are band directors and directly influencing young musicians. Thanks for welcoming MBIA into your schools and band rooms! And most of all, thank you for being an inspiration for some characters in this book! You know who you are!

A big shout out to all my early "beta" readers and proofers. Mom, you're the best! All my early readers on Wattpad, I appreciate every read, vote, and comment! Thanks, Sarah, for the pointers! Thank you ALL for spending your time to help Rigby's story come across the best that it could!

Thank you to my family for believing in this wannabe author's dreams. This completed novel is the realization of those dreams. The deepest and most heartfelt thanks to my wife for letting me spend extra hours at the coffeeshop to write and edit. Thank you for your support and for letting me chase this dream! Also, a big shout out to the two beautiful sons you gave me who want to be just like their daddy!

About The Author

Hi, I'm R.K. Slade. I am an eight-year marching band veteran. I marched trumpet four years in high school and four years in college. I love writing about all kinds of band and music. I am the founder of all the Marching Band Is Awesome communities on Facebook, Instagram, Twitter, Pinterest, YouTube, and Wattpad. These communities combined have over 100,000 fans and followers.

I have a beautiful family. My beautiful wife bakes the best lemon pound cake in the world, and I have two amazing little boys. They both want to be drummers and trumpet players, of course.

Whether I'm working on graphic design in my day job, or writing YA fiction like this one, I enjoy the music of Beethoven. I also choose epic film scores to be the soundtracks of my work time. I'm into gaming and I spend a lot of hours playing Minecraft, Battlefield and Clash Royale. I've always dreamed about writing a novel, and finally, with the publishing of this book, *Because,* that dream has become a reality.

More info at: marchingbandisawesome.com

59062482R00205

Made in the USA
Lexington, KY
21 December 2016